W9-AHA-977

Discard

)

SAFE
KEEPING

Center Point
Large Print

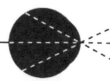

**This Large Print Book carries the
Seal of Approval of N.A.V.H.**

SAFE KEEPING

BARBARA TAYLOR SISSEL

CENTER POINT LARGE PRINT
THORNDIKE, MAINE

ISBN: 978-1-62899-228-1

Library of Congress Cataloging-in-Publication Data

Taylor Sissel, Barbara.
 Safe keeping / Barbara Taylor Sissel. — Center Point Large Print
edition.
 pages ; cm
 Summary: "When Tucker Lebay is targeted by the police in a murder
investigation after having been a person of interest in an unsolved case a
year ago, his mother and sister set out to learn the truth"—Provided by
publisher.
 ISBN 978-1-62899-228-1 (library binding : alk. paper)
 1. Families—Fiction. 2. Murder—Investigation—Fiction.
 3. Large type books. I. Title.
 PS3620.A985S24 2014
 813′.6—dc23
                                                              2014019458

For my sister Susan and my brother John.
And in memory of our parents, gone so soon.

My son is a murderer.

The words hovered in Emily's mind.

She said them aloud, "My son is a murderer."

But they sounded no more believable than when they were rattling around in her head. Why did her mind do this? Why did it conjure up the worst of her fears? One that was neither logical nor possible? So far, like Tucker, the girl, Jessica Sweet, was only missing, not dead, and whatever more dire connection might exist between them was a figment of Emily's overactive imagination, the result of too little sleep and too much worry. It was the uncertainty that was killing her. If only she could know Tucker was safe.

She stared over the foot of the bed, beyond the circle of lamplight, into new morning light that was as pale as a milky eye. Behind the closed bathroom door, the sound of the shower was a muted hiss. The sharp crease of light on the floor under the door assured her Roy was in there performing his morning routine. Even in retirement, he was a man of routine, of habits that were as predictable as moonrise.

Heart thudding, she looked at the telephone on the nightstand near her elbow and then at the bathroom door. Was she prepared for what would happen if she went through with it, if she dialed 9-1-1? Was there time before Roy was finished? The sound of the shower clattered in her ears. She lifted the cordless receiver from its base.

Impossibly his fingers closed over her wrist. "Don't, Em."

Her gaze bounced. A breath went down hard. "Someone has to—"

"No."

"Tucker's been gone almost two weeks, Roy. It's not like him."

"What do you mean? He pulls this stunt all the time, his damn disappearing act, and the hell with us left behind to worry."

"But never for this long. I think we should call the police."

"No," Roy repeated.

"What if he's been in an accident?" Emily asked. "What if he got mugged or someone took him? He could be lying somewhere hurt." Her voice picked up speed; it caught on her panic. "He could have amnesia."

"You're making yourself crazy." Roy sat beside her. "He's making us both crazy." Emily started to answer, but Roy talked over her. "He's thirty-four years old, for Christ's sake, a grown man. Why is he still living here? Why isn't he out on his own?"

"He's tried, Roy. You know he has." Emily stopped. They'd had this discussion so many times; she knew it by heart. If she were to go on and say the rest of it, that some children took longer to grow up, that if they were patient Tucker would eventually find his way, Roy would say she was making excuses. She would be moved to defend herself. They would go back and forth, making an endless loop of words that would resolve nothing.

He picked up her hand and met her gaze. The wan circle of lamplight silvered the gray bristle of his closely cut hair. With the tip of her finger, she traced a darker line of fatigue that grooved his cheek. He was exhausted from the stress; they both were. "I want some peace and quiet in our lives," he said. "Is that so much to ask? Haven't we earned it by now?"

"Yes," she said. "And we'll have it, you'll see. When we find Tucker, we'll sit down together—"

"God help us if it's happening again, Em." He looked hard at her.

But she wasn't having it and looked away. "Don't be ridiculous," she said, even though only moments ago, she'd been in the same place, entertaining the same anxiety. She thought of reminding Roy that Tucker had been furious when he left, and given his mood, it wasn't terribly unusual that he hadn't called. He'd walked out angry any number of times before, and while it was true that he didn't ordinarily stay away this long, it was still possible that was all this disappearance amounted to. Except it wasn't, and something inside her knew it, knew that this time was different.

It was like a crack in the earth, imperceptible to the naked eye, but there all the same, a warning, an omen. Setting the phone receiver on the nightstand, she pressed her fingertips to her temples. "I want him home," she said, putting her feet over the bedside. "I want to know he's all right."

"I think it's a mistake to call this his home, Em." Roy was in his closet now, pulling on a pair of jeans. "I think when he shows up, we need to set boundaries, set a concrete date that he has to be out of here. We've done all we can for him, more than most parents would."

"It might be different if you wouldn't lose your temper," Emily said. "If you could give him the benefit of the doubt the way you do Lissa. If you could just—"

"Just what, Em?"

She didn't answer; she was out of energy, suddenly past the wish to explain. She looked at the floor. *If he'd been our first, he might have been our last.* The old joke, one she'd heard other parents make, drifted through her mind. She didn't find it particularly amusing even though she'd resorted to it on occasion herself. Would she have had another child had it been Tucker and not Lissa who came first? No one could have asked for a lovelier or more obedient child than

10

Lissa, and Evan, the man she'd chosen for her husband, was a godsend. Emily and Roy relied on him, his steadiness, his kindness and good sense. Even Tucker seemed calmer and more content when Evan was nearby.

"What would you tell the police if you called them?" Roy emerged from the closet. "What evidence do you have—of anything wrong, I mean?"

"How do you know they don't have him already?"

"We would have heard."

"The girl who disappeared," Emily began, because it was impossible, after all, not to voice the fear that was uppermost in both their minds, "the one everyone is looking for, Jessica Sweet, I think I recognize her name. What if Tucker knew her, dated her like he did Miranda?"

"Like I said before, God help us if that turns out to be the case." Roy stuffed his shirt hem into his jeans and threaded his belt through the loops. "I'll tell you right now, I can't handle that again."

The drama, Roy meant, the horrible way it had ended—in Miranda's murder of all things. Emily picked at her thumbnail. She and Roy had welcomed Miranda Quick when Tucker first began dating her in high school; they'd grown fond of her. They knew her family from church, knew her to be a sweet girl, the very sort of girl Emily could imagine as a daughter-in-law, but after graduation Miranda changed, becoming restless and unhappy. She went out nights alone. Tucker had had no idea where she was or what she was doing, and when he found out, it devastated him. But he loved her, and he was determined to stay with her even after she proved herself unworthy of his devotion.

He remained faithful, while Miranda broke his heart over and over. Emily had never felt so helpless and frustrated. Then, just when she thought it couldn't get worse, Miranda went missing and Tucker was the one who found her body. A day later, the police came for him. They questioned him for hours. His picture was everywhere in the media; he was labeled a person of interest—in a murder investigation. How? Emily still couldn't wrap her mind around it, how her son had become involved in something so horrifying. She blamed Miranda. Miranda was the cancer who had gotten her hooks into Tucker. She was the blight of their lives, and if it was possible, Emily believed she hated Miranda more now that she was dead, and she truly didn't care if she went to hell for it.

Switching off the bedside light, she felt the mattress give when Roy sat down to put on his shoes, felt the heat from his palm when he flattened it on her back. He said he would make the coffee. "I'll bring it up to you with some toast and that marmalade you like. How about it?"

Ordinarily, she would have been delighted. Roy wasn't the sort of man who was comfortable in the kitchen. A construction site was more his domain; hard physical labor was his refuge, and providing a good living for his family was his contribution, his source of pride. Or it had been until last fall when he retired. Emily encouraged it. She imagined they would do things together, finish building the lake house, plant a vegetable garden. She'd dreamed of more exotic possibilities, traveling on the Orient Express or learning ballroom dancing, but in a very not-funny way, there was just something about having your son's name—their own Lebay family name—linked to a murder investigation that caused such visions to lose their luster.

Pushing aside the bed linen, she told Roy she would make the coffee, that she needed to get up, to be busy. But then she was sorry not to have accepted his invitation, because when they came downstairs, he didn't accompany her into the kitchen. Instead, he disappeared into his office.

Emily heard the door close, the click of the lock, and she sighed. Standing at the counter, she parted the checked curtains at the window over the sink. The view was as familiar to her as the image of her own face. Her great-grandfather had built this house, and it had come down to her through the generations. She grew up here and could recall the very year her parents remodeled the old carriage house to accommodate two cars and the work-shop, where, like her dad, Roy would go to putter. Beyond it, there was an alley. Closer in, a huge old elm tree centered the bit of backyard, housing a picnic table that Roy built and a wood-seated swing. After they were married in the spring of 1972, on his good days, Roy had pushed her in that swing.

"Higher!" she hollered at him, laughing. "Higher!" she shouted.

And later, he pushed her while she held their children as infants in her arms.

They had been happy, hadn't they? They weren't different from other families in the neighborhood. They shopped and vacationed and participated in community events. They attended church. And like their neighbors, they'd had their share of good times and bad.

Emily started the coffee, and while she waited for it to brew, she collected the Monday editions of the two newspapers they read from the front porch. Their small-town newspaper, the *Hardys Walk Tribune*, was lighter in weight and folksier in tone than the *Houston Chronicle*. On her way back to the kitchen, she paused at Roy's office door, and putting her ear against it, she listened and heard nothing. Only the sound of the tall grandfather clock on the landing in the front hall. The rhythmic *tock tock* was magnified like heartbeats in a row. Gunshots fired in evenly spaced salute.

She straightened. In her mind's eye, she could see Roy sitting at his desk, and on the wall opposite him, she saw the gun case that housed his collection. The glass front would hold a faint reflection of his image, doing whatever it was he did in there these days. She hoped he wasn't brooding. The guns worried her. She didn't like thinking it, and perhaps it was only a temporary effect of retirement, but there was something in his demeanor in recent weeks that was beginning to remind her of the wounded man he was when he came back from the war in Vietnam. He'd tried hard to hold in the horror, closing himself off from her, not wanting to burden her, he said. They'd worked through it eventually, but it had taken a near-tragedy to bring him around.

She tapped on the door. "Coffee's ready," she said through the panel, and she was relieved to hear his acknowledgment, to hear the leather creak as he rose from his chair. He followed her into the kitchen, and she thought the drag of his step sounded more uneven than usual. She wanted to turn and look, to ask if his pain was worse, but he didn't like her fussing over him.

She unsheathed both papers from their plastic wrappers and set them, still folded, on the table, and that's when she saw it—a piece of the face of the missing girl, Jessica Sweet. It was looking out from the front page of the *Chronicle*. Above it, Emily glimpsed two words: *found* and *dead,* and

15

her heart slammed into the wall of her chest. Any moment now, Roy would see it, too.

She brought the toast to the table and sat across from Roy. She was aware of the newspaper between them and was seized by a sudden, heated and irrational urge to tear it to shreds. She imagined Tucker coming through the door. He would put his arms around her; he would say how sorry he was to have caused her such concern. She would tell him about the dead girl, show him her picture, and he'd be sorry for her, too. But he wouldn't know her. He wouldn't have loved her or shared a messy, emotional history with her the way he had with Miranda Quick.

Emily picked up her slice of toast and then set it down, thinking if she had to sit here through another day without word from Tucker, or about him, she would come out of her skin.

She caught Roy's glance.

"What?" he said.

"Why don't we ride out there?"

"Where?" he asked, but she was certain he knew.

"Indigo Lake."

"What for? There's nothing to see," he said. "A slab, pipes, a frame. I ought to get Evan to send a crew out there to pull it down. I'll sell the land."

Evan had worked for Roy in the family construction business long before becoming Lissa's husband. Evan and Lissa ran the company now since Roy's retirement. Tucker would have had a share in running it, too, if he was in the least reliable.

Emily touched Roy's hand. "I think you should finish the house. It would take your mind off—" She didn't want to say Tucker, so she said, "Things, you know. You need a project. Once it's finished, if you don't want to keep it, you can always sell it then."

"Why the sudden interest? You've already said you won't move out there."

"I could change my mind."

"Why would you?"

Emily looked into her coffee cup. *For you,* she thought. But if she were to say that, he'd think it was out of pity. "A change of scenery," she said softly. "I think we need a change of scenery."

Roy made a sound that could have meant anything. He took his cup and plate to the sink, thanked her for the toast. It was only after she heard his office door close behind him that she realized he'd taken the Houston paper with him, and her head livened with a fresh buzz of anxiety. He was bound to see the photo and the article now, she thought, and she closed her eyes. It was happening again just as Roy feared. She could feel it to her core. And this time, when Roy insisted they cut their ties to Tucker, he would mean it.

2

Lissa pulled her pickup in behind her dad's truck and killed the engine, but she didn't get out right away. Instead, she distracted herself, looking along the sidewalk in front of her parents' house where the sharp morning light planked an angular path across the generously proportioned front porch to the door. How many times did she and Tucker paint that porch, all the balusters and assorted gingerbread trim? Tucker had resented every minute, but Lissa hadn't minded. She loved the house her great-great-grandfather, Hiram Winter, built. It was one of several of his designs in the neighborhood, a Queen Anne. He had favored the Queen Anne and Georgian styles. Deep porches, cornices, pilasters, colonnaded verandas and gingerbread were architectural details that Lissa loved, too. The classically fashioned bungalow she and Evan recently finished building on acreage west of town, in a newish subdivision, was a compromise. They were in the process of completing Lissa's art studio and a gazebo, too, in a style to match the house.

She gave the front porch another look. The newspaper was gone, which meant her parents had been up long enough to retrieve it. It would be lying open on the kitchen table, folded to show the dead woman's photo, and her mom and dad would be sitting over it in a worried stew of complicated silence, suffering the same nasty jolt of déjà vu as Lissa. It was inevitable given the eerie similarities between Miranda's and Jessica Sweet's deaths. According to the news report Lissa heard earlier, Jessica's car was found abandoned in the same strip shopping center where Miranda's car was found, and now Jessica's body had turned up in the same location, a mere matter of yards from where Tucker discovered Miranda's body a year ago. The manner of death was the same, too. Both women appeared to have been strangled. While the report hadn't mentioned Tucker's name in connection to Miranda's case, which remained unsolved, Lissa thought it was only a matter of time.

She looked out at her parents' house. She didn't need to see them to know they were as panicked by the news as she was. What could she say to them, anyway? It will be fine? She couldn't offer that kind of reassurance, not now. Maybe later. Maybe if she gave it a little more time Tucker would show up. She started the truck.

"Hey!"

Lissa froze, as if she could pretend she hadn't heard her dad's shout, hadn't caught sight of him from the corner of her eye, crabbing his way down the front steps. She looked through the windshield at her dad's pickup, at the license plate that had Disabled Vet printed across the top. He would allow the tag that labeled him a cripple, but if anyone were to suggest the use of a cane, he'd growl like an injured bear.

He met her at the gate, swinging it open for her. "Guess you came looking for your brother and thought you'd just skip on by if he wasn't here."

"No, Daddy, I was coming in."

"The hell you were."

"You look like hell," she said. Up close, she could see his face was sweaty and pale under his iron-gray buzz cut. His leg was bothering him again, or she should say the lack of his leg. The pain was worse, Lissa guessed. Ordinarily, he was never bothered by it. In fact, people who knew him often forgot he was missing a limb. According to her mother, though, the ill effects of her dad's amputation, the aching and tenderness, had resurfaced recently. Probably the result of stress, Lissa thought. He wasn't handling retirement very well, and there was Tucker, always Tucker. Lissa loved him—they all loved him—but the joke, the painful family joke, was that he could drive God to drink.

She followed her dad into his office. When she and Tucker were young, her dad kept it locked because of his gun collection. Of course, the precaution only heightened their curiosity; they had looked for ways to be in here, to handle the weapons, and their wish was granted. Over their mother's protests, Daddy schooled them—the same as their mom—in their use. He taught them to hunt and claimed Lissa had a dead eye.

She sat in a club chair across from him now, and she was wary. She couldn't quite sort out his mood. She asked if he was okay.

No answer. There was only the sound of his breath, the creak of the leather as he shifted his weight in the tall wingback desk chair.

Dropping her glance, she saw the morning newspaper folded on the desk's corner, the photo of Jessica Sweet staring out. It looked as if it had been taken from a high school yearbook of roughly the same vintage as Tucker's. Lissa thought she had read somewhere they were the same age, thirty-four, and it worried her. It made it seem more likely Tucker might have known her. She started to say something, to make some comment, or offer the customary reassurance, but then she saw the ledger—the old-fashioned, leather-bound business ledger that her dad insisted they keep the family company, Lebay-Winter's financial records in because he didn't trust computers, the ledger that was supposed to be at the office that she and Evan shared in town, but instead was sitting here, open on the desk blotter.

"What are you doing with that?" she asked.

"Not the right question," her dad answered.

"So, what is?"

"Oh, I think you know."

They sat, eyes locked, while silence rose, like a rigid wall. Lissa's dad, the former decorated United States Army drill sergeant, said a guilty man, a soldier in her dad's case, who had something to hide, couldn't handle the silence. Pretty soon, he'd break down, say whatever came into his mind just to fill the void. Eventually, he'd hang himself. Her dad was waiting for that now, for Lissa to hang herself.

She set her teeth together.

"I've been going over the numbers," he said finally. "You and Evan have been bullshitting me. We're not in good shape the way you said. In fact, this is looking like the worst year we've had in the past five. You want to tell me why you lied?"

"About the numbers?" *When had he gotten the ledger?* Lissa tried to put it together even as she said, "I don't know what you mean."

"Come on, Lissa!" Her dad smacked the desktop with the flat of his hand. "I'm retired, not senile."

"I understand that, Dad, but I assumed that since you retired and turned over control of the company to me, and to Evan, that meant you trusted us to run the place."

"I built that goddamn business from nothing, worked it thirty years. You can't push me out."

"Oh, Daddy, we're not trying to!" Lissa was nonplussed at the emotion in his voice, the way it slipped and caught.

He held her gaze, and she saw that his eyes

22

were dark with anguish and, amazingly, filmed with tears. In her entire life, she had never known him to cry; he counted a man's tears as weakness. It alarmed her; it hurt her heart. He could be gruff, even hard; he might take your head off if you made a foolish mistake. But the very same man had spent hours building her the exact replica of a dollhouse from an illustration in a book she'd fallen in love with, and she could still recall the shapes of the calluses that spanned his palm from all the times he'd taken her hand when he'd walked her to school. He'd taught her to drive and never once raised his voice, not even when she'd driven them into a ditch and he'd had to call a tow truck to get them out again.

"Look," she said quickly, "maybe we did overstate a bit. It's been tough the past several months, you know that, what with the economy, and then ever since—" She stopped before she could say Tucker's name, say how badly business had been affected by last year's notoriety, but her dad knew what was in her mind.

He inclined his head in the direction of the *Houston Chronicle* and said, "Yeah, well, it looks like the shit's about to hit the fan again."

"You don't know that, Dad."

A silence fell.

Her father broke it. "Your mother tried to call the cops to report him missing this morning. She would have, if I hadn't stopped her."

"She wants to find him, that's all."

He shook his head. "She's losing it."

Lissa didn't ask what he meant, whether he thought it was her mother's faith or her mind that was going. He looked at the newspaper, but she looked at him. She thought he was the one who was losing it. He looked so distraught. But he'd caused this, hadn't he? He'd put himself in this position.

As if he felt her gaze, her father looked at her and said, "What?" in that tone he used when he meant to prick a nerve.

"Momma said you told Tucker to get out and not come back."

"So?"

"So, you got what you wanted."

"He called me, his own father, a fucking bastard and said he was a grown man and could take care of himself, which I'd like to see—just once."

"Well, he could, if he had a job, if he had a paycheck. You cut him out of the business, Daddy! You basically disowned him. What was he supposed to do, fall all over you with kisses, his heartfelt thanks?"

"You know he blew another meeting with Carl Pederson."

She nodded. She and Evan were as irked at Tucker as her dad, as Carl himself, was. It wasn't easy to find a good cabinet man.

"If it was anyone else, screwing up as consistently as your brother has, I'd have fired them a long time ago," her dad said. "Even you and Evan would have. You know I'm right."

Lissa picked at her thumbnail. He wanted her to say he was justified in cutting Tucker from the business. And maybe he was. "Tucker is your son, not just some employee," she said.

"I've given him every chance, bent over backward. Like I said to your mother this morning, the boy needs to grow up. . . ."

And if that means he has to hit the bottom . . . Her dad went on.

Lissa tuned him out. Some things weren't worth fighting over.

"Where's Mom?" Lissa waited to ask until her dad was quiet.

"Upstairs. She's pissed because I won't go to the lake and see about finishing the house."

"What's going on with that, Dad? You always said after you retired, you were going to build that house and fish until you died."

"I've got no appetite for it anymore," he said, and his voice was raw. "You get a crew out there, pull the frame down, use the material somewhere else. Tell Evan—"

He stopped, but Lissa kept his gaze while a hundred thoughts crowded her mind. She could offer him comfort, but she didn't know how he'd take it. He'd never needed her comfort before.

He brushed his hand over his face, and the breath he took in was huge and ragged. "Go on, little girl, and check on your momma, will you? I'm worried about her."

"Daddy?" Lissa felt a fresh jolt of alarm. She could see his eyes were filmed with tears again. Her own throat constricted.

He waved her off. "Just let me be now."

"Tucker will come home soon. It'll be fine, you'll see."

"Sure," he said. "It always is, isn't it?"

She eyed him a moment longer, then left, pulling the door closed behind her. When she heard the click of the lock, she looked back, and the thought came that he shouldn't be alone now, not with all those guns, and it chilled her momentarily. She thought of asking him to let her back in, but he'd only refuse, if he answered her at all.

Her head throbbed with every step as she climbed to the second floor. She had wakened with another brutal headache this morning that had only gotten worse. She'd had a series of them recently. They had to be sinus related, she thought.

"Mom?" she called, reaching the upstairs hallway.

"Back here," she answered.

Lissa went toward the sound of her mother's voice and found her sitting on a footstool in the linen closet. Her mother looked up. "Honey, what's wrong? You're so pale."

"Headache," Lissa said. "I think it's sinus. I took some Advil, but it's not helping."

"Dr. White gave me something good for that last time I went to see him." Her mother went into the bathroom next to the linen closet and returned with a glass of water and a tablet. "It works, and it won't make you sleepy."

Lissa took the pill and a swallow of water.

"He said to remind you that you're overdue for a checkup."

"I know. I've been putting it off." Lissa drank the rest of the water. As much as she loved Dr. White, she wished she could see someone different for her exam, a doctor who hadn't known her since she was six. Someone who would only see her as a condition, not as a person. In case of bad news, she thought it might be easier if it were treated with clinical dispassion. Not that she felt as if she were seriously ill. It was only that she didn't feel herself. In addition to the frequent headaches, she wasn't sleeping, her appetite was low and, last week, she'd fainted. She kept telling herself it was stress. She wanted it to be.

Lissa's mother resumed her perch on the stool. "I didn't hear you come in."

"I wanted to check on you, you know, because of—"

"I've been rereading Dad's old letters," Lissa's mother interrupted. She half lifted a cardboard box from her lap. "Did I ever show you this

27

one?" She handed Lissa a sheet of onionskin paper, sepia tinged at the edges and covered in her dad's cramped writing.

" *'My Dearest Em,'* " her mother read, " *'my dearest one, my love, how will I tell you this news, the awful thing that has happened. I'm not the same, not your sweetest—not your sweetest honey—'* " She caught her lip, took a breath. " *'I'm not sure I'm even a man anymore.'* "

"Mom . . ." Lissa's murmur was half in sorrow, half in protest.

She hadn't read her dad's letters home from Vietnam, but she knew how he'd been injured there. Her mother had told her and Tucker the story, how in the aftermath of battle, he'd rescued a four-year-old North Vietnamese boy, an enemy's son, and run with him from a burning house, but before he could make it back to the location where his company was bivouacked, sniper fire had caught him in the meaty part of his calf below his left knee. Still, he'd kept running with the child; he'd brought the boy to safety against all odds, and sixty-one days later, they'd amputated the gangrenous, blasted remains of his lower leg. He'd nearly died from the infection.

Lissa was still in awe of the story. She couldn't imagine the selfless act of courage it had taken. She remembered socking a kid once in third grade who called her dad a cripple. She'd been sent home that day for fighting, but she hadn't been punished. Her mother only said the boy was probably frightened at the idea of her father having only one leg. It hadn't made sense to Lissa. Her dad wasn't different from any other dad with two legs. In fact, he was stronger than any man she knew. She never thought of him as handicapped. Most of her life, she'd scarcely been aware of it.

She gave her father's letter back to her mother. "Daddy doesn't look good, Mom. I'm worried about him. I don't think I've ever seen him quite so shaky."

"That missing girl—she's—"

"But it doesn't necessarily mean anything, you know?"

Her mother hugged her elbows. "They don't make linen closets with so much room in them anymore, do they? I played house in here when I was little, did I ever tell you?"

"Sure, Momma." Lissa went along. "We played house in here, too, remember? You and me and Tucker."

"It's just the right size. Your grandma let me have a little table. And dishes. Such pretty dishes. I loved being in here—I still do. The way the old floor creaks and how the sunlight comes through the door, and the smell—it's a comfort to me." She drew in a breath, eyes closed. "Some people think it's musty, but to me it smells safe. It smells the way love would smell, if love had a smell."

Lissa knelt beside her. "Tucker will be home soon, Momma, or he'll call. He always does." The assurance sounded no better now than when she'd offered it to her dad.

Her mother touched Lissa's cheek, lifted her fingers, trailing them across Lissa's brow. "You and your brother are so different," she said. "Tucker's blond, like me, like the Winters, but you favor your father with all that wonderful dark hair. You're strong, too, like he is."

They shared a silence.

"I want to help him, you know? But when he hits these dark places, when he retreats and goes into himself, I— It's hard to know what to do."

Lissa tucked a wayward strand of her mother's hair behind her ear. It added to her worry, seeing her parents so undone, so not themselves. Abruptly, she held out a hand to her mother. "Come with me to Pecan Grove. It will do you good to get out of the house."

"Oh, that would be lovely, but you've got work to do out there, and I'm fine. Dad and I both are. Don't worry about us." Her mother stood up making shooing motions, then suddenly she cupped Lissa's face in both hands. "Do you know how much I love you?" Her eyes were swimming with tears.

Lissa nodded; her own throat knotted.

"Sometimes, I think we get so focused on Tucker, we forget about you. Forget to tell you how special you are. Please say you know how much we love you."

Lissa slid her palms over her mother's hands. "Of course I do, Momma."

She gathered herself and gave Lissa's cheeks a final pat. "Don't pay any attention to me. I just need to hear from your brother. Once he's home, and he and your dad have mended their fences, we can get back to normal."

"What's normal?" Lissa asked, and she was glad when her mother smiled.

She stopped outside her dad's office door on her way down the front hall. "Daddy?" she called softly, but he didn't answer her, and she didn't call out again. Passing the dining room on her way out of the house, her path was diverted when she caught sight of the collection of family photos arrayed across the top of her mother's baby grand piano. Some were casual shots that her dad had taken back when she and Tucker were little. Others were formal studio shots. She picked one up, a five-by-seven framed in wood. It was of the four of them sitting on a sofa. Her mother was holding Tucker on her lap, and Lissa was leaning against her daddy's good leg, smiling, gap-toothed. Tucker was in shorts and had a Mickey Mouse Band-Aid on one chubby knee.

Setting the studio portrait down, she picked up

another, a shot her father had taken that her mother had framed in silver. It was from Easter Sunday. Lissa remembered the year was 1981. Tucker turned three that year, and she turned seven. They were outside on the front porch, dressed in their church finery. Lissa's outfit, a ruffle-hemmed sheath made of pink dotted swiss, with pink patent-leather Mary Janes and a purse to match, had been a favorite. Her mother had corralled her glossy, straight, dark hair into a French braid that hung midway down her back and ended in a tied puff of pink chiffon. Lissa wore it in a French braid to this day, to keep it out of her face, especially when she was working or painting. Growing up, Tucker called the braid her donkey tail to annoy her. He'd grabbed it and held it to his chin, letting the end dangle, making a long beard of it, teasing her. She'd wanted to clobber him.

She touched the tip of her finger to the image of his face, then put the photo back. Looking at it left her feeling some nostalgic mix of happy and sad. She guessed it was because life had never been as simple again after that year.

She was almost to the interstate when her cell phone rang.

"Where are you?" Evan asked when she answered.

"Why? What's wrong?" She knew what he

would say. Still, her heart paused when Evan said, "Tucker was here, at the office, and not fifteen minutes after he left, the police showed up, looking for him."

She put on her signal, turned right into a gas station and parked. "Do you know where he went?" she asked, and she almost couldn't hear her own voice over the hammer of her pulse.

"He didn't say. He wanted to see you, and I said you were at your folks', but I don't think he'll go there."

"No." Lissa pressed her fingertips above her right eye where the pain had settled into an ache dulled by the medication her mother had given her.

"He's driving some girl's car, an old Volkswagen. He says his Tahoe broke down on the freeway last night, and she helped him out. He said he's been in Austin."

"That's nowhere near—"

"Where the dead woman was found. Yeah, it's a relief."

"Can he prove it?"

"I don't know. He didn't say, and all the cops would tell me is that they wanted to question him, but not what it was about."

Lissa rested her head against the seatback. "Well, it could be anything. An unpaid speeding ticket. Lord knows he's gotten a slew of those."

"Yeah," Evan said, because, like her, he wanted

it to be that simple. They both did. And maybe it was.

"I wonder if he's called Mom and Dad," she said.

"I don't think so. He lost his cell phone."

"Figures. Is he getting another one?"

"He says he's busted."

"You didn't give him any money."

"No, and to his credit, he didn't ask."

"Did I ever tell you you're my hero?" Lissa ran the tip of her finger along the lower curve of the steering wheel, biting her lip, trying not to cry.

"Yeah," Evan said, "but I can always go for hearing it again."

They decided Lissa wouldn't call her parents until she knew something concrete. She was on her way to the office when her cell phone rang again. Glancing at the caller ID, she saw her own home phone number, the landline, and her heart faltered.

"Tucker?" she said when she answered, because it could only be him.

"That's me," he said.

"What are you doing in my house?"

"Hiding?" He laughed.

Lissa didn't. "Not funny. So not funny," she repeated, and the breath she drew bumped over the renewal of tears, the hot mix of relief, aggravation and outright fury that jammed her throat. If Tucker were here, she would pull off the road, she thought, and kill him.

"Can you come home?" he said. "We need to talk."

"What is it, Tuck?" Something in his voice deepened her sense of disquiet. Even when he answered that it was nothing to worry about, she wasn't mollified. Instead, what rose in her mind was the image of the two of them from that long ago Easter Sunday in 1981, and this time it brought with it a colder, darker memory of how quickly life could change, just the way it had then, in the space of one single, terrifying afternoon.

3

The I-45 interstate that bisected the heart of town wasn't really an interstate at all given that the entire length of it, some 294 miles, fell inside Texas borders. It was anchored on its northern end by the Dallas-Fort Worth metroplex and on its southern end by the bay-front city of Galveston. The drive down to the beach wasn't bad. If you started out early enough, it made a nice day trip. As children, Lissa and Tucker went with their parents, and when Lissa was older, high school age, she went with her girlfriends.

The last time was twenty years ago, the weekend after her high school graduation. She wouldn't ever forget it because it was the same weekend she realized Evan wasn't just some guy who worked for her dad. That weekend she went with a girlfriend to a party in a bay-front condo where cocaine was heaped in a bowl on the coffee table. It scared the shit out of her, but her girlfriend was all over it.

Lissa tried it, too, one tiny line—how could she not?—and then she freaked out. She was certain she was going to die of an overdose or become an addict. She felt wild, as if she had somehow crawled outside her own skin. In her mania, she went out to the beach to dance, alone, putting herself in even worse jeopardy as it turned out. She was fortunate, later, to escape behind the locked door of the bathroom, and when she spied the telephone hanging on the wall near the toilet, she did the only thing that seemed reasonable; she dialed her dad's office number. Thankfully—it still gave her chills to remember her luck—it was Evan who answered, Evan who came to retrieve her. Who knew what her dad might have done? He might have brought a gun or the police or both. He might have killed her, given his temper. He didn't often lose it, but he could, if the right trigger was pulled.

Instead, it was Evan who walked her up and down the beach along the water's edge, while she jabbered like a madwoman until the stuff left her system. He took her to an all-night café and bought her orange juice and a doughnut, too, and suggested she was probably not good drug-addict material, and then he drove her home. At some point before that, he called Tucker and alerted him. Lissa remembered now that it was Tucker who covered for her with their parents, who waited up for her.

It was usually the other way around, Lissa taking care of Tucker.

She sat at the I-45 intersection, waiting for the light to change, thinking of him waiting at her house to tell her God knew what. It wouldn't be anything good, not if the police were looking for him. When she had called Evan back and told him she was headed home, that Tucker was there, he said he would come, but as much as she might long for his support, she told him no. It was bad enough that she was missing work. She thought of her foolish behavior all those years ago, how she could so easily have fallen into harm's way and, instead, had fallen— She paused. Not in love with Evan, she thought, not at first. Something better, richer. It had been more like falling into deep and abiding friendship and gratitude. Love, the full-out passionate, can't get enough of you lust—Lissa's face warmed—that came later; it had been a slow, sweet progression, like the unfolding of a flower's petals into a fuller bloom. That long-ago day in Galveston, she hadn't had a clue about what she and Evan would come to mean to each other.

She'd still been woozy when he handed her carefully through the door to her little brother. Tucker had been all of fourteen, or fifteen, maybe. Lissa could see him in her mind's eye, hustling her up the stairs, leading her quietly by their folks' bedroom. He'd been upset with her, that she'd been drunk and strung out with people—men—she didn't know. Any one of whom might have been a psycho, he said. He brought her an aspirin and a glass of water, and because he wanted to make a point about the danger she'd put herself in, he gave her a folder full of newspaper clippings he'd been collecting about the girls from com-munities near Galveston who had been found dead around there. So many, dating as far back as the 1970s, that there were rumors of multiple serial killers working in the area.

Lissa knew of Tucker's interest in crime. During his short college career, he talked about studying criminology, but she didn't know much about the I-45 serial killings, or his fascination with them before that summer night when he took out all the contents of his folder and spread them around her on the bed and on the floor at her feet. There were photos of the victims and of the crime scene locations, most of which were strung along a battered stretch of I-45 the locals called the Gulf Freeway, an approximately fifty-mile stretch of the interstate that connected the unraveling southern edge of Houston to the Galveston Causeway. The land the highway bisected was riddled with tree-clotted, snake-infested bayous and the skeletal remains of oilfield equipment that sat forgotten and rusting in the mean shadows of smog-choked refineries. There were roads, too, old service roads made of chipped asphalt covered over with hard-packed dirt. They crisscrossed the terrain, and when the night wind was right, the smoke from the nearby refineries drifted down their rutted tracks like ghosts.

It was a murderer's paradise, the perfect dumping ground, one that over the years became known collectively as the killing fields. And the four-lane stretch of interstate that roped the crime scenes together, the Gulf Freeway, was referred to in other less flattering terms as the Highway to Hell, or the Road to Perdition, or the Killing Corridor.

Lissa remembered being spooked by Tucker's stories that night. She remembered thinking that while his interest did seem a bit obsessive and a little unusual for a kid his age, it hadn't struck her as weird. Not given his worry about her, that in her inebriated state she might have fallen prey to some monster killer. He told her he'd been reading up on the FBI, everything about criminal profiling he could find. John Douglas was his hero, he said, and when Lissa shrugged in ignorance, Tucker said, "Are you kidding? He's the guy who profiled the Green River Killer. That's how the FBI got him."

Tucker dreamed of being like John Douglas, of doing what Douglas did. Lissa thought he could have, too; he'd been one of the smart kids, at least through elementary school. But he'd also been labeled emotional, high-strung, ADD—whatever name the teacher du jour chose to assign to him, as if the label alone would be adequate to explain his behavior. Her parents sought help for him. Tucker was tested and counseled, but no

40

one could come up with a diagnosis that was definitive. It was frustrating, especially for her folks, but for Tucker, too.

He was a mystery even to himself.

Lissa pulled into her driveway now and parked behind the dented, yellow VW, eyeing it as she passed by, wondering about the girl it belonged to. Not a nice girl. Nice girls weren't in the habit of picking up stray guys from the side of the road in daylight, much less at night. Lissa was judging—she knew she was—but Tucker had a reputation for attracting the wrong sort of women, the kind who would lean on him and look up to him. He liked helping them; he liked it when they took his advice.

She found him in the kitchen sitting at the table. "Hey," she said, shrugging out of her jacket.

"Hey yourself." He found her gaze but let it go after only a moment.

"Evan says you were in Austin? You couldn't call?"

"Can you spare me the lecture, Liss? I already know I'm a fuckup, okay?"

She hung her jacket on the back of a chair, not saying anything, feeling her jaw tighten. Be something else, then, she wanted to say. *Please . . .*

"Look, I know you're pissed because I missed the meeting with Pederson, but I went by the office and gave Evan the plans, so it'll be fine now."

"God, Tucker, you're such an idiot! We were

already behind schedule out there. We're losing money hand over fist. Dad got hold of the books—he's about to have a coronary."

"What's that got to do with me? It's not like I work there anymore."

Lissa closed her eyes and took a breath. The work wasn't the issue. None of this—the schedule, Dad having the ledger, the fact that Tucker had been fired again—was important. But it was as if in some part of her mind she entertained a fantasy that if she concentrated on something else, she could hold off the calamity she could sense was shaping itself just beyond the periphery of her vision.

She watched Tucker's feet dance under the table. He looked rough, as if he hadn't slept or had a decent meal in any one of the twelve days he'd been gone. Mud rimmed the sole of one tennis shoe, the hem of one leg of his jeans. She noticed a cut beneath his right eye, a tiny, upside-down crescent moon inked in blood.

She leaned against the counter. "What were you doing in Austin?"

"Helping out a friend."

"What friend?"

"You don't know him. Guy's got a band—he's looking for a bass guitarist. I might go on the road with them."

Lissa kept Tucker's gaze, and he hung in with her, not letting hers go this time, and she was somehow relieved. Liars couldn't look you in the eye. She said, "A man with a band, huh? I figured it would be one of your stray-dog friends."

"Not this time."

Lissa went to the pantry. "Do you want something to eat?"

"Nah. Thanks. I stopped at Mickey D's on the way here. I'd take a cup of coffee, though, if it's no trouble."

"Since when do you drink coffee?"

"Since it got colder than hell outside." The grin he shot her was surface, a token meant to placate her. It didn't.

"You need to call Mom and Dad, Tuck."

"I'll call Mom, but I've got nothing to say to the old man."

Lissa could have asked him right then why the police were looking for him, but she didn't. Instead, she rinsed out the carafe while he told her about his Tahoe, that it had died coming back into town and that he'd gotten lucky when a girl pulled off the road to help him.

"Did you know her?" Lissa asked.

"I do now," Tucker answered, cocking an eyebrow. "I spent the night at her place."

"You're hopeless, you know that?"

"Yeah, but you still love me, right?" His smile now was pure Tucker, full of mischief and his affection for her. Full of so many small teasing moments they'd shared just like this one. Full of

43

all that connected them—family secrets, sibling histories, the ties that bind.

Lissa would tell people they were close, and in her next breath she would say they had nothing in common. Either way it was true. She'd taught him to read; she'd taught him to tie his shoes and how to color inside the lines. She'd read aloud to him and sung songs with him. "Itsy Bitsy Spider" was his favorite. He'd loved playing the finger game that went with it. At one time he'd even slept with a big, stuffed spider. It had been purple, and he'd named it Itsy. She wondered what had become of it. They'd played endless rounds of Clue and Monopoly on rainy days and shared a love of Bon Jovi and the first *Rocky* movie. Sometimes she understood Tucker completely; other times he was an enigma, a puzzle to which she was missing a vital piece.

She turned off the tap. "What happened to your face?"

He touched his cheek. "This? Cut myself shaving." His feet danced.

She looked out the kitchen window. The coffeemaker sighed. She said, "I hate what's happening, Tuck."

"It's not your fault Pop's an asshole."

He thought she was referring to the fight he'd had with their father, the latest blowout, and she was, but that was only part of it. The cup and saucer she handed him rattled in his big, work-roughened hands. He had strong, narrow wrists and long, tapered fingers that could measure an octave on the piano. Their mother had taught him to play, and he'd been a willing student until he picked up a friend's guitar one day in high school. He'd played in a couple of bands, and Lissa thought he was good, but she wasn't an expert. She only knew what she liked, and anyway, she kind of agreed with her dad. It wouldn't be reliable, earning a living that way.

Dad had wanted Tucker to play baseball, as if that would be a more stable occupation.

"The old man told me not to come back." Tucker blew over the top of his coffee cup. "So now, in addition to being jobless, I'm homeless."

"He didn't mean it. You know how he is. He's cooled off now. Trust me."

"I think I'm going to move in with Morgan, anyway."

"Who's Morgan?" Lissa sat across from him and stirred the sugar substitute from two blue packets into her cup.

"The girl I met last night. Her dad owns a car dealership. She thinks he'll hire me."

"What about the band? I thought going on the road with them was the plan."

"Whichever works out, I guess."

Where were you really? Lissa couldn't bring herself to ask. She was filled with foreboding, heavy with it. She cleared her throat.

45

"What?" Tucker gulped his coffee.

Too fast, she thought, because he grimaced as if he'd burned his mouth. When he asked for a Coke, she brought it to him, along with the *Houston Chronicle*. She unfolded it.

He popped the top on his soft drink. "What's this?"

"Do you know her?" Lissa sat down.

"This girl?" Tucker studied the picture. Nothing altered in his expression or in his voice. Lissa started to breathe, and then he said, "It's Jessica Sweet. Holy shit!" He brought his glance to Lissa's. "She's dead?"

"You knew her." Lissa's heart throbbed in her ears.

"Yeah. Miranda introduced us. They were friends."

"Oh, Tucker. She was a dancer, too? Did they work at the same club?"

"Yeah. So what? After Miranda was killed, we hung out together, but really, I hardly knew her. Jessica was Senator Sweet's daughter. You remember him, U.S. senator, back in the day? She was kind of wild, got into trouble with drugs and stuff. I heard she cost her old man his last campaign—"

"Tucker! She's dead!"

"Yeah, that's what it says here. I can't believe it."

"She and Miranda were friends. They worked at

the same club. You knew her. The police are looking for you. It's happening all over again. . . ."

"No, Liss. There's no history between us, no big soap-opera drama. In case you didn't notice, I didn't find her body."

Lissa didn't answer.

"Come on, you know I had nothing to do with this, right? I mean you're not stressing because you think I'm, like, guilty, are you? I didn't even know the chick was missing until this morning when I saw the news."

"A second ago, you said you couldn't believe it, as if you hadn't heard—"

"I should have known!" He tossed up his hands. "I should have guessed what you'd think. I bet Pop's all over it, too. I'm a killer, right? The family lunatic, the psycho. That's why Pop doesn't want me home." He stood up fast enough to rock the chair, grabbing his jacket, shoving his arms into the sleeves.

"Come on, Tucker. You have to admit it's weird. Twice? In two years? Jessica was found in almost the exact location where Miranda was. You knew both of them. You must see how it looks."

"Yeah. I see how it looks. I just never expected you would believe in how it looks. I thought you would believe in me."

"I do, of course I do!" Lissa picked up a towel, wound her hands in it. "It's just—"

"I'm only going to say this one time, okay? I didn't kill Jessica. I didn't kill Miranda. I've never killed anybody." His gaze was hard on hers.

She tented her hands over her mouth, said his name, fighting tears, fighting for breath.

"I've got to go." He shoved the chair under the table. "Thanks for the Coke."

"No, wait. Where will you go? The police—"

"Fuck 'em," he said, and then he was gone, slamming the back door behind him.

4

When Lissa called late that morning to say Tucker
was with her and seemed all right, Roy didn't
share Emily's relief; he acted as if it didn't matter
to him at all. He went out the back door and down
the steps, and Emily watched him cross the
backyard and disappear into his workshop. She
got out the ingredients to bake a chocolate cake,
Tucker's favorite. She wanted to have something
special on hand to feed him when he got home,
but she was irked at Roy. Suppose he wouldn't
even try and sort things out this time? She
creamed the sugar with the butter in the bowl, but
all at once, the mood to bake left her, and untying
her apron, she walked out of her kitchen and
around the corner to Anna Brinker's house.

They were lifelong friends, still living in the
houses they were raised in and that their mothers
had been raised in. Like many of the other historic
homes in the neighborhood, Anna's house, a pale
green, turreted Eastlake, was also a Hiram Winter
creation. When Emily and Anna were sixteen, a
new girl their same age moved with her family
into the Winter-built, red-brick, Georgian colonial
next door to Anna. Natalie's closet was crammed
with great-looking clothes she was willing to
share and she could use her mother's turquoise-

49

blue Cadillac convertible pretty much whenever she wanted it. She drove Anna and Emily everywhere, top down, radio blasting. They became inseparable and never really lost touch, not even after high school. It was their good fortune when as newlyweds they returned with husbands in tow to the old neighborhood, like migratory birds, to live in the homes of their girlhood.

They shared nearly everything: pregnancies and diapers, recipes, celebrations. They raised their children together. Emily and Roy had Lissa and Tucker; Anna and her husband, Harvey, had their son, Cory; and Nat and her husband, Benny McPherson, had their daughter, Holly. Lissa was the oldest, Cory was the youngest and Tucker and Holly were the same age, born only weeks apart. It was a good life, filled with good times.

But like all good things, those times ended. Not easily. Not in any way Emily cared to remember.

Stirring a teaspoon of sugar into her coffee now, she glanced at Anna. "I probably shouldn't have come. I'm not fit company in the mood I'm in."

"Nonsense." Anna patted Emily's arm. "Is Tucker coming home? Did Lissa say?"

"She didn't, and it worries me. I have a feeling they got into it, but it's not as if she'd tell me. You know how those two keep secrets." She was no different, Emily thought. She was keeping her own secrets. But when tempers were already strained to the max, sometimes keeping what you knew to

50

yourself was for the best. Sometimes, if you just gave a situation a little time, it would resolve itself.

"We need something to nibble on." Anna scooted from her chair and went to rummage in the pantry.

She was biting her tongue, but soon enough, she would speak her mind. She would give Emily her opinion, the benefit of her advice. In times of trouble, that's what friends did, but Emily didn't necessarily always want to hear what Anna had to say. As close as they were, and as much as they shared, Emily didn't feel that Anna understood about Tucker. How could she? His nature was so much more complicated than Cory's or Lissa's. Who knew how or why? Emily had used up Tucker's childhood trying to sort it out, to sort him out. It still mystified her that two children, who shared the same parents, could be so utterly different in almost every way. But it was watching Tucker struggle with those very differences, watching him try so hard to fit in, that made Emily want to defend him, to shield him. She could wish all she liked to have a son like Cory, one who fit the norm, a regular kid, but she didn't.

Perfect Cory, Emily thought, and then she was ashamed.

Anna turned from the pantry, holding out a box of Milanos, her favorite cookie. She smiled.

"I don't think those are on our diet, are they?" Emily smiled, too.

"Think of it this way. We can eat these or take Prozac. I think these are cheaper and better for us. Am I right?" Anna waggled her eyebrows, making a joke.

Emily laughed outright and then wondered how she could, given the circumstances.

Anna arranged the cookies on a plate and brought it to the table. "What has Roy said?"

Her casual tone didn't fool Emily for a moment. "Oh, you know Roy," she said just as casually, wanting to avoid contention, while at the same time knowing the impossibility, because she needed to talk this out, and who else was there but Anna? Emily flashed a glance at her and found her looking back.

"I know what you're thinking," Emily said, "but it isn't as simple as blaming Roy every time Tucker disappears."

"Did I say I blamed him?"

"You don't have to. I know you think he's controlling."

"I've heard you say it yourself."

"Yes, and you know why."

"Look, I'm as sorry as you that Roy's parents were tough on him and that he lost his leg in a war few of us wanted any part of, but you aren't responsible for that. If memory serves, you tried to keep him from going."

It was true. Roy had been two weeks into his first spring training camp with the Astros in

Kissimmee, and happier, he said, than any man had a right to be, when his draft notice came. The effect was devastating. He was terrified of losing her and his budding baseball career. She was the one who said they should go to Canada. She had often wondered since what would have happened if he had agreed. Who would they be now? He would have been granted amnesty eventually. Maybe he would have found a place to work in baseball again. One thing was certain: he would still have both his legs.

Anna said, "I'm not passing judgment, Em. You know that, don't you?"

Emily said she did, although Anna's opinion of Roy always seemed faintly condemnatory to her. She toyed with her teaspoon, feeling Anna's concern, and she was sorry for it. She regretted being the cause, and when Anna asked, "What is it?" she hesitated a long moment, drawing in a breath, before admitting that she was worried about Roy.

"He's so quiet and withdrawn since he retired, and this morning, he talked to Lissa about tearing down the lake house." She caught Anna's gaze. "What if it's coming back, all that old post-traumatic stress business?"

"You don't think he's drinking."

"No." Emily was definite.

"But you think he might—what? Hurt some-one, himself? Is it that bad again?"

"I don't know. I'm afraid to talk to him about it." She paused. "He's really had it with Tucker this time. I'm not sure what will happen when he comes home. I kind of dread it, actually."

"Oh, Em."

She stood up in the silence that fell and went to Anna's kitchen sink to look out the window. "I was foolish to think that because Miranda was dead the craziness would be over. I so wanted to believe Tucker would come to his senses, but he hasn't. He still associates with those people, her friends. Other women like her. It's as if she's still manipulating him, even from the grave."

"They were together a long time."

"I should have put my foot down at the very beginning. They were too serious about each other. But Roy said if we argued, if I made a thing of it, it would only make them more determined. How I wish I had listened to my own intuition."

"You can't blame yourself, Em. Miranda was a sweet girl growing up, remember? No one, not even her parents, knew why she went so far off the track. Tucker only wanted to help her."

"For all the good it did him, and still, he persists. If he's so determined to rescue the downtrodden, I'd much rather he'd become a missionary and render aid in some third-world country. It would be safer."

When Emily sat down again, Anna patted her

arm, and they shared a look deepened by years of familiarity and affection.

"The girl who was missing," Emily said, "Jessica Sweet, did you hear they found her?"

Anna nodded, and Emily sensed that Anna had been biding the time, waiting until Emily brought it up.

"I'm so worried she'll have some connection to Miranda. They were found in the same patch of woods."

"I heard that on the news."

"I need for him to come home, Anna. I need to look into his eyes, then I'll know—"

"Know?"

"Whether he—" Emily hesitated. *Whether he is a murderer.* She wanted to say it—to test out the possibility of it being true with Anna, her dearest friend in all the world—but even if she could have brought the words past the knot in her throat, they wouldn't be accurate. She couldn't really tell anything about Tucker by looking at him anymore. Now that he was grown, he was as much of an enigma to her as to anyone. All smoke and mirrors. Mercurial. Here and gone. All his life she'd sought answers, the key to understanding his nature. Had he come with a different temperament, one that was more tightly wired? Was it the fault of genetics, or had he been marked by early child-hood trauma, that handful of years when Roy had been so unstable? She didn't know.

Like Roy, Tucker suffered from night terrors. When he was a child, Emily had gone to him on those nights when he'd wakened, flailing and shouting out, and she had comforted him as best she could until he fell back asleep. But she no longer did that. He was a man now, and she imagined the man's fear exceeded the scope of her ability to reassure him; by now, its boundaries would be much larger than the mother-size shelter of her embrace. Or so she assumed.

He got his comfort elsewhere, in places she didn't want to think about. And that was the worst part of it for her. That in the wake of his random disappearances she was left to form assumptions based on nothing of substance, the fallout from a single childhood trauma, the failure to properly parent versus the heritability of a hotter temper. What, of any of it, was valid?

"Em?" Anna urged. "You can talk to me. You know that, right? You know nothing you tell me—"

A knock came on the back door, a sharp rapping, and they both turned to look in that direction. Anna went to answer it, and when she reappeared, Emily was alarmed to see that Roy was behind her. He was white-faced, and a muscle that might be rage or fear or both was darting like a minnow under the skin at the corner of his jaw.

Emily's heart closed as tightly as a fist. Her breath stopped. "Tucker?" she said faintly. "Has something happened to him?"

"The cops are questioning a suspect about that girl's murder," Roy said. "It was just on the news. It's Tucker, Em. They've got him."

She felt her knees weaken. Anna's palm slid under her forearm. Their eyes met. "Do you want me to call Joe?"

Emily's face warmed. Joe Merchant was a Houston homicide detective now, but once, while Roy was away fighting in Vietnam, Joe had worked as a security guard for her mother, and she and Joe had very briefly been lovers. The affair ended; the friendship didn't. Emily had needed for it not to end. When Roy came home from the war, he'd been so damaged in every possible way, and out of her grief for him, and feeling unable to cope with the magnitude of his injuries, she relied on Joe for his strength, his advice. Once Roy healed, the bond persisted, even though they would go months without speaking. Anna knew of their relationship, but Emily wasn't sure about Roy. He didn't ask, and it didn't feel wrong to her, keeping it for herself.

But Anna's mention of Joe's name now worried her. Not because of her history with Joe, but because of the legal bind Tucker had gotten himself into last November that Joe had helped her to resolve. Wanting to spare Roy the stress, she had said nothing to him about it, and she'd been afraid ever since of the consequences if he were to find out. She looked at him, but if he was aware of her gaze, her anxiety, he gave no sign. He was informing Anna sharply that since it was a Lincoln County case, he doubted they'd want interference from Houston.

"Is Tucker all right?" Emily knew her question was ridiculous, but she wanted Joe, the whole idea of him, banished, gone from the room.

"Oh, sure, Em. He's great. Jesus Christ." Disgust rimmed Roy's tone, but remembering Anna, he worked his mouth into something that was meant to resemble a smile, and taking Emily's elbow, he said, "We need to get home."

Leading her from Anna's kitchen, his gait was unsteady, and when he staggered, if it hadn't been for Emily, that she was somehow able to keep him upright, he might have fallen. She knew he knew it, too. She felt his humiliation, the blow leaning on her, even for a moment, was to his pride.

"Call me," Anna said after them, and Emily heard the apprehension in her voice.

"I talked to Lissa," Roy said once they were out of Anna's house and out of her earshot. "She and Evan are on their way to the sheriff's office to see what they can find out."

"Has Tucker been arrested?"

"I guess we'll know soon enough."

They climbed the back porch stairs, and going into the kitchen, Emily's gaze fell on the abandoned mixing bowl with the ingredients for a chocolate cake scattered around it; her apron was discarded over the back of a kitchen chair. The sight was so ordinary, and she felt out of place somehow, as if given all the brewing calamity she had no right to be here, to even think of baking a cake. And yet, it was all she wanted to do. "They shouldn't be the ones who have to go after Tucker every time," she said to Roy.

"You can't handle it, and you damn sure don't want me going down there," he answered. "That's what you told me last time," he said in response to her heated look.

She held his gaze, clinging to the hope that Roy was referring to the time in April when they'd given Tucker two thousand dollars to clear his traffic tickets, and not to the time in November when she'd contacted Joe for help after Tucker was arrested and charged with stalking. Keeping Roy in ignorance then had been out of concern for him, but he would likely not see it that way.

"You do remember telling me that?" Roy's stare was penetrating, unnerving.

"You always lose your temper. It doesn't help."

He didn't argue.

"Will they bring Tucker home?" Tying her apron around her waist, she crossed to the refrigerator. "I was going to bake a chicken for dinner. If I do two, there will be enough for all of us. We can sit down together when they get here."

"I don't want Tucker here, if they let him go."

"What?" Emily turned to Roy. "He's our son. Of course you want him here."

"Not if it's going to be the way it was when Miranda was murdered. Cops and reporters everywhere. Phone ringing all the goddamn time. I swear if Tucker gets pulled into this, if he knew this girl, too—" Roy pivoted on his metal foot, then pivoted back, locking Emily with his glare. "If that's the case, you and your friend Joe won't be able to pay his way out of this one, Em. None of us will. You do realize that?"

"I don't know what you mean." She didn't know how she managed to keep her voice level. Her heart was beating fast, so fast, she put her hand there.

Roy huffed his disdain and, leaving the kitchen, disappeared into his office, closing the door.

Emily followed him; she balanced her hand on the knob, and resting her forehead against the panel, she said, "I'm sorry, I was only trying to protect you." But then, lifting her head, she thought how badly she had failed, that in truth, she hadn't protected any one of them at all.

5

The sheriff's office and the county jail were housed in the courthouse, an imposing three-story, old colonial-style building on the Hardys Walk town square. Evan pulled into a space in the parking lot at the back, where parking was free. Out in front they'd have to feed a meter, and Lissa knew from previous experience there wasn't any telling how long they'd be.

Inside, the duty officer, a heavyset guy, didn't bother looking up when Lissa and Evan approached. He was engrossed in reading a magazine, or pretending to be, like maybe if he didn't look up, they would go away. Lissa steadied her breath. "I'm looking for my brother," she said. "Tucker Lebay?"

The officer took off his glasses, rubbed his eyes.

"We were told he was brought in here earlier this afternoon for questioning," Evan said.

"Wait here." The duty officer slid off the stool and headed for a door at the end of the counter.

Lissa turned to Evan, running her fingers around her ears. Her hands were shaking; she was shaking. Evan slipped his arm around her.

"I hate this," she said.

"I know, babe. Me, too."

"Daddy said not to bring Tucker home. What are we going to do? I can't tell Tucker that."

Before Evan could answer, the duty cop reappeared, resuming his post. "Sergeant Garza'll be out in a sec. You can sit over there on the bench, if you want."

Evan sat, but Lissa didn't. She paced and watched the big white-faced wall clock, marking the tiny jerks of the minute hand as it hooked each second, and when the door at the end of the counter opened again, she flinched. Evan stood up and came to Lissa's side as the woman approached them. She appeared to be Hispanic, dark-haired, slim, maybe thirty-five, dressed in a dark gray jacket and skirt, a pair of low-heeled black pumps. She looked businesslike, professional. Lissa couldn't read her expression. She didn't give it much thought other than to assume it was deliberate, that looking impassive was part of Garza's uniform. It didn't occur to her then there might be more to it.

The woman introduced herself. "I'm Detective Sergeant Cynthia Garza. Lincoln County Criminal Investigation Division. What can I do for you folks?"

"You're questioning my brother about Jessica Sweet's murder, is that right?"

"Yes, we—"

"Does he have a lawyer?"

"He hasn't asked for one."

"Well, I'm asking for one on his behalf." Lissa spoke strongly, surprising herself. In hindsight, it would seem laughable, her idea that she could control any of what was happening.

"I think it's a bit premature, but even if it weren't, it's actually his call," Garza said.

"Are you arresting him?"

Evan moved more closely to Lissa's side; she felt his warmth, his radiant calm. He said, "The family is understandably upset, so anything you can tell us—"

"Look, we're just talking to him. It shouldn't be too much longer," Garza added, walking away.

"Wait!" Lissa trailed in Garza's wake.

She didn't respond, didn't so much as glance back. She went through the door, and it snapped shut behind her.

Evan walked Lissa to the bench and sat her down. She put her face into her hands. She didn't want to feel the panic that was trying to stand up in her stomach. "Tell me this isn't happening," she said. "It feels like déjà vu all over again." Her voice broke.

Evan put his arm around her shoulders and pulled her against him. He murmured things, nonsense mostly. She felt his breath stir the hair at her temple. It both comforted her and made her impatient when he said it would be okay. Twenty minutes passed and when the door opened in the wall behind the duty desk a second time, Lissa straightened.

Her eyes collided with Tucker's; he lifted his chin, and his expression was at once chagrined and belligerent. But underneath, Lissa could see that Tucker was scared. Evan stood up and Lissa did, too, along with her panic. It made her feel light-headed and hot all at once. Her stomach rolled, and she put her hand there.

"Hey, guys," Tucker said. "Can you dig this? That I'm back here again? It's Sergeant Garza's fault." He jerked his thumb over his shoulder at the detective. "She can't get enough of me."

"Tucker . . ." His name when Lissa said it was protest; it was despair. She glanced sidelong at the detective. Garza appeared unaffected, but who could say for sure?

"Don't make any plans to leave the area, Mr. Lebay," she said. "We might want to talk to you again."

He raised his arm in acknowledgment. "Sure thing, sweetheart," he said, but he was looking at Lissa and Evan. "Where were you, anyhow? You get that mess straightened out with Pederson? You guys know I'm sorry, right?" He shifted his feet, lifting the faded red Astros ball cap he wore, slapping it against his thigh, resettling it. "This?" He pronounced the word as if they had asked for an explanation. "It's a bunch of shit. Big misunder-standing. Cindy here has got a bad case of the hots for me. She likes my company. Right, Cindy?" He turned to her and laughed, pushing the joke.

Lissa's throat narrowed with the threat of tears, the heat of exasperation. Tucker did this when he was frightened; he made an ass of himself, but she could hardly explain that to the detective. She took Tucker's arm. "Come on," she said.

"Yeah, okay," he answered. "I guess you better get me out of here before they change their minds and toss me in the slammer." He laughed, but when he lifted his cap again, his hand was shaking.

Lissa led the way to the door, and Evan held it open, so it was her and Tucker going down the steps, shoulder to shoulder.

"When are you going to learn to mind your mouth, Tucker?" Lissa asked.

"It's got nothing to do with my mouth, Liss."

"Your shoes are untied." She pointed this out as if it were important.

Tucker kept walking.

Lissa tried to catch Evan's eye as they got into the truck, but he wouldn't look at her. He never liked it when she and Tucker squabbled like children.

"You'd think someone from the media would be here," Lissa said.

"Maybe we got lucky," Evan said.

"Why?" Tucker glared at Lissa. "Because I'm a psycho?"

"I never said that, Tucker."

"You might as well have."

"Don't make this about me. Okay? Tell me why the police are talking to you about this."

"Because—" Tucker broke off, and Lissa heard him sigh as if he was reluctant but knew he wouldn't get away without answering.

Evan glanced at him in the rearview mirror.

Tucker said, "I was with Chantelle the Saturday night before she disappeared, okay? I was the last person to be seen with her alive, according to the cops."

"Chantelle?" Evan said.

"I thought you were in Austin," Lissa said at the same time. "I thought you said you hardly knew her."

"Chantelle is Jessica's—it was Jessica's stage name." Tucker tapped Evan's shoulder. "Dude, you should have seen the deck on her."

"Tucker!" Lissa turned around as far as the seat belt would allow. "Please tell me you didn't lie to me."

"I didn't. There was a party, okay? In Galveston. Before I went to Austin, I went down there with this other dude, and that's where I hooked up with Chantelle. I didn't want to tell you because you'd just give me shit about her."

"What other dude?" Lissa asked.

"Hooked up how?" Evan asked.

"Have y'all been home? I bet Pop is beyond pissed."

"Tucker, come on! This is serious." Lissa hit the seatback with the heel of her hand. "There's more to it than the fact you were with her, isn't there? Isn't there?" She insisted, because she could feel it. "Tell me," she demanded.

"Okay, okay. Chantelle was into some kind of bad shit."

"What do you mean exactly?" Evan looked in the rearview at Tucker again.

Lissa stifled an impulse to cover her ears.

"She did stuff just for kicks, like once she robbed a liquor store to see if she could get away with it."

"And you were dating her." Lissa didn't bother hiding her disgust.

"It wasn't dating, really. I just missed Miranda so damn much. Chantelle loved her, too. We helped each other."

Lissa might have scoffed at that, but Evan cut her off, and it was just as well, she thought.

"The stuff she did," Evan said, "you think there might be somebody who had it in for her, maybe bad enough to kill her?"

"It's possible. She was hooking—"

"As in prostitution?" Evan asked.

"Prostitution!" Lissa was stunned, but then she wondered why.

"Miranda never went that far. I know how it looks—you probably don't believe me, but just because you work for an escort service doesn't mean you're turning tricks. I tried to tell Jessica she was playing with fire. Looks like she got burned."

"Oh, Tucker." Lissa rested her head against the seatback. She had no idea what else to say. They passed several miles in silence.

Tucker broke it. "Bad thing is they got my DNA, got my prints, the works."

Lissa whipped around, finding his gaze, even in the dark. "You let them? Why? Why didn't you tell them you wanted a lawyer? God, Tucker! Didn't you learn anything last time?"

"It would have looked bad if I didn't cooperate."

Evan asked, "Are you saying you had sex with Jess—Chantelle, whatever her name is . . . was? They'll get a match?"

"They could, I guess, but one of the cops who ID'd her body works security part-time at Mystique. He knows Jessica and I hung around a lot together. You know the guy, Liss. Sonny Cade? I think he was in your class at Hardys Walk High, wasn't he?"

"I remember him, but he was a couple of years behind me. He was kind of a thug, always in trouble. He's a policeman now?"

"Yep. He's still a tough guy, but he's sharp. Runs his own security firm on the side. He knows a lot about the shit that goes on at the club."

Lissa and Evan exchanged a glance, and Lissa knew they were sharing the same sinking sensation of dread.

Tucker touched her shoulder and said he was sorry, and when she didn't respond, he settled back, but she was aware of him, of his distress, all the same. She knew his remorse was as real and true as her frustration. But he never changed; he just kept on making the same mistakes, again and again.

"Come on, Liss, it's going to be fine. Don't worry."

How? she wondered. But she didn't ask. She doubted he had an answer, or if he did, it would be one he'd invented, to placate her.

"I wish you guys had been with us in Austin." Tucker bent forward. "You would have loved it. That band I was telling you about? I knew the bass player. Me and the dude I was with—"

"What dude?" Lissa asked again.

"You don't know him," Tucker said. "The cool thing was we hooked up with these chicks, and we're sitting there in the club—we got, like, this whole backstage vibe going on, because of me. Because I knew the drummer and the bass player. The chicks were into it. It was great."

Lissa caught the flash of Tucker's teeth in the road light and knew he was grinning.

"What can I say?" he asked, having fun with it. "The women love me."

"Jesus, Tuck." Evan shook his head.

"Sorry."

For several moments there was only the sound of the tires, the hum of the truck's engine. The cab was washed in a dirty swirl of road light.

Tucker bent forward, touching Lissa's shoulder. "Look, all B.S. aside, I'm really sick about this. Underneath all that crazy shit, Chantelle was a nice girl. Not in the same class as Miranda, but she could have been if she hadn't gotten messed up on coke and meth. I was trying to help her."

"Oh, Tucker, when are you ever going to learn? Women like that don't want to be helped."

"Nobody deserves to die the way she did, Liss. To get killed and tossed into the woods like a sack of trash. I wish I'd been with her. I wish we hadn't gotten so pissed off with each other."

"What do you mean pissed off?" Evan asked.

"It was nothing, really. We had a—a discussion, you know?"

"A fight, you mean," Lissa said.

"That's why I left the party," Tucker said. "I'm sorry as shit now." His voice wobbled, and Lissa felt her own tears rise in her throat.

"Was Todd Hite there? Did he know Jessica?" Evan asked. "Could she have been involved with him the way Miranda was?"

Lissa turned to Evan. "Oh, my God," she

murmured. It had been a while since she'd thought of him. Todd Hite had been the other person of interest in Miranda's murder case besides Tucker —someone else's brother, son, uncle, source for heartbreak. Lissa had been convinced Todd was guilty. The whole family had thought so. Todd Hite was—or he had been—a stockbroker until a police undercover operation exposed him as the ringleader of a white-collar gang, composed mostly of his clients, who were involved in everything from money laundering and drugs to prostitution. Somehow, because Miranda attended several of the gang functions as an escort, Todd got the idea she was a police informant. He was overheard threatening her life. A month later she was dead.

"Why are you asking about him?" Tucker sounded wary.

Lissa knotted her hands.

"Because, he blamed Miranda when he got arrested, remember?" Evan said. "He accused her of ratting him out. He got fired because of her. He was pretty pissed off. Maybe it was the same with Jessica."

"Hite's full of shit."

"You don't think Miranda or Jessica were working with the cops?" asked Evan.

"Hell, no. Miranda would have told me," Tucker said. "Look, there were a lot of people at the party in Galveston. A lot of guys. Hite could have been there, I guess, but I doubt it." He

71

sounded forlorn now. Pressing his palms together, he knifed his hands between his knees. "God-damn it, I do not want to see Pop. Do you guys?"

"We could get something to eat," Lissa said. She wasn't hungry, but she didn't want to face their folks, either.

"I could go for a burger." Evan pulled into the parking lot of Ace's Grill, a diner and pool hall near Lissa's parents' house, and while Evan and Tucker went inside to order their hamburgers and beers, Lissa called home. She was relieved it was her mom, not her dad, who answered, even though she had to reassure her mother a dozen times that Tucker was fine, everybody was fine.

"We're just getting a hamburger, Mom," Lissa said.

"I roasted two chickens," Lissa's mother said. "There's plenty for everyone."

"Oh, I'm sorry. We didn't know. The guys are already inside ordering. Will it keep until tomorrow?"

Her mother said she imagined it would get eaten one way or another. She said, "You're sure Tucker's okay now, he's in the clear?"

Lissa said she hoped so. She said they'd be there within the hour.

Tucker and Evan were already eating when she joined them. She unwrapped her burger.

"Your folks okay?" Evan asked.

"Mom made dinner for everyone," Lissa said.

"Uh-oh. Should have known." Tucker took a swallow of his beer. "Is she mad?"

"No. You'll have it for lunch tomorrow." Lissa set down her burger; she wiped her fingers on her napkin. "Listen, Tucker, about this morning, at the house, I didn't mean anything."

"I know. It's all right," he said, but he wouldn't look at her.

"It isn't that I don't believe in you."

Now he met her eyes. "I said I know."

Lissa held his glance a moment, then picked up her burger again. "Where did you go, anyway, after you left? Where did the police find you?"

"Morgan's apartment. I was taking her car back to her. They got me in the parking lot there."

"Who's Morgan?" Evan asked.

"There wasn't any reason not to go with them," Tucker said, as if he hadn't heard Evan, or maybe, Lissa thought, Tucker was ignoring him. Maybe, for once, he was embarrassed to admit he'd been picked up by yet one more woman, a total stranger, and spent the night with her, in her bed.

"I don't understand why you would talk to them, though, without a lawyer, Tuck." Lissa rewrapped her burger. She couldn't finish it, or her French fries, or her beer.

"You're done?" Evan asked. "Was it bad?"

"No, it's fine. My head hurts, is all."

"It's hurting all the time lately," Tucker said.

"Too much of the time." Evan wiped his mouth, wadded his paper napkin and tossed it into his empty burger basket. "Do I have to make an appointment with Dr. White, or will you?"

"If you don't do it, Liss, I will," Tucker said. "You can't whip up on us both."

She dipped her glance; she didn't want them to see that she was afraid.

Their mother wasn't more than a silhouette, a dark sketch under the porch light, when they pulled up in front of the house. Still, it seemed to Lissa that she could feel the worry rising off her in waves, or maybe she was conditioned to expect it from long experience. She wondered how many hours her mother had logged on the porch, looking up and down the street for Tucker, consumed with anxiety for him, praying for any sign. Lissa had done time on the porch, too. Hard scary time. She could name the day it started, the first time Tucker disappeared. It had been the week after they were to have celebrated his fourth birthday.

Dad hired a circus clown for the occasion. He bought a movie camera. Unable to sit still, Lissa's mother dropped her at a friend's house to play. Lissa ended up spending the night there, and the following day when her mother picked her up, she wasn't the same. Nothing was. She tried to explain it, how Daddy's mind broke from all the terrible things he went through during the war, and somehow this made him lock Tucker in a closet. She said she needed Lissa to be very brave, because Daddy was gone for a while to the hospital, and Tucker was still so badly frightened, he wasn't talking. Lissa remembered her own panic. She remembered Tucker's hollow stare and the grim set of her mother's mouth.

She remembered the day a week after her father left when she walked out onto the front porch, hunting for Tucker, anxious about him and her parents, her dad's absence, her mother's and Tucker's terrible quiet. She expected to see her little brother playing in the yard, but instead, she saw the front gate hanging open, idly squeaking on its hinges, and beyond it, nothing.

A white aching space.

As if along with Tucker the whole world had vanished. The police were called in, and they found him just after nightfall, after everyone was good and scared, none the worse for his adventure, in a ravine nearly a mile from their house. The story he told was that he'd been trying to catch a dog, a little puppy. He said he followed it because it looked so sad and lost, and he wanted to bring it home and take care of it.

Lissa remembered Tucker hiding from their dad on his return from the hospital weeks later. Even though he was calmer and seemed to keep a better grip on his temper, it took Tucker a long time to warm up to him again. Thinking back now, Lissa didn't remember the movie camera ever making it out of the box. It was probably packed away somewhere along with Momma's habit of humming and Dad's laughter, which was rare even then.

She didn't know exactly, because even as a child she'd been reluctant to ask, to talk about her dad's absence at all. She had always thought there was more to it; she still did.

Evan took her hand, and they followed Tucker up the sidewalk.

Their mother came to the top of the steps. Tucker joined her, and she took hold of him, bending her forehead to his chest. She wasn't crying, but she was close to it, and Lissa was glad when Tucker slipped his arms around her.

"Come on, Ma. It's nothing," he said. "It's over."

"Are you sure?" She tilted her gaze to look at him.

"They wanted to ask me some questions, that's all."

"You didn't know her, then? Jessica Sweet? You told the police you didn't?"

Lissa's heart sank. She ought to have warned her mother, but there hadn't been time, and truthfully she hadn't wanted to. "Mom? I think he's going to need a lawyer."

"No, I told you—"

"You talked to the police without an attorney, Tucker. They know you had a relationship with Jessica. Nothing's over. When they find her killer, then it will be over."

6

Tucker said Lissa was making too much of it, that it was no big deal. This time he had an alibi—witnesses, receipts, proof that he was nowhere near here when Jessica Sweet was killed and dumped in the woods. Emily wanted to believe him; she did believe him. She gathered herself. "I baked a cake," she said.

Tucker grinned his foolish puppy grin. "Chocolate?"

She nodded, patting his cheeks, happy to have him home, to have her family together. She didn't miss Lissa's sigh of exasperation but chose to ignore it. "Why don't we all go inside?"

Lissa asked for a rain check. "I'm worn out, and Evan and I have an early day—"

When she broke off, Emily didn't have to turn around to know that Roy was standing in the doorway. She froze. She had tried talking to him at dinner, forcing herself to say Joe's name. She had said, "Please, let me explain," but Roy answered there wasn't a need, and his voice had been low with hurt. She had no idea what he thought he knew, or where he could have gotten his information, if he had any, and she was beside herself with the worry of it. But there was no way they could pursue it now, in front of the

77

children. She hugged her arms around herself.

Tucker lifted his cap, whipped it once, then again, against his leg, saying nothing.

The silence thickened. Someone in the neighborhood called for their dog and now the night breeze carried the sound of a train whistle from the edge of town.

"Roy?" Emily lifted her voice. "I was just saying we should all come inside and have some cake." She paused, and when he didn't answer, she turned to him, and she was relieved and not a little amazed when he didn't argue, when instead, he backed out of the doorway, leaving it open. Gesturing at Tucker and Lissa and Evan, she followed Roy down the front hall and into the kitchen. The cake was centered on the table, underneath a glass cake dome. It had turned out beautifully, and Emily was glad she hadn't abandoned making it.

"Mmm, looks yummy." Lissa opened a cabinet and lifted down five dessert plates.

"I hope it's not too dry." Emily gathered forks and napkins, taking a moment to circle Lissa's waist as a way of thanking her for staying, for being amenable.

Lissa tipped her head to Emily's. They were often the peacemakers, the buffer between Roy and Tucker.

"Is coffee all right? There are soft drinks and milk." Emily looked around at the men, and she thought it wasn't only Roy who was humoring her. Every one of them was. Even Lissa was likely wondering if Emily truly believed she could serve them slices of cake like doses of medicine and somehow defuse the tension. She knew better, of course. But she wanted her family to see that regardless of the circumstances they could still come together, just as they had in the past, to share in the sweetness of dessert.

When everyone was seated, she said they should join hands. It seemed important to offer a blessing. "Roy, would you do the honors?" she asked, and her heart almost broke with love and gratitude when he bowed his head, and taking Tucker's hand in his left and Lissa's hand in his right, he thanked God for them and for Evan, and for the cake, and Emily, who baked it.

After they said their amens, she squeezed Tucker's opposite hand. "Thank you, God, too, that our son is home safe." She smiled at him.

He kept her glance and her hand, and there was something wounded and fraught caging the shadows of his eyes. Some quality or essence had come over him—was it despair? Remorse? She didn't know, had never seen it before.

"I've been a bastard," he said.

Emily frowned.

"I'm sorry," Tucker said.

"It's all right, honey," Emily said, but panic knotted her stomach.

"It isn't all right," he insisted. "It hasn't been right—*I* haven't been right, not for a long time."

"What do you mean, Tucker?" Lissa asked the question Emily couldn't find breath for.

"I didn't murder Jessica Sweet." Tucker looked hard at Lissa. "Or Miranda. I tried telling you earlier, Liss. The cops can dog me into hell, and they probably will, but they've got it wrong."

"If they're so goddamn wrong," Roy said, "why do they keep coming after you?"

Emily tensed, waiting for Tucker to say something ugly; she waited to hear the scrape of his chair, the clatter of his plate when he dumped it into the sink. She waited for him to walk out in a huff, or walk out yelling. But for what seemed an eternal moment there was nothing.

And then Tucker said, "I want to come back to work."

Emily looked at Tucker in astonishment.

But he had eyes only for his father. "I'll do whatever it takes, Pop. You can cut my salary, put me on any kind of job. I don't care. I just want a chance to make it up to you, to get it right."

A tremor rocked Tucker's voice, stalling Emily's heart.

"I meant what I said before," he went on, "about being a bastard. I'm sick of myself. Sick of living this way. Sick of being so fucked up— Sorry, Mom. There's no reason you should believe me, but I swear this time it's different. If you could just let me try—if you could just give me one more shot."

Roy drew his napkin from his lap. "The only job we've got going on is Pecan Grove, and Pederson's made it clear if he sees you out at the site, he'll quit. We can't afford to lose him. I think your sister and Evan would agree."

"Maybe if we talked to him," Evan said.

"If we reassure him he won't have to work directly with Tuck again," Lissa said. "Either Evan or I can meet with Carl from now on."

Emily clenched her fists, willing Roy to see the possibility.

He didn't. "That's not going to fly," he said. "If he even sees Tucker out there, he says he's done. I had to tack five percent onto his original bid to get him to stay as it is."

"Dad!" Lissa protested. "We're already upside down on that job."

"Yeah, well, do you think losing Pederson is going to put us right side up?"

"Look," Evan said, "we could use Tucker's help out at our place, right, Lissa? He could lay the floor in your art studio, for one thing."

"That would be great," Lissa said. "I'm dying to have a real place where I can paint again."

Evan found Tucker's gaze. "We can't pay you much."

"I don't want any pay. I'll just be glad for a job, the chance to show everyone I mean what I say."

"It's a deal, then," Evan said. "You want to start tomorrow?"

"Is eight o'clock too early?" Tucker said, sounding as eager as a child.

Evan laughed, and Lissa said it was fine. She said, "The floor tile for the studio is at the office," and a discussion ensued among the three of them about the logistics of transporting it to the house.

Emily looked at Roy when he shifted his fork from one side of his plate to the other, the noise drawing her attention. She knew what he was thinking, that this was another of Tucker's empty promises. He would say people don't change, that they were incapable of it. She didn't know how much he based his opinion on his own experience, the ongoing war he waged with his own demons. She didn't hold his gaze when their eyes met. She couldn't. She was too afraid of what she might reveal. Why hadn't she told him immediately when Tucker was arrested last fall? A confession now would sound so much worse. She stood up, and began stacking plates, pausing when Evan mentioned the lake house.

"I think I know how we can engineer the deck off the master bedroom to extend over the water the way you want it to," he told Roy. "If you've got a set of plans here, I can show you."

Emily exchanged a wondering glance with Lissa, who shrugged.

Catching them at it, Evan grinned. "Roy did say he wanted to be able to fish from bed."

"Please tell me that's a joke," Emily said, feeling a warm surge of delight mixed with relief. Suppose Evan could convince Roy to take up his project again? Suppose Tucker did even half of what he promised? Suppose he was right and the police were finished with him? Suppose her worry over what Roy might or might not know about Joe Merchant was needless? Then life might be as it had once been. She wondered if she was asking for too much.

Tucker said the house plans were upstairs, that he'd get them.

Lissa stored the leftover cake.

Emily carried the dishes to the sink. "I don't have a clue how Evan can fix the problem with the deck, but I'll be beyond ecstatic if he can get your dad back to work on that house."

"Me, too. Evan's as worried as we are about him. He thinks Daddy's in a lot more pain than he's letting on."

"He is, but we both know how he feels about seeing a doctor. He won't even let Dr. White look at him."

"If only Tucker would get his act together, that would help."

"Maybe he will this time. I've never heard him sound quite so—" Emily paused, hunting for the right word.

"Committed? Contrite?" Lissa supplied two. She dampened a dishcloth and wiped the countertop. "He has to grow up sometime."

Emily opened the dishwasher. "He said he has receipts, proving he was in Austin over the weekend when Jessica was murdered. Did he give them to the police, do you know?"

"They're in his glove box. He has to get his car back first."

"That should take care of it, right?"

"Maybe, but you know, if it doesn't, if the police insist on pursuing him, we'll have to get a lawyer."

Emily wouldn't say it aloud; she didn't want Lissa to worry, but she wondered where the money to pay a lawyer would come from. She wondered why the police focus on Tucker continued. It was as if they wanted him to be guilty. A year ago, when the police fixated on him, the media raised the outrageous possibility that whoever killed Miranda had likely killed the other two victims who'd been found at the same location in previous years.

More than one reporter speculated that the I-45 serial killer had moved his base of operations from the Galveston area north, seventy or so miles, to the piney woods. They associated the location with Tucker's home—her home—by describing it as "near where Tucker Lebay, a person of interest in the murder of Miranda Quick, lives."

It horrified Emily, the very idea that her son's name was forever linked in some people's minds to such brutal crimes. And it was complete insanity, anyway. The math didn't work. Tucker wasn't old enough to have committed the first two murders. He wasn't capable of such violence in any case. These crimes were the work of a monster, one who was still out there, still on the loose, which could only mean more women would disappear, more bodies would be found. And more families, good families, like the Quicks, would suffer heartbreak and loss, while the police wasted time hounding Tucker, while they drove him even further back into the black cave of his unhappiness and frustration.

Lissa came to stand beside her.

"I wish Tucker could be more like Evan." Emily was sorry even as she said it. Even as she felt Lissa's arm slip around her waist, the surge of her love was tainted with regret. She shouldn't compare them, these three who would always be children to her.

She had mothered Evan, too, the same as Lissa and Tucker, ever since Roy gave Evan a job when he was barely seventeen, nothing more than a scrawny boy. As a nine-year-old, Tucker almost instantly idolized Evan. But even Lissa, at thirteen, was drawn to him, although she had pretended the opposite. Still, the seed of their attraction for each other had been visible from the beginning. Tucker's admiration was less self-conscious. So often when he needed someone strong, when he needed a sure and steady guide, Evan was there.

He possessed every admirable trait a parent could want in a son, despite his own complicated upbringing, which involved a father who'd walked out and a mother who was indifferent. Emily would never understand it. Evan's parents were so careless with him, and yet, he never caused them, or anyone, one moment's worth of worry or doubt.

"Some people seem to lead a charmed life, while others struggle," she said now, and there was a bite in her voice that was unintentional, and she rued it.

Lissa moved away. "Evan hasn't led a charmed life, and neither have I. Tucker has the same opportunity as anyone to make better choices. Not even Daddy can stop him."

"I didn't mean—"

"I know, Momma. It's okay."

Emily glanced sidelong at her daughter. "I know you've pretty much decided not to have children, but if you were to change your mind and become a mother, you'd understand. There's just this drive to protect, especially when your child is—" Emily shrugged. She didn't want to say *impulsive* or *high strung,* or *oversensitive* or—she didn't know. Just hardwired, differently, in some nameless, unfathomable way.

● ● ●

Lissa and Evan had left, and Roy had gone upstairs to bed, when Tucker found Emily, as she had hoped he would, outside on the porch, tucked into a corner of the swing.

He sat down beside her. "What are you doing out here? It's cold."

"I think that woman is calling your dad," Emily said without preamble.

"What woman?" Tucker asked, as if he didn't know.

"The one who had you arrested for stalking her last fall," Emily answered shortly. "Revel Wiley."

"What makes you think—?"

"I've been getting calls on my cell phone from her number, and I've ignored them. Now, in the past few days, the same number has started coming up on the landline caller ID. When I answer, she hangs up. But if your dad answers, he talks away. He's acted odd when I ask about it. I'm afraid it's her, that she's stirring up trouble again." Emily couldn't keep the edge from her voice. "Every time I think how you involved me in that mess, Tucker, I'm angry all over again. I wish you hadn't put me in the middle of it."

"I'm sorry, Mom. I didn't know who else to call."

"I posted your bail. I paid Revel a thousand dollars to drop the stalking charge altogether

87

because you said that would end it. I should have known better."

"I'll talk to her."

"No! For heaven's sake, Tucker, if you can only do one thing for me, please, please promise me you'll stay away from those women, the clubs, that life."

He scrubbed his hands down his thighs, shifted his feet, jarring the swing.

Emily's initial jolt of exasperation was softened by her regret for his inadequacies and his struggles, his aura of unhappiness. It was the constant war of her own emotions that weighed on her, that rendered her nearly useless when it came to making a stand. At one moment she would feel she didn't love Tucker enough, or in the right way, and then at another, she would feel as if she loved him and catered to him too much. She slid her palm over the back of his hand. "You know I want to believe what you said earlier, that you want to change, to take responsibility, but for that to work out, you're going to have to stay away from Miranda's friends—"

"Revel misunderstood me, Mom. I only wanted to help her get out of the business and out of the rat hole she was living in."

"Yes, but she and the rest of those girls aren't your responsibility. You can scarcely take care of yourself."

Even in the half-light, Emily could see his

shoulders sag. She saw his defeat and his aggravation written into the line of his jaw, the crease of his brow. He hitched forward, setting his elbows on his knees. "I'll be up a shit creek with Pop if he finds out."

Emily was worried, too, for the possible consequences, which was why she'd talked to Joe and solicited his help. She felt as though the slightest pressure could send Roy reeling off an edge. A breeze kicked a hash of dried leaves mixed with road grit along the curb, making a ruckus, and she looked in that direction. "He's done so well for so long," she said.

There had been episodes of irrational behavior as the result of lingering post-traumatic stress, but none so terrifying as what occurred on the occasion of Tucker's fourth birthday. That awful day when she left Roy and Tucker napping to run last-minute errands, only to come home and find Tucker locked in a closet, and Roy pacing the house with a loaded gun, drunk, and raving about shelling from the enemy. When she tried to reason with him, he angrily informed her that she was a fucking idiot if she didn't realize they were at war in a country where even the women and children carried weapons. Couldn't she see that he had secured their position to save her and their home? It took every ounce of her strength and diplomacy to convince him to hand over the key to the closet and scoop Tucker, eerily quiet, alarmingly covered in blood, into her arms.

Weary by then, and sobering, Roy slumped to the floor. He allowed her to take the gun, his old Colt service revolver that he'd carried in Vietnam, and to bring Tucker around the corner to Anna's, where they found he was bleeding from a cut on the heel of his bare foot. When Emily asked how he'd gotten hurt, he only stared at her, eyes stunned, uncomprehending. He didn't speak again for six days.

The single saving grace that came out of the whole ordeal was that it frightened Roy badly enough that he finally sought help. It wasn't until after his six-week stay in the VA hospital that Emily found out Tucker inadvertently set off the whole tragic sequence of events when he wakened before Roy and went into the bathroom for a drink. It was the sound of the water glass exploding against the tile floor when it slipped from Tucker's small hand that jerked Roy upright. Caught in the throes of one of his war dreams, the nightmare came with him as he rose, terrified, into an altered reality.

For him the house was a battleground, Tucker the enemy.

To this day, Emily couldn't bear to think what might have happened had she not come home when she did. She would have taken the children and left Roy then, and he knew it. He stopped drinking entirely. He packed away his collection of guns, only getting them out again, years later, when Lissa and Tucker expressed an interest in learning to shoot. As a family, they took every recommended step, and eventually they mended. Normal life resumed.

A new normal, Emily thought now, scarred by a feeling that, as parents, she and Roy had failed Tucker, failed to protect him, to keep him safe. She flattened her palm on his back, remembering the awful days when he hadn't spoken, remembering, too, the sore number of weeks that passed before he would stay even for a moment in the same room with his dad. Tucker's trust had been broken, and it had made her heart ache, watching Roy work to regain it, watching his hope fade a bit more each day that Tucker didn't reach out to him. They hadn't forced it; they'd been advised to give it time. And then one day, Tucker wasn't a little boy anymore, and Emily realized he wouldn't ever reach out to either Roy or her in the way that small children do again. They were out of time.

She rubbed a circle between Tucker's shoulder blades. "Maybe I'm wrong, and it isn't Revel who's calling your dad. She did tell me she was going back to Oklahoma, where her folks live. That's what you wanted, isn't it?" Emily didn't know why she was saying any of this when she knew perfectly well Revel was the caller, and while Revel had made a promise about leaving Texas, Emily had no real hope she'd kept it.

Tucker didn't look as if he believed it, either. He said he didn't really care anymore what Revel did.

"The trouble with people like her is that when you give in to them, it's only the beginning." Emily repeated a line from the lecture Joe had given her when she'd called him for advice after Revel made a second, nerve-jangling demand for more money. He'd gone with her to meet Revel, and flashed his badge at her, warning her not to contact Emily or Tucker again or there would be legal consequences, all of which was completely false. Even Emily knew Joe acted outside his authority. He claimed it was nothing, but Emily was still angry at herself and at Tucker that Joe had put his career in jeopardy for them.

She wanted Tucker to know this, to know the cost of his actions to others.

But neither Tucker, nor Lissa for that matter, knew much about Joe. Emily's friendship with him was hers, her island of peace, the ribbon of sanity she could hold fast to through the hard times, the times of calamity. It didn't diminish her love for Roy; in fact, she thought it might make it possible.

She met Tucker's gaze again. "Let's just hope she's gone, okay?"

Tucker blinked up at the porch ceiling. "Yeah, because I'm dead if Pop finds out about this on top of everything else. He'll never give me another chance."

He sounded so despondent Emily put her hand on his knee. She felt an urgency to ask, to press: *What about Jessica? Who do you think killed her? Will the police be back? What are you going to do with yourself?* She wanted to have it out once and for all, but she knew that nothing with Tucker was ever once and for all.

She surprised herself when she opened her mouth and all that came out was that she hoped he wouldn't leave again. "At least, if you do," she added, "I hope you'll stay in touch. It's scary when you disappear, Tucker."

He said he knew it and promised he'd do better.

"I feel as if our family is falling apart," she said, and she was sorry for it when her voice caught, when tears stung the undersides of her eyelids.

Tucker slipped his arm around her shoulders. "It's not, Mom. We're fine, okay?"

Emily hugged herself. "You mean everything to me, you, Lissa, Evan and Dad."

Tucker tightened his grasp. "I know," he said. "Don't worry. Nothing's going to happen to our family."

Emily felt an urgency to put her arms around him, to gather him into her embrace and hold on to him, but she resisted it, still aggravated and worn out, and even when a small, wise voice in her brain advised her she would regret it, she sat with her arms folded.

7

The next morning when Lissa fainted, it happened suddenly. She sat down on the side of the bed to tie her bootlaces, and the next thing she knew she opened her eyes to find herself lying facedown on the floor. It took her a few moments to realize that she had passed out—for the second time in as many weeks. She rose slowly onto her knees, blood throbbing on the right side of her face, black dots eating the margins of her vision. She was thankful she was alone. Evan had left for work, and Tucker wasn't coming by with the floor tile until later.

Checking the clock, she didn't think she'd been out long, less than a minute, she guessed. Still, it wasn't as easy to ignore this time. If Evan were here, he'd probably take her to the emergency room, and maybe he'd be right. Using the mattress, she levered herself to her feet and went into the bathroom. The pain in her head was hot and searing, and she fumbled through the contents of the medicine cabinet, finally finding the Advil, helping herself to three.

Cathy, the receptionist at Dr. White's office, was new and seemed only superficially interested when Lissa explained she'd been a patient from the time she was six and that she was suffering recently from continual headaches. It wasn't until she mentioned fainting dead away that Cathy perked up.

"When?" she asked.

"A little while ago. It wasn't for long, and I feel okay now. Maybe a bit woozy, but I haven't had anything to eat yet." Not since the cake last night, Lissa thought, which, unlike the hamburger and fries, she had managed to get down for her mother's sake.

"Is this the first time?"

"No," Lissa said. "It happened one other time, week before last. It was nearly the same experience. I got out of bed and keeled over. My husband was with me. He said I wasn't out more than a minute."

"Can you come in later this morning? Say around 10:45?"

Lissa said she would be there.

Evan was already out at the site when she called to say she'd scheduled the appointment. She didn't mention that she'd passed out again. He'd only worry, and she might as well wait until she knew something definite. "I'm going to come in to the office, but I have an errand to run first, if you won't miss me for another half hour or so."

"I always miss you, babe," he said.

"Uh-oh. What did you do?" she teased.

He laughed. "I'm just glad you made the appointment. Tucker and I had a plan to drag you there if you didn't."

"Not necessary."

"What's the errand?"

"Diane Merrill called and asked me to drop by." It wasn't implausible as invented stories go. Lebay-Winter was building Diane and Doug Merrill's house, and the Merrill's were also friends. Diane was a close enough friend that she would cover for Lissa if she asked.

"Is there a problem?" Evan asked.

"No, I don't think so. They got the tub install done yesterday. She wants me to look at it." Lissa bit her lip; she hated lying, but Evan would argue if she told him the truth.

"Why? Because it's butt ugly?"

Lissa laughed. "I guess that means you aren't going to be happy when I tell you I ordered one just like it for our bathroom. Black porcelain with gold fixtures. I'm thinking of repainting the walls, too. A nice dark shade of red? What do you think?"

"You're a funny girl," Evan said. "Tell Diane hi for me. Maybe she and Doug will want to get together later this week. We could grill steaks or something."

"I'll ask," Lissa promised, but by the time she got into her truck she'd forgotten all about the Merrills. She didn't give much of a thought to whether or not she ought to be driving, either. She felt fine; she would be fine, she had to be.

• • •

At the Lincoln County sheriff's office, when Lissa said who she was and that she was there to talk to Detective Sergeant Garza about her brother, Tucker Lebay, the duty officer, a woman this morning, picked up her phone and spoke to someone—Garza, Lissa guessed—and then said Lissa should follow her. They went through the door behind the duty desk into a cavernous room crammed with an assortment of battle-scarred desks. A row of tall, metal filing cabinets was pushed against a far wall, blocking most of the natural light that came through the only windows.

Phones rang in discordant harmony. Overhead, wire cages housed light fixtures that buzzed and sputtered.

The room smelled vaguely of mold and sweat, of burned coffee and stale fast food, with an undercoating of fear, of boredom and hopelessness. Lissa's pulse hammered in her ears. She wondered how anyone could stand working here, day after day, up to their neck in other people's despair.

Garza walked out of a cubicle in one corner to meet them, and the duty officer muttered something unintelligible, and left.

"What can I do for you this morning, Mrs. DiCapua?" Garza dropped into her desk chair.

Lissa perched on the edge of the only other

chair, a wood-seated relic that looked as if it had come out of the schoolroom. "I came to talk to you about my brother."

Garza sat back and crossed her arms. She was dressed again in gray, a suit jacket over a starched white oxford shirt. Her chin-length dark hair was neatly tucked behind her ears. Besides the skirt and low heels, the only concession to her sex was her lipstick, a shade of deep red-brown, the color of mahogany.

"I don't want to cause trouble for Tucker." Lissa kept Garza's gaze, trying to get a read on her mood, but the detective was as inscrutable this morning as she had been yesterday. Lissa had no clue how to play this, how to get across what she needed to, whether she even could.

"You and your brother are close?"

"He's a good guy. But sometimes he doesn't exercise the best judgment."

"How do you mean?"

"I didn't really come here to talk about him."

"But you just said—"

"I know." Lissa touched her right temple; the pain was centered there and fanned out behind her eyes. Her mouth felt dry. She wondered about asking for some water. Suppose she passed out again? Suddenly, she didn't know why she had come, what she hoped to accomplish. "I didn't know Jessica, but I knew Miranda, and I just wanted you to know that Tucker really loved her.

He wouldn't have hurt her. I thought maybe he didn't explain it."

"Were you and Ms. Quick friends? Did she confide in you?"

"Not friends exactly. We lived in the same neighborhood, but she was younger, Tucker's age. My parents know her parents, though. When she and Tucker were in high school, Miranda was at our house a lot. Her folks still live a couple of streets over from ours, but you must know that."

"Did she ever mention a man named Todd Hite to you? Did she ever say he threatened her?"

"You're talking about the stockbroker. He did threaten her. It was in the paper. They quoted him, saying something like, 'I'm going to get that bitch,' only the word *bitch* was edited out. He thought she cost him his job and his broker's license, that's what the article in the paper said. But he was just blowing off steam, wasn't he? Isn't that what the police said? Isn't that why you people cleared him?"

"We haven't cleared anyone." Garza's gaze was penetrating. "Were you aware that Ms. Quick was working with us at the time on that case, involving Mr. Hite?"

"Really?" Lissa was taken aback. She said, "I heard that, but I—" She faltered to a stop. She couldn't imagine Miranda in the role of an infiltrator.

"You didn't know." The tilt of Garza's head, her narrowed eyes, suggested disbelief.

"No, it's hard to believe."

"What about your brother? Did he know?"

"When we talked about it he—" Lissa broke off, feeling set upon, somehow under fire. She had a sense there was some game being played, but only Garza knew the rules. She decided to turn the tables. "Was Todd Hite involved with Jessica?" she asked. "Is he a suspect now, in her murder, too?"

Garza bent forward, leaning her weight on her elbows. "These women were strangled, Mrs. DiCapua. Do you know what the experts say about strangulation? That there's a sexual element to it. It's a very personal way to kill someone."

"So it's true what they said on television. Jessica was strangled the same as Miranda." Lissa straightened.

"Mr. Lebay's relationships with these women were sexual, right? You would characterize them as personal, wouldn't you?"

"What are you getting at?"

The detective waved her hand as if her meaning was of no consequence. "Your brother— So far he seems unable to account for his whereabouts on either occasion when these women were murdered."

"He was in Austin when Jessica was killed. He has receipts."

"Really? He didn't mention those. Have you seen them?"

She hadn't, she realized, but that didn't concern her as much as the fact that Tucker hadn't mentioned them last night when Detective Garza questioned him. "He was probably so stressed he forgot to tell you." It was the only explanation she could think that made any sense. "But he has them," she added.

"So he was in Austin when Ms. Sweet was murdered and in Dallas when Ms. Quick was murdered, but he's got no witnesses. No one can vouch for him. And so far it appears he was the last person to see either of these women alive."

"Have you questioned the band members he was with in Austin this past weekend?"

"We will if we can find them."

"What do you mean? He's given you their names and their phone numbers. Maybe I should contact them myself."

"I would advise against that. Leave the investigating to the professionals—"

"My brother didn't hurt these women, Detective." Lissa persisted even though a part of her was appalled that she would continue to talk in the face of Garza's apparent circumspection, if not her outright suspicion.

"Do you know that when we asked him if we could get a look inside his car yesterday, he told us it was in the shop for repairs?"

"It is. It broke down on the freeway when he was coming back from Austin."

"You know this for a fact?"

"I know that's what he told me, and I believe him."

"We asked Tucker to bring the car by here when the repairs were done, we'd get a look inside then, but he refused. He told us to get a warrant."

"That is his legal right, isn't it?"

Garza nudged the edge of the desk blotter with a considering fingertip. "We'd like to see a little more cooperation, is all. You can tell him that, if you like."

Lissa stood up, shouldering her purse. "I can see I wasted my time coming here, that you've already made up your mind. But just so you know? If you arrest Tucker, if you so much as bring him in here again, we'll get a lawyer. We're not letting you people grill him for hours on end like you did last time."

"Who said anything about an arrest, Mrs. DiCapua?"

"Thanks for taking the time to talk to me, Detective Sergeant Garza." Lissa headed for the door.

"My pleasure. I appreciate you coming in. Say—"

Lissa paused, turning to face Garza, brows raised.

"One more thing before you go—you don't happen to know where your brother's car was towed, do you?"

"Didn't Tucker give you that information?"

102

"I wondered if *you* knew, Mrs. DiCapua."

"I don't. I'm sorry," she said, and wondered why she apologized.

"Oh, no worries." Garza's smile was still in place, enigmatic, and lasted just enough longer to deepen Lissa's alarm and her regret over the impulse that brought her here.

Garza thanked her for coming. "You be sure and let us know if you think of anything else."

"Oh, you can count on it, Detective. Trust me." Lissa didn't know how, but she managed to keep the agitation she was feeling out of her voice. She managed to sound as if talking to a detective about a murder investigation was normal, one more item to cross off her to-do list. But walking away, her heart slammed against the wall of her chest, and her head filled with a horrible sense that showing up here was the worst mistake she'd ever made. If Tucker did get arrested, it would be her fault.

It would be because she had put the idea into Detective Sergeant Garza's head.

She got into her truck, slammed the door and sat staring through the windshield, feeling blank with disbelief. This couldn't be happening, and yet it was. The police were fixed on Tucker; they had no one else, and they were serious, deadly serious. Unshouldering her purse, Lissa dug out her cell phone. Tucker had mentioned Sonny

103

Cade, that he was a policeman, that he worked at the club. Lissa hadn't really known Sonny in school; he'd been two years behind her. But Sonny knew Tucker. Maybe there was something he could do. She didn't know what exactly. Turning on her phone, she did a Google search for his name.

She remembered him having a reputation as a troublemaker in school, always in detention for fighting, for mouthing off. She remembered him having the face of a crow with a long beak of a nose and small, glossy black eyes set close on either side of it. He'd combed his dark hair back from his forehead, making a sleek, shiny cap. She imagined he would end up in prison, but the last she heard, he enlisted in the army and served two tours of duty in Afghanistan, or somewhere like that, overseas. It must have turned his life around, she thought, because here it was, an article from a few years ago all about his military career, and alongside it was a photograph of him, wearing a Houston police officer's uniform. The article said nothing about a second career, working security at La Femme Mystique, nor did it give a hint about how she might reach him.

She continued scrolling through the search results, and her heart rose when she saw it, the bold line of text that read Security Firm Opens, Hardys Walk, TX. Clicking on the link, she read the short announcement. Sonny's name was there along with the contact information for the firm, and even as Lissa programmed it into her cell phone, the prospect of speaking to him loosened a bolus of panic from the floor of her stomach. It wasn't as if they would be sitting around revisiting their glory days. For all she knew, he wouldn't talk to her at all.

Pulse tapping, she went back to the news article and studied his photograph. His eyes were still set close together and the look in them was still mean. He was bigger than she remembered. She couldn't imagine approaching him, much less asking him for— What exactly? *He knows Jessica and I hung around a lot together. Knows a lot about the shit that goes on at the club.* What Tucker said about Sonny went through Lissa's mind. What else could Sonny know? She glanced up, her stare drifting.

Working security he would see a lot; he would see the men who frequented the club. He would know the troublemakers, the ones who might have given Jessica Sweet a hard time, the ones who would be capable of hurting her. Garza had warned Lissa to stay out of it, to let the professionals handle things. But how could she when Tucker was in so much trouble, when even his life could be at stake? How did Garza's warning or her fears compare to that?

Lissa stowed her phone in her purse. If she didn't hurry, she'd be late for her appointment with Dr. White.

8

The instant Emily wakened, she was aware that every fine hair on her body was standing on end. Roy's presence was tangible; she could feel him towering over her, willing her to open her eyes, but she didn't. She feigned sleep, buying time, trying to discern his mood from the rasp of his breath, the hesitant scrape of his steps as he gave up on her and walked away. The snick of the bathroom door when it closed behind him was soft.

It was automatic, this daily mapping of Roy's emotions. It wasn't any use resenting it, but today she did. Today it aggravated her.

Her mother had predicted it, that Roy would make Emily unhappy. But she would have said anything, done anything, to prevent Emily from marrying Roy. And the more she worked against the idea, the harder Emily fought her. He wasn't their kind, her mother said. "You have no idea what you're getting yourself into," she warned.

Emily had so wanted her mother to stop her constant diatribe. She'd felt sick enough over her suspicion that she wasn't really in love with Roy. At least, not the kind of love you're supposed to be in when you agree to marry someone. It took Roy being half the world away for her to discern the truth of her feelings, and it seemed so natural when her heart's path found its way with Joe.

Emily was drawn to him from their first encounter. There was something in his gaze, a gentle intensity that made her feel she was important to him, as if he valued what she had to say. The first time she gave herself to him was after they shared a picnic on a remote beach in Galveston Bay. As they sat listening to the ocean's hushing whisper, she became chilled in the cooler evening air, and Joe brought a blanket from the trunk of his car and covered them both. She remembered lying back in his arms, the night sky flung like a lush, velvet cape overhead, a jeweled rain of glimmering stars, falling all around them.

She didn't suffer a moment's regret for their intimacy. Some soul-deep intuition told her Joe was her man; he was the one for her, and she would have followed her instinct without hesitation if Roy had come home safe and in one piece. She would have suffered her mother's gloating gladly. But Roy didn't come home in one piece. He was horribly wounded, inside and out. The loss of his leg cost him almost everything. His dreams were in shreds. He would never be the man he'd planned to be, and Emily couldn't bear to hurt him more. It wasn't in her.

She grew to love Roy in her way. And Joe married someone else, too, a woman with whom Emily thought he'd been very happy until her death from ovarian cancer six months ago. They had no children. Emily never asked Joe why. On the rare occasions they met, they almost never discussed their personal lives. Outside of Tucker.

"I don't want Tucker living here anymore, Emily." Roy's voice above her was low. "I don't believe any of his bullshit about wanting to change. He's only saying what he thinks we want to hear."

She opened her eyes. "He's our son," she said.

"He's a grown man. We've done all we can for him."

"He just needs a little more time, Roy." Emily was unflinching now. But so was he. She saw the flint edge of his will that hardened his expression. She saw his pain, too, that was never better, fighting in the shadows of his eyes, and it broke her heart. It always broke her heart.

"If we don't cut him loose, he'll end up taking us down, too," he said.

She shook her head. Anxiety was like a snake uncoiling, racing through her mind, looking for a gap, a way out.

"You wouldn't keep a dog you couldn't trust in your house, would you? You would put that dog down."

Her eyes widened. "My God, Roy!" She sat up, flinging aside the bedcovers. "What a thing to say!"

He left her, rounding the foot of the bed,

disappearing into the closet. She heard the sounds as he pulled on a shirt, buckled his belt. "I'm going out to the lake house," he said when he reappeared.

"Really?"

"Evan's idea about how we can build the deck over the water might just work. I want to check it out."

Roy sounded inspired. Evan's strategy had worked, Emily thought, and she wanted to give in to the pleasure it would be to watch Roy take up his pet project again. If circumstances had been other than what they were, she might have asked him whether he planned to finish the house. She might even have offered to go with him, but he had aggravated her with his talk about Tucker moving out. If only he would finish the damn house. He could move into it then, she thought. Alone, for all she cared. It was what he wanted, wasn't it? To be rid of them all? She settled her breath and said she would make his breakfast.

The mattress sagged as he sat beside her on the bed. He trailed the tips of his fingers across her cheek, rubbed the pad of his thumb gently across the fullness of her lower lip. "I'll get something on the way," he said. "When Tucker gets up, you tell him to clear out. I want him gone by the time I get home."

"He doesn't even have his car, Roy."

"He said last night it's supposed to be ready

this morning. You can run him over to the shop to get it, then he can be on his way. I mean it, Em."

It's him or me. Emily waited for Roy to say this. But he didn't.

Leaving her, he went to his chest of drawers, pulled out a pair of socks, and sitting again on the end of the bed, he slid one over the metal foot of his prosthesis and the other over his flesh-and-blood foot. Emily watched his shirt shift across his back, and she warmed with her desire for him that like her heartache had never faded. The still-strong, muscled contours of his shoulders and arms, the notched blade of his spine, the narrow plane of his hip—all were a familiar landscape to her after so many years, a territory both loved and despaired over. She felt his power and the power of his anger, and she knew why it was there and the effort it had taken to keep it leashed all these years. He came into her sometimes and he was a battering force, a pounding fury. It was as if he meant to cleave her in two, and afterward, when he was spent, he held her so tenderly, and she would feel his tears against her breast.

They seldom speak of it, his tears, their meaning—those battle-shocked children: his own small son whom Roy himself had terrorized, and that other boy, the one he'd rescued, left behind in another country to who knew what sort of fate.

110

The awful memories are always present, haunting Roy's eyes. Emily could never look at him without seeing them, however unconsciously.

"You'll talk to Tucker?" Roy stood looking down on her.

"We can't just put him out." Emily slid her feet into her slippers, reaching for her robe. "He has no place to go."

"He isn't going to learn any other way. It's called tough love, Em. We should have done it years ago."

"Why can't you give him a chance? Give him the benefit of the doubt?"

"I've done that. I've jumped through hoop after hoop. Now he's back in hot water, and not just some Mickey Mouse bullshit, either, Em. It's murder, for Christ's sake."

"There's no evidence tying Tucker to Jessica," she said. "The police have nothing, just as they had nothing when Miranda was killed. Even Lissa says—"

"He's considered a person of interest. She said that, too."

"But you can't possibly believe—"

"What I believe doesn't matter. The cops have other ideas. I can't go through it again. Can you?"

"What choice is there? He's my son. It's what I have to do."

"Do you remember the last time?" Roy sat down

again, taking her hand in his, looking earnestly at her. "Do you remember how the police and the media came through here and tore the shit out of the neighborhood, parking all over folks' yards and the street? People were pissed. We got a fucking brick tossed through our window. Somebody wrote *murderer* on the garage wall. Do you think they're over it?" Roy didn't wait for her answer. "Hell, no. They want Tucker out of here. They don't care how it happens. If they have to take the law into their own hands, they'll do it."

"Our neighbors aren't like that."

"Hah! Like I've always said, Em, you live in a different world from me. Always seeing the good that isn't there. If we're tolerated, it's because of your family. People around here still respect the Winter name."

She looked at Roy in surprise. She hadn't thought he was aware, or that he cared about her family's name. She had always thought he resented it.

"But even that'll go unless Tucker does, then where do you think we'll be? They'll run us out of the business. Probably run us out of town. I don't like it any better than you, but if we protect him again, we'll lose everything. Is that what you want?" Roy stood up.

Emily studied her hands folded in her lap.

"We have a daughter, too. We have to think of

her and of Evan. You and I aren't the only ones who would be affected. God knows I wish it wasn't true. I wish you and Liss weren't involved in this nightmare. But the cord's got to be cut, Em, if you want to eat, if you want to keep a roof over your head and Lissa's."

She didn't answer.

"It's for Tucker's own good."

"You should believe in him." Emily flung the words at Roy. "You're his father." *You know what you put him through, what he's suffered because of you.* That part of it hung unspoken, but Roy understood her meaning nonetheless. Emily knew, by the way his shoulders dropped, by the way he pinched the bridge of his nose. Rubbing her upper arms, she stared at the floor, feeling anxious and sorry that she had raised the specter of that awful day. She didn't like reminding him, but he had driven her to do it. For several long moments neither of them moved, and then Emily heard the sound of his steps as he left her and the decided click of the door when he closed it behind him.

It wasn't until after she showered and dressed that she found the gun. The toe of her shoe encountered the barrel of the Colt service revolver Roy had brought back from Vietnam when she was straightening the coverlet on his side of the bed. Going to her knees, she lifted the hem of the dust ruffle and picked up the weapon, then gingerly, she stood with it balanced across the cup of her palms. The safety was on, but it was loaded. She could tell by the weight. Still, she checked, carefully lowering the trap door and spinning the cylinder, the way Roy taught her, and then closing it again, she aimed it at her shadow on the opposite wall.

"Bang, you're dead," she said.

She waited until Roy left to call Joe, and hearing his voice, hearing him say her name, she was instantly steadied.

"I heard about Tucker," he said. "That he was questioned about Jessica Sweet's murder last night."

"Yes." She paced to the kitchen window and looked out. "He seems to think that was the end of it."

"It's hard to say. I sure hope so."

In the background, Emily heard the sound of a siren, a tangle of voices. A woman's laughter. "You're busy. I shouldn't have called," she said.

"No, it's all right. I'm on a break, actually, getting coffee."

"I'm so worried, Joe. It's scarcely been a year since we went through this with Miranda's death, and there's the other thing now with Revel Wiley."

"Have you heard from her again?"

"She's called, but I haven't answered. I think she's calling the house now, the landline, and talking to Roy. He's acting funny, not himself. . . ." She fell silent.

"Maybe I'll take a run by the club after I get off, see what she wants."

"No. I've already put you in enough jeopardy."

"You let me worry about that, okay?"

Emily ran her fingertip along the countertop's edge, remembering the day she drove into Houston to see Joe after his wife died. She brought him chicken miso soup and a small loaf of home-made wheat bread, and when he opened the door, her heart shifted hard in her chest on seeing the shadows of his grief so dark in his eyes. She followed him into his kitchen, setting the soup and bread aside, and spent the rest of their short, awkward visit fighting an urge to move her fingertips over the lines sadness had carved on his face. She would have given anything to be able to soothe him, to bring him peace. He had done the same for her more times than she could count. When she expressed her regret over this to Joe, he took her hand and, folding it, pressed first her knuckles and then the inside of her wrist to his lips. She left him shortly after that. Neither one of them had mentioned her visit to him since.

"Have you ever heard of anyone named Darren Coe?" he asked her now.

She straightened. "His family lives in the neighborhood. Why do you ask?"

"His name came up back when Miranda was murdered. Nothing developed on that score so I didn't follow up on it, but now, I'm hearing it again in relation to Jessica's case."

"Is Darren a suspect?"

"More a person of interest. Word is he knew Jessica, and he knew Miranda, too."

"He did. They went through school together. Tucker and Miranda were the same age. Darren was two years ahead of them."

"What about recently, in the year before she was killed?"

"If they had a relationship then, I never heard about it. Besides, he's married."

A silence came, one just long enough for Emily to realize her folly in assuming men were always faithful to their wives. She sensed Joe's smile.

"Were Coe and Tucker friends?" Joe asked. "Are they now?"

"No, I don't think so, not anymore. Something happened—" Emily paused. The incident she referred to was years ago now, but the old disgust and regret lingered, like specters.

"Emily?" Joe prompted.

"A girl, Holly McPherson, who lived in the neighborhood then, accused Darren of assaulting her. He denied it—he claimed she misunderstood. She was so young, only fourteen at the time. It was awful."

"You didn't believe Darren?"

"No. Holly was shattered over what happened, so much so, she and her parents moved out of state." *It was never resolved.* Emily could have said that, too. She could have said the neighborhood was never the same again. She could have said she'd never liked Darren even as a child. There was something off about him, something false and too glib in his demeanor, his speech. He was arrogant, a manipulator. But people found him charming; they fell for him. Women fell for him. Emily thought how Roy would disagree with her. He didn't see Darren in the same unflattering light. But not many in town did.

She said that to Joe now, that Darren was well respected in the community. "He's the head baseball coach at the junior high. Roy was telling me the other day how he's turned the team around, that because of him they've won a state championship the past five years in a row."

"Interesting," Joe said.

"Why? You say he's a person of interest. I'm not sure I know what that means. Is there evidence connecting him to these murders?"

"No, nothing confirmed. I'm sorry, I shouldn't have said anything, at least not until I had the facts. Let me look into it some more, and I'll call you if I find anything."

Emily bit her lip. "I don't know how I can ever thank you."

"No, none of that now. I'm not even sure there's

anything helpful here. You realize these cases are Lincoln County's business. Working in Houston/ Harris County, I've got no jurisdiction, no influence and damn few friends up there."

"That's just it. I feel as if you're risking your job, and I don't know how I'd live with myself if you lost it."

"You let me worry about that. You said Tucker and Coe aren't friends, is that right?"

"I don't think so, but honestly, I'm not sure." She remembered when Tucker was younger how she'd done everything she could to discourage their association. After the incident with Holly, Darren stopped coming around, and she'd been relieved. She couldn't remember now the last time she'd seen him.

"Well, just in case, tell Tuck to stay away from Coe, okay? The guy's bad news, for one thing, and for another, he's got an uncle who's a deputy sheriff on the force up there. He's the kind of guy—" He stopped.

Emily heard static, a voice, a staccato burst of words that sounded as if it was coming from Joe's police radio. He came back in a moment and said he was sorry, he'd have to call her later, and that quickly he was gone. She clicked off her cell phone, wondering at his mention of Darren Coe, feeling troubled by it.

She felt the same sense of helpless aggravation she'd struggled with when Miranda was alive and causing Tucker so much heartbreak. Darren had manipulated Tucker, too, and bullied him, and Emily's attempts to intervene, to guide Tucker away from Darren, had been as ineffective and frustrating as the ones she'd employed in Miranda's case.

The experts claimed that under the right conditions everyone was capable of murder. But it would take more than the right conditions, wouldn't it? A murderous person would have a certain kind of personality, Emily thought. They would have an aura, a darkness at their center, something almost tangibly evil. The sort of twisted deviancy she had sensed in Darren Coe even as a child with his smiling ways and slippery tongue. And whatever the pathology was, it would have grown up now, wouldn't it, in the man?

9

"So, you have a sinus infection, and Dr. White thinks it's stress related?" Evan wasn't buying it; Lissa could tell from his voice.

Keeping her cell phone to her ear, she rested her head against the truck seatback. She was still parked in front of Dr. White's office. It was lunchtime and people were deserting the building. They were like ants, streaming across her view, threading their way to their cars.

"What was his advice? Drugs, meditation? A gas mask?"

"He gave me a prescription to take care of my sinuses," she answered. "He said too much stress can weaken your immune system." At least this part was true. Dr. White had really said that.

"Where are you?" Evan asked.

"I'm headed your way."

"You told him you fainted a couple of weeks ago, right?"

"I did." She caught her lip. She should say she had passed out again, and she would tell him, later, when they were home together.

"Well, is stress to blame for that, too?"

"It could be. He took some blood to see if I'm anemic or something. He didn't seem all that concerned." Lissa caught her glance in the rearview mirror and looked away.

"When will you get the results?"

"A few days. Cathy said she'd call."

Lissa could have filled the small pocket of silence that opened between them with the rest of everything that Dr. White had said, but she didn't. Instead, she held her breath against the words and the tears that were packed behind her eyes, and when she could trust her voice, she said, "Have you heard from Tucker?"

"Wonder of wonders, he's picking up the floor tile for your studio."

"He got his car back?"

"Yeah. Your mom dropped him off at the shop. The alternator was out."

"Evan?"

"What, babe?"

The words, the ones that would convey another of Dr. White's suspicions about what ailed her, were still stacked against her teeth like small stones, but she couldn't say them. Instead, she blurted out, "I talked to Detective Sergeant Garza," which was the second in a list of items better left unspoken.

"What? Why?" he asked. "Did she come to the house?"

"No," Lissa admitted. "I went to her office before I came for my appointment."

"I thought you were at the Merrills'."

She closed her eyes. The Merrills. The first of the three lies she'd told Evan and all of them in one day. "I know. I'm sorry, but I didn't want to tell you before because I knew what you'd say."

"That talking to the cops was a mistake?"

She didn't answer.

"It's hard," Evan said. "I know it is. You just want to defend Tuck, and so do I, but you need to stay out of it, Liss."

She rubbed her temple, thinking about Sonny Cade, her intention to see him. Evan would be against that, too. "I don't think Detective Garza paid much attention to what I said, anyway. She seemed more interested in whether Miranda ever talked to me about Todd Hite. It turns out she really was working undercover."

"You're kidding. Wait until Tuck hears."

"It's crazy, isn't it?"

Evan laughed. "Yeah, you could say that," and then he paused, and Lissa knew why, that he was unwilling to speak ill of the dead, to say what he'd said before Miranda was murdered, that she was the reason blonde jokes were invented. But maybe he was wrong about her; maybe they all were, and there was more to Miranda, more to her life, than they gave her credit for.

"It gives Hite one hell of a motive to murder her, doesn't it?"

"Yes, but how does that explain Jessica? She

was murdered the same way, found in nearly the exact same place."

"Could be two different killers."

"I don't see the police looking at anyone but Tucker. What if they never do and he ends up getting arrested? I can't let that happen." She waited for a response, more argument, a solution. "Ev?"

"We'll get a lawyer, or a detective, someone who knows what they're doing."

"With what, Evan? We don't have the money—" She stopped, conscious again of her fear and the cold, irrefutable fact that Tucker was in danger, real danger. The police went after the wrong man all the time. Innocent people ended up in prison; they ended up on death row. *Her brother could—* She bit the inside of her cheek, afraid she might scream.

Evan said they shouldn't get ahead of themselves, that they'd find the money if they had to, and it was the sound of his voice more than his words that calmed her. "We've got no reason to believe the cops won't get it sorted out, and this'll blow over."

"Garza wants Tucker to let them look inside his car," she said.

"She should get a warrant, then."

"What if I made it worse for him?"

"I doubt that you could. What if Jessica was part of the same sting operation? Did Garza say?

If these women were police informants, it seems to me there'd be no end of suspects."

"Listen to us, Ev. You're using words like *sting operation* and *police informant*. We sound like a cop show on TV. How? Stuff like this doesn't happen to people like us."

Evan was silent. What could he say? That they were the exception? That maybe they'd get their fifteen minutes on *48 Hours* or *Dateline*? But now it occurred to Lissa that Sonny Cade, in his capacity as a police officer, might know about the sting operation. He might know how Miranda was involved and whether or not Jessica had also been a part of it. The more Lissa thought about it, the more she felt there had to be a connection between their murders and that police action. If anyone could confirm that, it was Sonny. She had to talk to him. She started to say something about Sonny to Evan—she wanted to know what he thought—but he was talking about lunch, and it was fine, really. Better, in fact, to wait until after she saw Sonny to say anything. "I'd love to meet you somewhere," she said.

"Me, too, but I'm at the site, waiting for the painters. Carl showed up, too, finally."

"Really? Is he over his snit?"

"Seems to be. He says they'll make the deadline if he has to work his guys overtime. He damn sure should since Roy tacked on the five percent."

"It's going to be hard to recoup that. I wish Dad hadn't done it."

"Yeah, but maybe he's right, and it'll light a fire. The faster we can get these models ready for the opening, the faster we can get potential buyers in here and start making money instead of spending it."

"When I talked to Mom earlier, she said he was gone to the lake house. Whatever you said to him last night, Mom thinks it made a difference."

"He's just scared, Liss. I think since he retired he's got too much time on his hands."

"Hmm." Lissa traced the lower arc of the steering wheel with her fingertip.

"Things haven't exactly turned out for him the way he thought they would, or the way he wanted. We should cut him some slack."

Lissa's throat narrowed, and she blinked away a fresh threat of tears. She was turning into a regular crybaby, she thought.

"Babe? You there?"

"Yep," she managed.

"What's wrong?"

She thought of everything she could say, and then said the only thing that made sense to her. "I just love you so much. My family is so weird, but you take it in stride." She laughed.

Evan didn't. "They're my family, too, you know. Your dad especially has done a lot for me. He went out on a limb for me."

"I know, Ev, but still." Lissa ran her finger along the steering wheel. She wouldn't argue because it was true; she wouldn't say out loud that it rankled that Evan felt so beholden. Sometimes she resented it, too, that her dad and Evan were so close. They shared an understanding that Lissa couldn't. But even more, it hurt Tucker. He was the real son, the blood son, but of the two of them, her dad favored Evan. She knew why; she knew her brother wasn't half the man Evan was. Tucker would never be as grounded; he lacked Evan's discipline and quiet, inner strength. It wasn't that Tucker didn't try. Sometimes he tried too hard. Her dad tried, too. When he'd offered to pay for Evan's night classes at the University of Houston, he'd offered Tucker the same deal, but Tucker had flunked out there the same as he had at Texas Tech, even though Evan spent hours tutoring him. And Evan had gone on to graduate—with honors. It was the way Evan did everything—with honor.

"God knows where I would have ended up if it wasn't for your dad giving me a job," he said. "But I also know you guys had a rough time on his account—" Evan stopped.

Lissa heard his breath go out. Her dad was a complicated man. His heart was a mystery; Lissa seldom knew how he felt about things, about her. Loving him wasn't easy, not for Evan, either. She started the truck, saying she'd meet Tucker at the house and help him unload the tile. "I don't know how long it'll take." She was thinking of her intention to see Sonny, that she needed to give herself time. She would tell Evan afterward.

"Don't forget to fill your prescription," Evan said.

The nonexistent prescription. Was that lie number four? Lissa put the truck in reverse, but then set her foot on the brake when Evan asked if she'd seen that day's newspaper. "No," she answered. "Why?" She cut the ignition.

"There's an article in the Metro section. It says the cops have a suspect, that an arrest is imminent."

"What? Why didn't you tell me before? Is Tucker's name mentioned? Does he know? What if he takes off again?"

"No one's name is mentioned," Evan said. "It probably doesn't mean anything. That's why I didn't say anything."

"Still, I better find Tucker and check on my folks. They'll be thinking the worst." There went her plan to stop by Sonny's office, Lissa thought. But maybe her parents would be fine. Maybe Evan was right, and it was a false alarm.

"There might be reporters," Evan said.

Lissa felt her hope flatten. She restarted the truck, promising Evan she would call if she needed him.

"It's probably nothing," he repeated.

But she thought, *No.* It was starting all over again.

10

Emily and Anna spent Tuesday afternoon at the church sorting through clothing donations for the local battered women's shelter, and while Emily was glad enough for the diversion, for the respite it gave her from the worry that darkened her mind, she was relieved when they were finished and could leave. She wasn't as foolish as Roy thought; she knew she wasn't welcome. Despite Anna's protests that Emily was imagining the chill in the air, the reality was that their wider circle of friends—the ones Emily and Anna had, in the past, shared church socials, lunch dates and birthday parties with—had closed, leaving Emily outside its arc.

Because of Tucker.

None of her friends' children had a habit of disappearing. They hadn't fallen in with the wrong sort of people; they hadn't grown up to distinguish themselves as murder suspects.

Not that anyone had brought it up, the fact that Tucker was under police scrutiny again. No one mentioned it or his or Jessica Sweet's name, at least not in front of Emily. Still, she felt their scrutiny and enough of their judgment that she'd been provoked to the point of defending Tucker even if only to herself. *Whatever happened to innocent until proven guilty?* she had wanted to ask.

She was driving out of the church parking lot when Anna commented that everyone had seemed friendly enough.

Emily signaled a right turn at the corner, and said, "I called Joe this morning."

"Really? How come?"

Emily changed lanes. "Roy wants me to put Tucker out of the house, and I'm not going to do it. If he wants him gone, he can see to it himself."

"Good for you. Let him do his own dirty work."

"Maybe he's changed his mind. Maybe a day at the lake—"

"Why did you call Joe?"

Emily wished she hadn't mentioned it. Now Anna would worry it to death. "What would you think if I told you I might move into the lake house when it's finished?"

"I'd think you were crazy. What about your great-grandfather's house? You wouldn't sell it, surely."

Emily felt the weight of Anna's gaze, her consternation, and kept her attention on the road. "If Roy would give Tucker the chance he's asking for . . . maybe. I don't know. . . ." Although in her heart she did know; she would do whatever it took to keep her family together.

A few blocks later, when Emily turned down Anna's street, she slowed as she passed the house next door to Anna's, a red-brick, Georgian colonial, where the McPhersons had once lived.

"Do you ever hear from Nat?" she asked Anna, peering past her, at the house.

"Not in several years. I used to get a Christmas card, but no one seems to do that anymore."

"I wonder how she and Benny are, how Holly's doing, if they're all right now." *If Nat has forgiven me . . .* The conversation with Joe, recounting for him what had happened to Holly, had brought it all back.

Anna admitted that she wondered, too. When they were parked in her driveway, she said, "Come in for coffee."

"All right," Emily said, but even as she followed Anna into the kitchen, she felt the drag of reluctance. She didn't necessarily want to talk to Anna about Joe or the McPhersons, and anyway, she still had grocery shopping to do. "I told Joe what happened with Holly," she said, and it was as if none of her reservations was worth further consideration.

Anna turned from the cabinet, holding two mugs. "How did that come up?"

"He asked me if I knew Darren." Emily brought the sugar bowl and spoons to the table and sat down.

"Why?"

"I'm not sure. The whole conversation was sort of strange." Emily realized the truth of this. She met Anna's glance. "He said I should tell Tucker to stay away from Darren."

"But they're not still friends, are they?"

"I didn't think so, but now I wonder. Why would Joe say that?"

Anna filled the mugs and brought them to the table. "Just hearing the name Darren Coe makes a knot in my stomach. When I think of what he did to Holly and then turned around and acted like he was the injured party, the poor, suffering victim. It kills me that people fell for it, that they still fall for his act. It's as if he walks on water in this town."

"What if it turns out there's a connection between him and these girls' murders?"

Anna looked dismayed. She said, "Oh, Em."

"He had such a mean streak as a boy, remember?"

"But the idea that he could be a murderer is just so— He grew up playing with our kids. They all hung around together nearly every day. It's scary." Anna stirred sugar into her coffee.

"After what Darren did to Holly only Tucker would have anything to do with him. Do you remember how furious Natalie was?" Emily had been upset over Tucker's misplaced loyalty to Darren, too. She'd tried talking to Nat, tried apologizing, explaining. "Nothing worked with her," Emily said. "I never talked to her again. It still shocks me that we aren't friends anymore. We three were so close."

Anna said, "Anger is how Nat dealt with everything back then, Em."

"I know. I don't blame her. I'm just sorry." Emily fiddled with her teaspoon.

Anna said, "You're going to drive yourself insane, you know. Nat's gone—it doesn't matter what she or anyone else thinks. You, me, the people who matter, know Tucker has nothing to apologize for in regard to Holly's situation, and as far as Miranda and Jessica are concerned, who knows who killed them? There could be any number of people . . . men who—"

"Tucker being one of those men." Emily thought how deeply ashamed she was that Tucker was lumped into such a category, and then she was ashamed at herself, that she could be so judgmental of her own son. It made her no better than the rest of the neighborhood.

She thought of the things she had come to know, the world she'd been introduced to as the result of being Tucker's mother, a world far removed from her dreams for him when she'd held him as a baby, warm and sweet smelling from his bath, in her arms, a world where her son fell for the wrong sort of girl and got dragged into a dark and dirty life. At least, that's how she viewed it, but then her generation had been raised differently, in a time when the lines between right and wrong, and moral and immoral behavior, were much more well-defined.

Anna was quiet, turning her mug in a circle, keeping her eye on it.

"That woman Revel Wiley called again this morning before I left the house." Emily hadn't meant to say it, to burden Anna with more of her family's drama that increasingly was a source for shame.

Anna looked up. "She talked to Roy? Because I'm not sure it would be a bad thing."

"No, he was already gone, and when I answered, she talked to me, instead of hanging up. Who knows why. She said she has Tucker's phone."

"His cell phone? How did she—?"

"She was at a party in Galveston, where Tucker was. She found it there. She says there's evidence on it that proves he wasn't in Austin." Emily took her mug to the sink and rinsed it.

"What sort of evidence? Did you tell Joe?"

Emily said she hadn't, that Revel had called after she talked to him.

"She's harassing you, Em. I think you should call the police on her. This has gone on long enough."

"She warned me not to. She said if I told anyone, there would be worse trouble." Emily broke off. Panic mushroomed. It jammed her throat, heated the space behind her eyes as if now she'd mentioned the source for it, it had only been waiting for the opportunity.

"Em? She could be lying, you know." Anna laid her palm on Emily's back.

"She wants five thousand dollars, Anna, or she'll take the phone to the police. Where am I going to get that? If I take any more out of the account, Roy will know. He'll find out I paid her before to get Tucker free of that stalking charge, if he doesn't know already."

A silence fell, and Emily would always think she sensed it, the awkward shape it took on before Anna spoke, before she said, "I could do it, Em. I could lend you the money."

Emily felt the flush of humiliation heat her cheeks. "No, Anna, I didn't mean—"

"I know, but I want to help."

"Thank you, but no." She pushed away from the countertop, shouldered her purse. "I have to go. I still haven't been to the store."

Anna looked confused, even hurt, Emily thought. But it was too difficult trying to explain how it felt to be the one in the friendship who was always in trouble somehow, always in need —or to have the child who was.

Emily left Anna blindly; she left wondering if she would lose Anna's friendship and her respect the same as she'd lost Natalie's. She wondered if in the end, when this was over, she would have no one left, not even Tucker.

Swiping away her tears, she decided on her way to the grocery store that she would make chicken Parmesan for dinner, and she was glad to have a plan. Cooking was her solace, a form of meditation, a source of satisfaction and comfort. It kept her grounded, and she needed that now. If nothing else, at least she could get a good, hot meal on the table. It was something, wasn't it? It was better than giving in to the hysteria she felt pressing hard against her ribs. Better than listening to her mind relentlessly asking why. Why was this happening to her son, to her family? Why were they always the ones life chose to test?

She was standing next to her half-filled grocery cart, admiring the fresh-cut chicken breasts, when her cell phone rang. The sound jarred her; she didn't want the interruption, but seeing Joe's name in the caller ID window, she changed her mind.

Rushed through a greeting, telling him where she was, what she was making for dinner, stopping when he said her name, "Emily?" and then, "Maybe you want to wait until after you've checked out to hear—?"

"No," she said faintly, but she was conscious of the other shoppers, the lack of privacy.

"The thing is, I found a report," Joe said. "Well, not the actual report, but some notes that were made, regarding a complaint Miranda filed against Darren Coe, here in Harris County."

"What sort of complaint?" Emily maneuvered her cart and herself as far as she could out of the aisle.

"It was the month before she was murdered. She

135

alleged that Darren assaulted her sexually and that he battered her and threatened to kill her, if she told. The report mentions photographs, but if there were any, they're missing."

"What are you saying? Do you think he could have—?"

"I'm not saying anything, okay? Not yet. But you should check this out with Tucker. Ask him what it's about."

"Why?"

"Because his name is mentioned in the duty officer's notes. Evidently, when Miranda came in to report the assault, he was with her. The photographs of Miranda's injuries were on his phone. They should have been printed and put together in a file, but it doesn't look as if anything like that happened."

The silence was problematic, lingering.

"Joe?" Emily prompted.

"I don't know—I'm just unsure about this. The report's incomplete. I only found it because— But never mind that. Ask Tucker, okay? See what he knows. I've got to go now, but I'll call if I hear anything else."

Emily thanked him, and when he asked, she said she was fine, but she wasn't. She left the grocery store, left her half-filled cart parked beside the meat counter and drove home, her mind churning, feeling bewildered, panicky, and yet somehow hopeful. If Darren Coe did this . . .

But she was afraid to go any further with such a thought.

Parking the car in the garage, she got out and opened the trunk, then stared, uncomprehending of the emptiness, before recalling that she'd left the groceries in the cart at the store. Calamity ruined everything, she thought, even something as ordinary, as mundane and simple, as dinner on a Monday night. That was the thought in her mind when she closed the trunk.

And while she did register the sound of a car passing slowly by in the alley behind her, enough so that she turned to look, to see it was a midsize sedan, neutral in color and unfamiliar to her, her observation was little more than cursory. Even when the car returned, coming into her view again as she was climbing her back porch steps, she felt no sense of alarm, and she would find that amazing in hindsight, that under the circumstances she paid so little attention.

11

Lissa turned the corner onto her street half expecting to see her house and driveway staked out by reporters, but it was blessedly vacant of all but Tucker's Chevy Tahoe. She found him out in back, sitting on the bench in the gazebo, and she sat down next to him, scooting close. She wanted to tell him about Miranda working for the police, but then she'd have to confess she met with Detective Garza, and she wasn't sure how he'd react. It might not mean anything, anyway.

"You got your car back," she said instead.

"Yeah, it about took my last dime." Tucker sat forward, bracing his elbows on his knees. "You want to show me how you want the tile laid in your studio, then I can get started unloading it."

"What about those receipts, from when you were in Austin?"

"What about them?"

"They're in your glove box, right? You need to give them to the police, so they can check them out."

"I will, in the morning."

Why are you waiting? Lissa jammed her hands into her jacket pockets. If she asked, it might lead to more of a discussion than she wanted. "Have you seen today's *Chronicle*?"

138

Tucker said he hadn't. He looked wary now and impatient. When she didn't elaborate, he said, "I guess there was something in there about me. . . ."

"Not you specifically, but it looks like they're about to arrest someone for Jessica's murder."

Tucker sighed. "Jesus."

Lissa patted his knee. "It could be anyone. Todd Hite. Who knows?"

"What a shit storm. I'm really sorry."

"I know."

"I didn't do it."

"I know that, too," she said.

"You're sure it didn't give my name?"

"No, so maybe—"

"We both know there's no maybe. It's me the cops want, for whatever fucked-up reason."

"If that's true, you're getting a lawyer this time, Tucker. No argument."

"It'll have to be a public defender. The old man sure won't pay for it, and I'm not about to ask you and Evan."

"We'll worry about that when—if—something happens."

Tucker picked up a small stone near the toe of his work boot and chucked it out the gazebo door.

Lissa followed the arc of its path until it fell into the grass. "I'm thinking of talking to Sonny Cade."

"What for?"

"Maybe he saw something like someone getting rough with Jessica. Or maybe he knows about that sting operation Todd was involved in, or some-thing about Todd, or one of his clients."

Tucker didn't say anything.

"You think it would be okay?"

"Okay how? I don't think he knows shit, if that's what you mean."

"He was kind of rough around the edges in high school."

"Who wasn't screwed up back then? Cade is a stand-up guy. He did time in Afghanistan, came home with medals. Talking to him about his experience over there made me wonder why I didn't sign up. Maybe it would have straightened me out, too."

"Dad didn't want you to have anything to do with the military," Lissa said.

"Oh, yeah." Tucker laughed, and the sound was hurt. "I forgot. I was supposed to be the next Nolan Ryan, do my old man proud."

Lissa didn't respond. Tucker's failed baseball career was still such a sore part of his history. He'd been coached by their dad to be the best, and it had earned him a full ride scholarship to play for Texas Tech, but then, in his freshman season, he'd injured his knee permanently, sliding into second base. Lissa didn't think their dad had ever gotten over the disappointment. "I remember you and Sonny were friends in school," she said after a bit.

"Yeah, so?"

"I bet he'd want to help you, and maybe he can."

"I doubt it, Liss, really."

"C'mon, Tuck, when Evan and I picked you up from the jail, you said he knows what goes on at the club. You acted like he had your back."

"I guess." He lifted his hat, resettled it. "Pop's at the lake, working on the house. Did you know?"

Lissa said she did, feeling the bite of exasperation at the way he'd changed the subject.

"This morning when Mom said he was going out there, I thought maybe it was a sign, that things would be all right. I thought how I could help him, if he'd let me."

Lissa let her stare loosen into the middle distance. She flinched when Tucker jerked to his feet, when he shouted, "Goddamn it! Why can't they leave me alone?"

She touched his hand.

He looked down at her. "Let's get the stuff for the floor out of my car, okay? I need to get to work."

She nodded, and led the way up the path toward the driveway.

Tucker came around her to the back of the Tahoe and opened the hatch. Three boxes of the clay floor tiles Lissa had ordered were wedged into the space with the tile saw, a tool kit and several buckets of grout and sealer.

"I'll get the handcart," she said, heading for the garage. It took her several minutes to find it, and by the time she returned, Tucker was sitting on the Tahoe's bumper, having already taken everything, except the tile, to the studio.

"Move over, tough guy." She knocked him with her hip and, reaching into the hatch, dragged out the box nearest to her and loaded it on the cart. "Want some iced tea when we're finished?" She stacked a second carton on top of the first.

"That would be great." Tucker whipped his hat off his head, armed the sweat from his brow.

Pulling the last box toward her, Lissa froze. "What is that?" She stared at the stain she'd uncovered. It looked like blood, old blood, a largish spot roughly the size of a breakfast plate, dark reddish-brown in color. Glancing around the interior of the hatch, she saw other, similar stains, a broad brushstroke, a smattering of smaller dots. The hair on her neck rose. Her heart dropped like a felled bird.

Tucker looked where she was looking. "It's blood," he said matter-of-factly, resettling his hat. "A couple weeks ago, I was driving out of the neighborhood, and there was a dog lying in the road. Some asshole hit him and didn't stop."

"Was it alive?"

"Barely. I took him to that clinic, the one that just opened on Tenth and Pin Oak? The vet there did everything he could, but the poor little dude died two days later. Cost me a hundred seventy-five bucks."

Lissa glanced at him and away, and for some reason, she thought of the people she had seen on television, the ones with family members who were charged with crimes and then found to be not guilty. In interviews they would say they believed implicitly in their loved one's innocence despite the accusations or the evidence. They would say they never suffered a moment's doubt. She admired that, but even so, she questioned whether it was possible. To never have a moment's doubt? Not one fraction of one second's wonder? She wished she could feel that certain of anything or anyone, and it wasn't that she suspected Tucker. Even the thought filled her with guilt.

She looked back at him, and he smiled. He held her gaze.

It was enough.

There was no sign of the media at her mother's house, and Lissa was relieved. She found her mom in the kitchen, starting dinner.

"Meat loaf," she said when Lissa asked what she was making. "Cherry pie, I think, for dessert." She seemed unsettled, distracted.

143

"You saw the article in the newspaper." Lissa was guessing.

"No," her mother said. "I haven't had time to look at it." She got out a small bowl and began sifting the flour she'd measured for the piecrust into it.

"Well, it's probably nothing." Lissa glanced around and saw the *Chronicle* in its plastic sleeve on the counter. She picked it up, taking it to the table. "Evan said there's something in the Metro section about Jessica's case, that they're on the verge of making an arrest."

Her mother went still, her shoulders dropping as if someone had pulled the pin that held them in place.

Lissa flipped through pages until she found the story, and even though Evan had warned her it was there, she winced at the headline. Arrest Imminent in Sweet Murder Case. She thought of her meeting with Detective Sergeant Garza, who had told her nothing, given her nothing.

Her mother dusted her hands and came to the table. "How imminent is imminent, do you think?"

"Who knows," Lissa answered.

Her mother went back to her pie making.

Lissa folded the newspaper. "I saw Detective Garza this morning."

Her mother looked at Lissa over her shoulder. "Whatever for?"

She repeated what she'd told Evan, leaving out the part about Tucker's refusal to allow the police to search his Tahoe. Her mom didn't need an additional worry.

"I have a hard time believing Miranda was working for the police," her mother said when Lissa finished. She cut cold pats of butter over the top of the flour. "At the time, I thought that was just media hype."

"Me, too. I'm still not sure I believe it. I feel like Sergeant Garza was playing some sort of game. The way she talked to me, the questions she asked. I got the feeling she thinks I have information, and I'm hiding it, trying to protect Tucker. It was weird."

Her mother turned, wiping her hands on a kitchen towel. "Well, I found out something myself about Miranda, from Joe Merchant. You remember Joe—"

"Sure." Lissa crossed her arms, feeling a flutter of unease. Her mother seldom mentioned Joe. Lissa had met him a handful of times; once when her mom took her and Tucker to a park in Houston, he had pushed them on the swings. On the occasions when Lissa asked about him, her mother would only say that Joe had helped her over the years. *He's a good and kind man, a dear friend,* her mother would say, and Lissa believed her. She had liked Joe the times they'd met. But he was a cop, Lissa thought, a *homicide* cop.

"He ran across a report about Miranda having been assaulted the month before she was murdered."

"Not by Tucker?" Anxiety jolted up Lissa's spine.

"No, no. You won't believe who."

"Someone we know?"

"Darren Coe."

Lissa's heart stalled.

"Joe didn't have many details, but he did say Tucker was with Miranda when she went to the police station. Something must have happened to the report, though, because— Lissa what's wrong? You're as white as a sheet." Her mother came and sat her down. She brought Lissa a drink of water.

But the mention of Darren Coe's name had badly shaken her, and setting the glass down, she bent her face into her hands, trying to take it in, saying, "I don't believe it," repeating herself, "I don't believe it," even as the kaleidoscope of images from that long-ago, horrible night in Galveston careened through her mind.

Pulling her hands from her face, she stared at her mother. "Are you sure? What exactly did Joe tell you?"

"Nothing much, honey. Just that Miranda came to the police station and said Darren had assaulted her."

"Sexually." Lissa wasn't asking, and she could see that her mother was mystified by her certainty.

"Yes, she was sexually assaulted and battered. Those were the words Joe used. He said she made the statement that Darren threatened to kill her if she reported him."

"Momma! It must be him, then. He murdered her!"

"Well, it does sound as if— But I don't know. It was a little confusing. Joe said the paperwork indicated Tucker took photos of Miranda's injuries with his cell phone, but they're not in the file."

"Why didn't Tucker ever say anything?"

"I don't know. I've felt ill, though, ever since I talked to Joe, thinking of how often Darren was in this house, pretending to be Tucker's friend."

Lissa shook her head. "He was never anyone's friend. I'm not sure he knows the meaning of the word."

"You know who I thought of right away."

Lissa met her mother's gaze. She knew precisely. "Holly McPherson," she said, and looking away, she felt the weight of old guilt and remorse.

"It makes me wonder if there are others, who else he might have—"

"Me."

"What? What do you mean?"

Lissa twisted her hands in her lap, trying to find the words, the way to answer, uncertain if she could. She had prayed this day would never come.

"Lissa, honey, you're scaring me." Her mother

pulled a chair out from the table and sat across from Lissa, their knees almost touching.

"You're going to be so disappointed in me," she said.

"No, sweet. Never." She took Lissa's hands, locking her gaze, making her feel trapped.

"There was a party in Galveston, the summer after I graduated from high school," Lissa began, and as she went on, telling her mother about it, her foolish behavior that night, she felt as if she were describing someone else. "A girl with no sense," she said to her mother. "I don't know why I was so stupid. I never took any drugs before. Never did again, either."

Her mother touched her cheek, dabbing at Lissa's tears. "I'm so relieved you were okay, that Evan came for you. Thank God for him."

Lissa nodded and looked away.

"So Darren was there? Were you with Courtney?"

Courtney was Darren's older sister and Lissa's one-time best friend. It was logical for her mother to assume they'd gone to the party together, but they hadn't. "I don't remember now where Courtney was."

Lissa had always wondered what would have happened if Courtney had been there. What she would have done if she'd seen her little brother, the brother she idolized, a Hardys Walk High School star athlete, bent over the coffee table sucking cocaine up his nose. He'd grinned when he caught sight of Lissa. She had yet to try the cocaine, but she'd had enough to drink that she wasn't as affected by his behavior as she might have been. She wasn't on her guard against him.

"If I'd been sober," Lissa said to her mother, "I might have tried to get him out of there. Mostly, though, I ignored him. I couldn't figure out what he was doing there, anyway. It was a college crowd."

"What were you doing there?"

"I was invited by a girl who was in my summer art class. Her cousin was a sophomore at UT, and he and a few of his buddies were renting a condo on the beach. Come to think of it, that might be why Darren was there. Maybe UT was trying to recruit him for baseball even then."

"But he was doing drugs."

Lissa made a face that let her mom know she was being naive.

Her mother was still appalled. "He was what? All of sixteen?"

"Yep, but obviously, I wasn't thinking about that or much of anything at all. The place was packed, and the music was so loud." Lissa remembered the sliding glass door had opened right onto the beach. She remembered sitting in the hot tub at some point. When night fell, they'd planted tiki lights in the sand, a row of them that led to the water. She'd been out there, near the shoreline, dancing, alone, when Darren came up to her.

"It was right after I tried the cocaine," Lissa said, not looking at her mother. "He wanted me to come with him. I didn't want to go, so he started pulling me. He got behind me and was kind of hustling me along, back up the beach, toward the condo." She paused, swallowing, biting her lips. She felt shrouded in the thickness of her shame, the half-remembered pall of her panic. "He pushed me behind the building, where the AC compressor was. . . ."

She remembered her sense of the place, that it had been walled in, the size of a largish closet, built out of brick, with no ceiling. The hot air blasting from the compressor had carried the stench of road tar and fainter undercurrents of salt and fish. Darren had pinned her body beneath his against the building. She remembered his breath on her neck, rank with the smell of beer. Her stomach had rolled; she'd been sure she would be sick.

"I couldn't move," she told her mother. "I could barely breathe. I was so scared."

She felt his mouth hard on hers, her pulse banging in her ears. He'd shoved his knee between her thighs and said she looked as if she could use a good fucking from a real man. She'd squirmed against him, fighting him, but that had only seemed to inflame him, so she'd gone limp, and he'd loosened his grasp enough for her to tell him that if he didn't let her go, she'd report him. He'd laughed like he couldn't believe it, like he'd never heard anything so stupid. "Bitch, please. You think anyone's going to believe you didn't want it, that it wasn't consensual?" he'd asked.

"Oh, Lissa," her mother said, cupping her cheek.

But Lissa shrank from her touch, saying, "No, Mom. Please."

Her mother lowered her hand, but her eyes were bright with righteous anger and her own tears for Lissa's suffering.

"I told him I meant I would report that I saw him doing coke. I said I would tell his coach. That's when he slammed my back against the building again and put his hand around my neck. If you could have seen the look on his face, Mom. It was evil, pure evil, so twisted, I didn't even recognize him. He was no one I knew."

"Please tell me he didn't—"

"Rape me?" Lissa said the words her mother couldn't. "No, thank God. This other guy came around the corner then. I think he was looking for a secluded spot to pee, actually, and when he saw us, he yelled out something about it being a hell of a party. I don't think he even realized— Anyway, it distracted Darren, long enough for me to get free of him."

That was when Lissa found her way, staggering,

half-witted and jibbering, back into the condo and into the bathroom. She'd spied the phone and called the office number, getting Evan instead of her father.

"Does Evan know what Darren did to you?"

"No," Lissa said. She hadn't been able to bring herself to tell him that part. The rest of what he knew she'd done that night had been bad enough. She remembered her shame, corrosive and raw, and she remembered somehow feeling, through all the ugly mélange of her emotions, the first inkling that she might love Evan and want him to love her. And she'd been panicked to think she would lose her chance to find out about him. She had been so afraid he would think she was nothing better than some wild, stupid girl and dismiss every thought of her. And so she hadn't confided in him. Now she wondered if she would have to. He would be so angry. Not because it happened, but because she'd kept it a secret. She hadn't trusted him. But she had an even worse regret: that by not speaking up, she had protected Darren, allowing him to assault other girls. Holly and now Miranda, and who knew how many others? Lissa put her face in her hands again.

"It breaks my heart that you went through it alone," her mother said.

Lissa lifted her gaze. "There's more, Momma. Darren threatened to hurt Tucker if I ever said anything."

"He was serious?"

"I was such a chicken, I believed him, and all I could think was how I was leaving for college at the end of the summer. But Tucker still had two years with Darren in the same school."

"Oh, Lissa—"

"Aaghh. It's been so long since I thought of any of this! It was only a matter of weeks after I left for A&M that Darren assaulted Holly. I was sick when Tucker called and told me."

"Does Tucker know that Darren—?"

"I've never told anyone, Momma. I was too ashamed. I still am." Tears coursed down Lissa's cheeks.

Her mother found a tissue and brought it to her. She held Lissa, and the murmur of her voice was soothing, a lullaby, and Lissa found comfort in it, enough so that she regained a semblance of composure.

She drew back, blowing her nose, dabbing her face. "What Darren did to Holly was the same as what he did to me. That's how I knew she was telling the truth. If only I'd said something before, but I was afraid for Tucker and for me. Now there's Miranda. If he did murder her, it's my fault."

"No! Honey, you can't blame yourself. When I think what could have happened. Oh, I always knew there was something the matter with Darren—"

"Would you have been as sympathetic if you

had known then? Would you have even listened to me?" Lissa was suddenly furious, as if Darren's assault and the terrible consequences of her silence about it were her mother's fault. But Lissa couldn't stand to think of the harm she'd done, or the harm Darren had done because she had been a coward; she had allowed herself to be victimized. Being angry with her mother was easier. "You always had your hands full with Tucker," she said, and her tone was hotly accusing.

Her mother stared, and Lissa saw that she was bewildered and clearly hurt, but Lissa went on, anyway. "His issues were so huge," she said. "They took up every room. They sucked the energy right out of this house. I couldn't add to that. You needed me to be good, to keep to the straight and narrow, and except for that one night in Galveston, I pretty much always did. This probably isn't the right time to say all of this—" Lissa pressed her fingertips to her brow, wondering at herself, the agitated jumble of her feelings.

"I'm so sorry," her mother murmured, "for what happened to you, for not being there for you, for your feeling that Tucker took precedence. I never wanted that, but I know it's true, and I'm sorry for that, too." She left Lissa and, finding the kitchen towel, blotted her face. "But you must realize how much harder on him your dad was. I always felt I had to compensate."

At first Lissa was so astonished all she could do was stare at her mother, and when she did finally speak, her resentment was back to sharpen every word. "I didn't ask to be favored, and honestly, I never felt Daddy spared me anything."

"He bought you a car for graduation. Tucker got a savings bond."

"Please correct me if I'm wrong, but that car was given to me so I'd have a fast way to get home from A&M if Tucker got into trouble. I'm always the one who has to bail him out."

"That isn't true, Lissa. Trust me, I've done my share, more than my share. You'd be surprised."

"What is that supposed to mean?"

"Nothing. Never mind," her mother said, but her eyes were troubled, and her hands when she reached to straighten her hair were shaking. "I'm just upset for what happened to you and everything else. I don't half know what I'm saying."

"No, Mom, there's something more." Lissa was certain of it. She wiped her eyes, settled her breath. "You were telling me about the report Joe found. Did he say Darren is a suspect in Miranda's murder?"

"He said he'd call when he had more information."

"Well, I can believe it, can't you, that Darren could kill someone?" The words sounded bald and cold, but Lissa felt their truth in her bones, in the core of her heart. "When I remember how he looked that night . . ." She suppressed a shudder.

"You're right, you know, about the car."

Lissa looked at her mother.

"We did want you to have a way home, just in case."

"Momma, don't worry about it. I don't know why I brought it up."

"No, let me finish. I always knew it was too much, that we shouldn't ask it of you, that you shouldn't be burdened with the responsibility of your brother, but things have been different for him, harder, because of your dad, his expectations, as much as you don't want to hear—"

"I do want to hear, if you mean you're finally going to tell me the whole story about Dad, what happened to him in the war and what really happened that day he put Tucker in the closet."

"You know all of that."

"No. I don't. I know the gist of it and that's all. It's like this big thing, a big jagged knife, came along and opened a wound in our family, and we've been pretending ever since that nothing happened."

Her mother's stare drifted.

"Mom?"

"Now isn't the time."

"Then I have to go."

The pause they shared was impatient and sad, and Lissa regretted it. She thought of Dr. White and his upsetting suspicions and how badly she wanted to confide them to her mother. She needed her mother's support and advice before going home to tell Evan. But this was the perfect example of Lissa's complaint. Her mother was already stressed, already disturbed enough over Tucker and all this new business about Darren Coe. Lissa couldn't add to that. It wouldn't be right or fair. She went to her mother and hugged her. "I'll call you tomorrow, okay?"

Her mother held her close, then let her go.

On her way to her truck, Lissa passed Tucker on the sidewalk to the alley. She thought of stopping, of asking him why he'd never told her about the assault charge Miranda had leveled against Darren, but Tucker looked upset. He looked as if he was in a mood, and she couldn't deal with it. He called her name and asked her to wait, but she waved him off.

"Later," she said, "okay? I have to go home now."

In hindsight, she would be sorry she didn't stop to speak to him, to soothe him, not that it would have changed anything. It was just the last time either one of them would be free.

12

Emily was still thinking about Lissa, still disturbed, when she sensed his presence, and closing the oven door on the cherry pie, she hesitated before turning to greet him. She needed a moment to switch gears, a moment to find the right way, if there was one, to tell Roy that she hadn't ordered Tucker to leave, that, in fact, if Roy wanted it to happen, he would have to do it himself. She was thinking of how to word it: *Tucker's working at Lissa's just as he said he would. Doesn't that say something, mean something?* she would say. *He just needs a chance, our support, a roof over his head until he can get on his feet. . . .* She was holding this very speech in her mouth as she turned, but it died on her tongue when she saw that instead of Roy it was Tucker who had appeared. One look at him, at his dark, disgruntled expression, and her heart fell, and for no reason she could name the smallest electric jolt of panic rocketed through her veins.

"I thought you were at Lissa's." She forced a smile.

One that he didn't return. He was in a mood she knew all too well, the one where he wanted her to know he was unhappy. He would want her to fix it, whatever was wrong. All his high-flown talk last night, the promise that he'd changed, his sincerity, had been real, but only in the moment. She ought to have known better than to buy in to it. Hadn't she heard it before, a thousand times? Didn't she—she more than anyone— know Tucker's temperament was more fickle than the south Texas weather?

Emily picked up the kitchen towel and folded it in half, smoothing the crease. She knew everything about him and almost nothing about her own daughter. She thought of all that Lissa had confessed, terrible things she'd known nothing about. Emily couldn't stand it, thinking of how desperately her daughter had needed her, and she hadn't even noticed. She'd been too distracted with worry over Tucker, too busy running interference for him, trying to stay one step ahead, trying to make up for—what?

Lissa had been there through the dark and blessedly brief number of years when her father drank, when he ranted and raved. She'd been wakened by his shouts in the night. But she hadn't drawn her father's attention like Tucker had. Roy loved his daughter with his whole heart, but he had poured his soul into his son, only to watch him fiddle away every last opportunity. Roy would accuse Emily of overcompensating for Tucker's shortcomings. He would say she made excuses for him. But Roy was so impatient with Tucker, so ready to blame him when it was Roy's own mistaken sense of failure as a man, a soldier and a father that lay at the root of his misery.

They had erred so horribly as parents, Emily thought. Perhaps it would have been better to have left Tucker to Roy, to his firmer hand, then Tucker might have grown up tougher and stronger. He might have more confidence now. But how could you know what was right, what was in a child's best interests? It wasn't as if making a mess of your children was the same as making a mess of dinner. It wasn't as if you could order up another baby or two and start over.

"Pop called me."

Tucker drew Emily's attention.

"He said you don't want me living here any-more."

"No, I never— I didn't—" Emily felt blindsided, even though she had planned to make Roy initiate the discussion. "It isn't what I want, Tucker."

"Yeah, I know. It's what he wants. I'm supposed to be gone before he gets home. I guess he's on his way in from the lake now." Tucker pulled a chair out from the table and dropped into it. "I'd damn sure leave if I had anywhere to go."

"I've made a cherry pie, it'll be done soon. You'll have some while it's still warm. It would spoil anyone else's dinner, but not yours, not the way you eat." She laughed, and even she was disgusted at how perky she sounded. Setting aside the towel, she retied the apron she was wearing over her slacks, and going to the sink, she began rinsing the dirty bowls and utensils. Outside, the air was blue with the onset of evening. The empty swing hanging from the thick limb of the old elm tree shifted idly in the breeze. The pair of cardinals that nested every year in the mock orange bush called to each other. Their song was punctuated by the raucous cry of a mockingbird.

"I don't know how I'm supposed to get an apartment without the money for a deposit. Plus a lot of places want the first and last month's rent, too."

Emily heard the plaintive sound of Tucker's voice over the water's rush and wished she couldn't.

"Mom? What am I supposed to do? How can I go when I have no money to live on?"

She turned off the water, facing him as she dried her hands. "What do you do with it, Tucker? I just wrote you a check—"

"That was two weeks ago."

"You're paid a salary, too, the same as Lissa—" She broke off, seeing his mouth harden, the look in his eyes that was mutinous and hurt. It was a mistake to compare them. She knew that.

"I was fired, remember? Booted out of the business on my ass. Now he's booting me out of my house right when I've got all this shit going on with my car. Getting it fixed pretty much wiped out my savings. And for the record? Pop never has paid me what he pays Lissa and Evan."

161

"Oh, Tucker, I don't think that's true." Emily wasn't sure. She didn't keep up with the business anymore. "What about everything you said last night, doing whatever you could—"

He talked over her. "Pop says it's because I live here, I'm freeloading, don't have a wife, a new house, responsibilities, blah blah. It's bullshit."

"I guess I can help you," Emily said, reluctantly dragging out the words, as if that would somehow cause either of them to look at the mistake she was making and stop it. She found his gaze, and said, "But please, promise me this will be the last time."

And his face when he turned it up to her was alight and set in the expression of the perpetually drowning man, the man who has once again spotted the means that will save him, buoy him, bear him to shore. Emily dropped her glance, both sickened and relieved at the upward shift in his mood. It won't last, but for the moment, he was happier. He would be on his best behavior. Roy would arrive, and they would share a nice dinner, after all.

"Will a thousand hold you?" she asked. "I know Lissa and Evan can't afford to pay you for whatever you're doing for them over there, so we'll call what I'm giving you your salary for that work. All right? Just between us."

He shrugged. "Sure. Whatever."

"My purse is on the counter over there." She

gestured. "If you'll hand me my checkbook . . ."

He went to get it.

She said, "I found out something today, about Darren Coe and Miranda, that I need to ask you about."

"What's that?" He had his hand in her purse fishing for her wallet, and watching him, Emily forgot her concern over Darren and Miranda; instead, thinking how often Tucker had taken her money, with her permission and without it, and it was almost surreal when she saw fingers, Roy's fingers, close strongly, menacingly, around Tucker's wrist. Her gaze rose to Roy's face, which was reddened and angry. Where had he come from? How was it she hadn't heard him? Her heart plummeted as quickly as a hailstone fell from a thundering sky.

"What do you think you're doing, boy?"

"Jesus, Pop." Tucker tried to jerk free and grimaced when Roy's grip tightened.

"I said he could, Roy."

Roy shot her an exasperated look. "We can't keep giving him money for nothing, Em. It's not helping him or us."

"It's not for nothing. It's for the work he's doing at Lissa's."

"Come and get your purse."

"But he should be paid, shouldn't he? And Lissa and Evan don't have it to spare—"

"Now!"

163

"All right, but let Tucker go, will you? Please?" She went behind Roy and snatched the purse.

"Take it upstairs."

Emily backed into the doorway that separated the kitchen from the front hall, but she couldn't go any farther. She didn't dare turn her back. She whispered his name, "Roy?" and she was weak with relief when he let Tucker go with a shove.

They stood, glaring at each other, chests heaving. Their breath in Emily's ears was rough and hurtful like sandpaper on her flesh.

Tucker rubbed his wrist. "You ever lay a hand on me again, old man, you'll regret it."

"You think you can go against me and win?"

"Push me again and see what happens."

Roy beckoned. "C'mon with it, then, tough guy. You think you're the man, take a shot."

Tucker's hands balled into fists. His eyes flattened.

Emily caught her breath.

"Well?" Roy asked. "What are you waiting for?"

The silence spun out, tinsel thin. Tucker found her glance. "Momma?" he said, and the sound of him, the bewilderment that had so suddenly seized him, caused her heart to lurch even more heavily against her ribs. He was a child again, that long-ago boy, the one she had scooped out of the closet, mute in his terror. That little boy had blinked at her in just this way. He had said, "Momma?" then, too, as if he wasn't sure.

"What's the matter, big-time? You scared? Scared of a one-legged old ex-army sarge like me?"

The talk was tough, but there was a tremor in Roy's voice, a certain tentativeness in his posture, and Emily knew he was remembering that day, too, when he had menaced his son, and instead of acting the part of a loving father, he had become a monster to be feared. She could taste his anguish over this as well as her own, and the flavor was corrosive, like acid, and it burned. She moved to Tucker's side. "That's enough," she said. "Leave it alone now, both of you."

"Asshole," Tucker said without heat.

"Hah!" Roy made a dismissive motion with his hands. "You're nothing but another punk mouth thinking you're a big hoss. I dealt with your kind in the army all the time." He took Emily's purse from her and headed down the front hall. "You're not getting any money off your mother," he said over his shoulder. "Not this time. Hear me? You know what's good for you, you'll keep out of my sight. You'll get clear away from here."

"How do you expect me to do that?" Tucker yelled after him, and he'd recovered his temper, his adult belligerence. "You'd give it to Evan or Lissa, no questions, but not me. Right, old man? I'm the loser, the fuckup, the one you wish was never born!"

His voice cracked, and Emily laid her hand on his arm, murmuring his name.

165

He brushed her off. "He thinks more of Evan as his son than he ever has me."

She wanted to speak, wished desperately to reassure him, but her throat was tight and swollen with her grief, her misgiving.

"I'm out of here," Tucker said in a low voice. "I'd rather live on the street than live another fucking second with that asshole."

"No! Tucker, you can't leave like this." Emily's voice broke on the words.

"Watch me," he said.

And then he was gone, up the stairs, and the ceiling creaked as he moved roughly around his bedroom, slamming drawers, jerking things off shelves from the sound of it.

Moments later, the timer rang, and Emily took the cherry pie from the oven and set it on a folded tea towel to cool. Methodically, she set about mixing the ingredients for the meat loaf she'd planned for dinner since she'd left the makings for chicken Parmesan in the grocery cart she'd abandoned at the store. She was glad, really. Tucker loved meat loaf. He would stay and eat, she told herself. Roy would calm down, and they would talk sensibly. They would work out something. It was a ridiculous dream; she knew it was. Nevertheless, within half an hour, she had popped the meat loaf into the oven, peeled the potatoes that she intended to mash and serve with butter and set a pot of fresh green beans over a burner to simmer. Going to the pantry now, she shifted things around until she spotted the one remaining jar of red sauce she'd made from last fall's tomato crop.

She had it in her hands when the thud of something hitting the floor overhead in Tucker's room startled her. Her gaze jerked upward, and that quickly, the jar of sauce slipped from her grasp, shattering on the tile floor. She froze, her anxious stare fixed to the ceiling, waiting for a sign that Roy had reacted badly to the noise, but there was only silence.

Lowering her gaze, she studied the mess on the floor. Her slacks were splattered, too, and she thought how much all the red, puddled and dripping, looked like blood, and the sight of it disturbed her on some level she couldn't name.

13

When Lissa stopped by Sonny's office after leaving her mother's, no one was there. The door was locked. It was the same at Lissa's own office. Everyone, including her and Evan's assistant, was gone. Retracing her steps to her truck, Lissa's mind was on Evan, the notion that he was probably at home, wondering where she was, and she didn't see the woman, not until she spoke.

"Excuse me, are you Tucker Lebay's sister?" The woman picked her way around the front of a new, red Lexus.

Watching her approach, Lissa wasn't alarmed, only curious, wondering who she was.

"My name is Revel Wiley. You don't know me, but your brother and I are friends—or we were once."

Now a small pulse of anxiety did dart up Lissa's spine. "What do you want?" she asked. She couldn't see the woman's eyes. They were hidden behind sunglasses that reminded her of Jackie Onassis. Lissa could see herself mirrored in the lenses.

Revel hitched her oversize handbag higher on her shoulder. "I work at La Femme Mystique."

No surprise there, Lissa thought, given how the woman was dressed—in a fitted, purple jacket over a matching pair of skinny jeans so tight they clung like paint. "Is there a problem?"

"Well, yeah, it's your brother, he's—" Revel stopped, seeming to consider. Then she said, "Never mind. I'm really sick of trying to deal with you people. I should take this to the cops. It's what I should have done in the first place." She started to walk away.

It was pure reflex when Lissa grabbed her arm. "You've obviously got something on your mind that concerns Tucker. What is it?"

Revel looked pointedly at Lissa's hand; she let go.

"I guess it runs in the family." Revel took off her sunglasses. Her eyes were as heavily made up as her mouth, and full of malice, a kind of twisted pleasure, as if she were enjoying herself.

"What does?" Lissa asked.

"Grabbing. Hanging on when no one wants you to."

"I don't know what you're talking about."

"Your brother. That's what he does. He hangs on, always trying to tell people how to live, always playing the role of savior. First he tried that shit on Miranda, then he pulled it on Chantelle. Now they're both dead." Revel looked hard at Lissa. "Doesn't that worry you?"

"Should it?" Lissa didn't know where she found the breath to ask, the will to stand her ground. She had a sensation similar to the one she'd felt at the meeting this morning with Sergeant Garza, that Revel wanted something from her, that she sus-pected Lissa of hiding something.

"I could tell you things about him." Revel's eyes were bright, probing.

"Such as . . . ?"

"Oh, no, no, no." She wagged her index finger in front of Lissa's face. "I don't talk for free."

It was a moment before Lissa registered it, that this was some kind of blackmail attempt, in near-broad daylight, in her office parking lot. "You're asking me for money?"

"I don't give it up for free, darlin'."

"No," Lissa said. "I'm sure you don't." Her truck chirped when she hit the button to unlock the driver's-side door.

"Does the name Darren Coe mean anything to you?"

A smattering of gooseflesh rashed Lissa's skin. She turned to look at Revel. "Why are you asking?"

"Son of a bitch worked Miranda over pretty good the month before she was killed. He might have done it to others. Does that fit with what you know about him?"

Lissa was momentarily astonished, and she worked not to show it, to keep her voice casual when she asked how Revel knew.

She shook her head. "Only other thing I can say is that's pretty much how and when all this shit got started—with those two losers."

"You mean that's all you can say for free."

Revel laughed. "You're smarter than your brother."

"I think I've heard all I want to—"

"So, you're saying you want me to talk to the cops instead, is that it? Because I want to be clear here, give you a fair chance."

Lissa set her booted foot on the running board, using it to boost herself into the driver's seat. "You're bluffing," she said with more bravado than she felt. "If you knew anything substantial, you would have already gone to the police."

Revel stepped in close enough to the truck to keep Lissa from closing the door. "You know, I never did get what Chantelle saw in your brother, or Miranda, either, for that matter. He gave them nothing but shit about the dancing. He was always on them to quit, to find a better life. If it had been me, I would have told him he could park his opinion up his ass."

Something in Revel's tone of voice made Lissa look sharply at her, made her say, "You have a thing for him."

"Hell, no!" Revel was quick to deny it, but everything else about her posture, her expression, said she had feelings for Tucker.

The tension in Lissa's shoulders eased a bit. She said, "I need to go," pulling the door toward her, narrowing the gap.

"All right, but you should talk to your mother," Revel said, backing away.

"My mother?" Lissa flung the door wide again. "Why?"

"When you talk to her, give her my regards, will you? She's a nice lady."

"What are you talking about now?"

"She knows. Ask her about Tucker's cell phone. Tell her she's got three days to pay up, or I'm handing it over to the cops."

"You have Tucker's phone?" Lissa was thoroughly confused. "Where did you get it?"

Revel didn't answer; she disappeared into her car and drove out of the parking lot without a backward glance.

Evan turned from the stove to smile at Lissa when she came into the kitchen. His eyes filled with warm affection, his delight at seeing her. He held out a spoonful of his famous chili, offering her a taste, totally caught in the moment, and she opened her mouth dutifully, like a bird, taking in the food, talking around it, nearly breathless, jittery in her impatience to spill the details of her encounter with Revel.

"Revel," she said when she'd finished filling Evan in, "what kind of name is that?"

"A stage name," Evan said. "How's the chili?"

"Fine. Delicious. I'm still trying to figure out how she knew I'd be there when I didn't even know myself I was going there until I left Mom's."

172

"She took a chance obviously. We should make a salad, hmm?"

"Come on, Evan. How can you be so blasé? She has Tucker's phone. She said she knows things."

"Did you see the phone?" His gaze on hers was steady.

"You think she's lying?" Lissa hadn't considered that possibility.

"She said she knew your mother, too. Do you believe that?"

Lissa thought about it. "No," she said after a moment. She realized she couldn't imagine her mother knowing anyone like Revel. "She threatened to go to the police, though."

"The Revels of this world don't usually talk to the cops, trust me. She's just some hooker out to make a buck, or it could be like you said—she's got a thing for Tucker. Maybe she's trying to get to him through you."

"Get his attention, you mean?"

"Yeah. Did you call him?" Evan helped himself to a bite of his chili, savoring it.

Lissa said she had tried calling him, and her mother and dad, on the way home, but no one had answered. She'd left messages at each number and on the landline. She was thinking of the article in the paper, the one that had mentioned an arrest was imminent in the Jessica Sweet case, when she said, "What if something's happened?"

Evan set down the spoon he'd been using to

stir the chili and pulled her into his embrace. "Somebody would have called. Let's have dinner, then we can run over there and check on them if you want."

Lissa nodded. She went into the mudroom to hang up her jacket and bent her forehead to the wall. She wanted so badly to tell him about Darren, that Miranda had been assaulted and threatened by him, that even Revel knew it happened. It could be such good news for Tucker. But it would mean reliving that night in Galveston again for the second time in one day, and she would have to admit that Darren attacked her, too, and she had said nothing, done nothing. She couldn't face Evan's reaction, his anger that she'd kept it a secret, the disappointment in her that seemed inevitable.

"Chili's ready, Liss. Can you make a salad?"

Pasting on a smile, she emerged from the mudroom, and she was glad Evan was concealed from her behind the open refrigerator door. She took the head of lettuce, fresh spinach and the cucumber he passed to her. She plucked a tomato from the windowsill and agreed with him when he said he'd be glad when they could put in a vegetable garden.

She carried the salad to the table.

Evan brought the chili and crackers, and they sat down.

He groaned when he took a bite. "I swear to

God I make the best chili in the state of Texas, maybe in the entire world."

"Hah. Let me see." Lissa spooned a bite onto a cracker and popped it into her mouth, closing her eyes, savoring it. "Not bad," she said, playing the moment, drawing it out, wishing with her whole heart it never had to end.

Mock hurt rode his expression. "That's all you can say?"

"You already have a big enough head," she said.

"Speaking of heads, how is yours? Is whatever Doc White prescribed working?"

Lissa dipped her gaze into her bowl. Here it was, the moment she'd been dreading.

Evan said her name. "Lissa?"

She met his gaze. "The truth is he couldn't prescribe anything stronger than Tylenol, and that hardly touches the pain."

"You said he gave you— What's going on?"

"I might be pregnant, Evan."

"What?"

His expression was comical. He couldn't have looked more astonished if she had handed him the maybe-baby alive and squirming across the table.

"The urine test was negative, but he said the other symptoms I have—"

"Passing out?"

"Umm, and my breasts are tender and I'm peeing more."

"Why didn't you tell me?"

"What? That I'm peeing more?"

"You know what I mean!"

"Well, anyway, he did a blood test. He'll call me tomorrow, or the next day, or sometime, I guess." *Never? Could it be never?*

"Oh, my God!" Evan half stood. He sat back down. "Oh, my God."

"This was never supposed to happen, and anyway, we don't want children, right? That's what we said."

"Dr. White said it *probably* couldn't happen."

"We should have been using protection."

"Not even the pill is a hundred percent, Liss."

She got up from the table. "I guess how it happened doesn't matter, does it? The result is the same, and so is the answer."

"You can't get an abortion."

She looked at him. "Are you forbidding me?"

"Well, no, what I mean is—is that really what you want?"

"Don't you? Haven't you said a gazillion times you had enough of fathering, helping to raise your siblings after your dad died?"

Evan was the oldest of five, and he'd stepped in to help his mother care for his three younger sisters and a brother after their father walked out. He'd told her in the very first conversation they ever had about children that he would be fine in a marriage without them. Lissa knew there were people who thought choosing not to have a baby was un-American or irreligious—her mother-in-law, for instance—but she didn't care what anyone thought. She was smart enough to know that motherhood was not for her. She didn't have the courage for it. Suppose she was given someone as difficult to handle as Tucker? She didn't know how her mother stood up to it, the worry and frustration; Lissa only knew she couldn't. And until this moment, she had believed Evan felt the same. She met his gaze. "Am I remembering wrong?" she asked him. "Was it not a joint decision?"

"Yes, it was, but this is our baby. We made this baby. How can you just—"

"*I'm* not doing anything. I thought *we* had an understanding." She sat back down. "We should finish dinner."

"We should have our baby."

"We don't even know if there is a baby."

A cell phone sounded.

"Must be yours," Lissa said. "Mine's dead."

She watched Evan leave, nervously rubbing her upper arms. She heard the murmur of his voice, and then it rose, taking on an edge.

"Okay," she heard him say, and then, "Yes, we'll come right now."

Lissa's arms fell to her sides; her heart picked up its pace. "What is it?" she asked when he appeared in the kitchen doorway.

"That was your mom. A reporter called a while ago and asked her if she knew her son was being arrested for Jessica Sweet's murder."

"Oh, no—"

"Now there's a sheriff's car parked out in front of the house. She said she can't see who's inside."

"They're going to arrest Tucker? Does he know?"

"She said the cops are just sitting there. She wants us to come."

The silence as they drove was anxious, gnawing. Lissa couldn't stand it. She glanced at Evan, taking in the rigid line of his jaw, the knot under his ear that jumped like a tiny piston. She said, "I'm sorry this is happening," and she thought he would say he was sorry, too. She thought he would pick up her hand, kiss the tips of her fingers, her palm, the way he often did when they were driving. But he didn't. He only looked at her, and his eyes were baffled, as if he wondered who she was.

What about you? she wanted to ask. *What about how you blindsided me? How could you decide you wanted to be a father and not tell me? When did you?* The questions ran a heated circuit in her brain, but she was too panicked about Tucker to ask them. Her heart thudded in her chest. She wanted to get to her parents' house; she wished they would never get there.

When they arrived, the deputy sheriff's car that sat at the curb was empty.

Evan said, "Come on. They must have gone in already."

The ruckus of loud voices coming from the kitchen was audible the moment they opened the front door, and they went quickly toward it. Lissa halted on the threshold, her glance shooting across the room to Tucker and the man who had him up against the wall. "You aren't arresting him?" she asked, and it was stupid, a stupid question. Clearly they were arresting him, but it was as if her mind refused to accept it.

Her father got up from the table, thrusting his napkin aside. She felt the heat coming off him when he brushed by her. She heard the sharp snap of his office door when he closed it.

"We have a warrant, Mrs. DiCapua."

Lissa's eyes collided with Detective Sergeant Garza's eyes. "But when I saw you this morning, you said nothing about an arrest."

"Things have changed."

"What things?"

"I'm not at liberty to say."

"Can they do this?" Lissa's mother was appealing to Evan. She was white-faced. She looked as if someone had struck her full force from behind. Lissa went to her and took her hand.

"They can do whatever they damn well please," Evan responded.

They both flinched when Garza's partner snapped the metal bracelets around Tucker's wrists.

"He hasn't had anything to eat," her mother said, as if that were the worst of it.

"It's okay, Mom." Tucker looked at Lissa. "Tell Pop it's nothing, will you? Tell him I'll be back before he can miss me." Tucker laughed now, but not as if it were funny. "Maybe somebody should call me a lawyer," he said. "Who's that guy in Houston, Ev? We built his house, remember? Loomis? Mickey Loomis, wasn't it?"

"I'll call him. Don't worry, squirt," Evan said.

It had been a while since Lissa had heard Evan call Tucker by that name, and it sounded almost like a term of endearment. It sounded laden with love and regret.

Garza and her partner ushered Tucker into the front hall.

Lissa's mother ducked into the laundry room and emerged with Tucker's jacket.

Evan and Lissa fell in behind her.

Outside it was dark, but someone had switched on the porch light, and in the glow, the sidewalk was a dull gray seam wedged between the darker rectangles of grass. Evan and Lissa stopped where the glare bled into shadow, but her mother followed closely behind Garza, finally catching her elbow, thrusting Tucker's jacket at her. "There's no sense in my son being cold."

Garza took the jacket and pushed Tucker ahead of her through the gate.

"Hey, Ma," he hollered, "keep my dinner warm, will you?" A pause ensued while he was stuffed into the backseat of the sheriff's car, then he called, "Don't rent my room out, okay, 'cause I'll be back."

Lissa's heart lurched. She slid her arm over her mother's shoulders.

Tucker bent forward as the car pulled away from the curb, and the last they saw of him before it disappeared from view was his frightened, white face framed in the rear passenger window.

14

The phone was ringing when they came back into the kitchen. Emily darted a glance at Lissa and saw her own shock and bewilderment mirrored in Lissa's eyes.

"Don't answer it," Evan said, but Lissa already had.

"Hello?" She was tentative, wary.

"Who is it?" Emily asked.

Lissa put the caller on speaker and upped the volume.

"I'm Vincent Treadway with the *Lubbock Avalanche-Journal*," a man said. "I'd like to ask you about Tucker Lebay. Are you a family member? Is it true he's been arrested?"

Emily's breath went down hard.

Evan muttered, "Just what we need."

The man went on, talking fast, his words running together. "I've heard he may also be charged in the strangling deaths of other women who've been found murdered along I-45. Can you comment?"

Lissa didn't bother; she punched the off button.

"Why would a reporter call from Lubbock?" Evan took off his jacket. "How did he find out so fast?"

"Maybe because Tucker went to Tech. He played baseball there, remember?" Lissa docked the receiver.

182

Emily went to the table. The setting was undisturbed.

Eerily pristine.

She looked at the dished plates, each one bearing a slice of meat loaf with mashed potatoes and buttered green beans. There are yeast rolls, a tossed salad. All of it was waiting for a family that wasn't coming, that might never again be together in a way that was familiar or ordinary. Her throat knotted. She wanted the dinner gone, out of her sight, but the idea of so much good food going to waste defeated her.

As if they could read her thoughts, Lissa and Evan took over the task of clearing the table, and when the phone rang again, Emily answered it.

It was another reporter, from a newspaper in Huntsville this time. There was a prison there, Emily thought. The one where the state executed men for their crimes. She hung up even as the reporter was firing his questions.

But the flow of calls didn't stop, and in the next hour she answered the telephone so often, the questions blurred: "Are you Tucker Lebay's mother sister wife daughter?" "Are you a relative neighbor detective cop?" "The police won't confirm it, but the rumor is they have enough evidence to charge Mr. Lebay for the murder of Miranda Quick as well as Jessica Sweet. Did you know her father was the late U.S. Senator Erwin Sweet from Lubbock? Do you care to comment?"

"No." Emily repeated it over and over.

"I didn't remember the senator was from Lubbock," Evan said at one point.

"That must be why the reporter called from there." Lissa was twisting the dishtowel in her hands.

Emily wanted to go to her and stop her from doing it, but she couldn't leave the telephone. She was waiting for it to ring again, waiting for some other reporter to mention the other killings the way the Lubbock reporter had. She was afraid to ask Lissa or Evan about it. But maybe she heard wrong, or maybe the Lubbock reporter was into sensationalism. She traced the feathered lines of her eyebrows with her fingertips. Only God knew what they would read in the newspapers, or hear about themselves on television tomorrow and in the coming days.

The phone rang again, and she was reaching for it, but suddenly Roy was there, pushing her aside, grabbing the cordless from its base, shouting into it, "Who is this?"

Emily stared at him.

"Well, here's my comment, asshole," he yelled. "You call here again, and I'll sue you and everybody at your fucking paper to hell and back."

"Dad!" Lissa said.

Emily put her hand on his arm. He shook her free. He was having none of their protest if he was even aware of it.

His voice rose. "You won't have so much as a ballpoint pen to write down your precious fucking facts, do you hear me?" Jerking the receiver from his ear, he banged it once hard against the counter before slamming it back onto its base, looking around at them. His face was dangerously red. His eyes were wide, and the irises, which were usually a pale shade of blue, were as dark as bruises. He was like a maddened bull, Emily thought.

"Dad!" Lissa tried to get his attention. "This isn't helping Tucker."

"You think we can help him? Are you crazy? You think the cops arrested him for kicks? They've got something on him, something strong, like DNA, or who knows what. Enough to make their case. Enough that he's going down."

The phone rang again, and before Emily could stop him, Roy grabbed it, ripping the cord out of the wall. The receiver skittered across the floor, but he dangled the base from his fist like a trophy, grinning, enraged.

Emily took a step back. She was acting on old instinct when she took several more steps, crabbing her way around the table, putting it between her and Roy. Her ears were ringing, her breath all but stopped. She found Lissa's frantic gaze and knew Lissa was remembering those long-ago days, too, when Roy had broken, when his control had collapsed. Reaching out her hand, Emily said, "Lissa, come. Come here to me."

But she didn't move; she seemed paralyzed. The silence spun out, mute, yet electric.

"Roy, come on, why don't we sit down." Evan's was the voice of reason, and Emily thanked God for him.

Roy looked in Evan's direction, but his face was drained of expression, as if he didn't know where he was. And he very well might not, Emily thought. She kept her gaze on him. They were each one staring at him. He might have been a live bomb or a grenade someone had tossed into their midst.

The grandfather clock on the stairway landing tolled once, marking the half hour. The telephone rang again, and the sound from the other extensions in the house was eerily distant.

"Dad?" Lissa took a tentative step toward him, and Emily gripped the back of a dining chair. "Daddy, we have to call Mickey Loomis. Tucker needs a lawyer."

"No," Roy snapped. "I'm not asking one of our clients—"

"Technically, he's not a client anymore," Evan said.

"I don't care. I'm not asking anybody for help, and I'm not paying any lawyer to bail out a killer."

"Dad!"

Emily was as shocked as Lissa. "Tucker is our son, Roy."

"No." He swung his glance to her; his finger

rose. "He's *your* son. *You* coddled him. You let him do whatever he damn well pleased, and now I hope you're happy with the result."

"Don't you dare blame me for this! I'm not the one who drank myself nightly into oblivion. I didn't scare him to death and throw him into a closet. I should have left you then. I should never have listened when you said you could make it up, make it right!"

"You're never going to let me forget that, are you? You'll blame me for every fuckup in this family until the day I die! It'll never matter how many times I say I'm sorry, will it?" Roy crossed the floor toward her, kicking aside the chair that stood between them. Emily flinched, and somehow Evan was there, blocking Roy's advance, telling him to stop, and Roy did stop.

He bowed his head.

Lissa crossed her arms, and Emily could see that she was shaken. She knew so little about her father's struggle. Maybe they'd been wrong not to be more open about it, but a man's pride was important. Roy had so desperately wanted to be the hero his children had believed he was.

"You know Tucker isn't capable of murder, Roy." Emily spoke to him from the circle of Evan's embrace, over the thudding of her heart. She was sorry for their harsh words that she knew were the result of shock and terrible fear. She would take them back, if it were possible. She knew Roy, knew better than anyone how torn he was by guilt and utter despair. They had brought Tucker into the world. Roy, perhaps even more than she did, had welcomed a son. They had raised him together with the highest hope, the greatest joy, only to see him flounder and fail again and again.

"We can't leave him in jail, Dad." Lissa drew Roy's glance.

"What do you suggest?" Roy pushed the chair gently, methodically, under the table. "Where do you think I'm going to come up with the cash for bail? The dead woman's a U.S. senator's daughter, for Christ's sake. The goddamn politicians will be all over it. Bail's bound to be sky-high."

"Whatever it is, we just have to come up with it, that's all," Lissa said.

"Bullshit! You and Evan and your damn brother have already sunk the business into more debt than it ever carried when I was running it."

"I guess it's a good thing the bank takes my signature on the business checks the same as yours," Lissa told him. "I can arrange bail for Tucker myself."

Emily waited for Roy to forbid Lissa, but he didn't.

"It's just a loan, anyway, Dad, until the charges against him are dropped."

"Ah, Liss." Her name from Roy's mouth was a sigh.

"Tucker is my brother, Daddy, and I'm going to help him. I don't care what the politicians, or you, or anyone else in the whole state, the whole world, think. He's not a murderer!"

"Take my advice—let the cops sort it out. I told you, I'm done."

"Roy! What is the matter with you?" Emily spoke almost without thinking, but she was appalled. When was a parent ever done? Regardless of the trouble a child brought home, or their age when it happened, they still belonged to you. You couldn't deny blood, or refuse it, much less be done with it. "There are other suspects. That stockbroker, what's his name, Hite. There must be dozens more given the line of work the women were in. Or are you just that determined to believe your own son is responsible?" Emily threw Roy's question to her from a few days ago into his face. A moment passed before she added, more quietly, "If that's the case, I'm sorry for you."

"Darren Coe could have done this," Lissa said. "Mom? Tell him what Joe said."

"Merchant?" Roy's glance jerked to Emily.

She'd been afraid to mention Joe, but now that Lissa had, she was relieved. "He found a police report, Roy, that says Darren Coe assaulted Miranda and threatened to kill her the month before she was murdered. There may be more to it that will connect Darren to her death. I don't know, but Joe's looking into it."

"Well, he's looking in the wrong place. Coe's a fucking hero in this town. Everyone looks up to him."

"That doesn't make him incapable of violence." Emily crossed her arms.

"He did it to me, Daddy." Lissa looked at Evan and apologized. "I didn't tell you everything about that night."

"What night?" Roy asked.

As Lissa explained, Emily moved to her side and took her hand, and when Lissa was finished, she reminded Roy of Holly McPherson's accusations against Darren that had come only weeks after his attack on Lissa.

"That son of a bitch," Roy muttered. "How does he get away with it?"

"Friends in high places, I think." Emily was convinced of this. "His sister, Courtney, is married to a Houston city councilman, remember?"

"Jesus, Liss." Evan sounded stunned.

Emily felt badly for him, for the shock this was, and the way he'd had to hear about it.

"Darren threatened to hurt Tucker if Lissa told," Emily said.

"That's no excuse, Momma. I should have said right away what happened."

Emily gave her hand a reassuring squeeze. "Joe mentioned Tucker took photos of Miranda's injuries with his cell phone so if we can just—"

"That's all well and good," Roy said, "but he

190

was arrested for Jessica Sweet's murder, not Miranda's."

"Where are they?" Evan asked. "The photos?"

"I'm hoping they're still on his phone," Emily said, "if that's possible."

"Where is it?" Roy's gaze rested on Emily. "Did you ask him? Let's have a look and then we'll see."

"He said he lost it, but—" Breaking off, Lissa found Emily's glance. "Mom, I met this woman today. . . . You don't know anyone named Revel, do you? Revel Wiley?"

Emily gave her head a slight shake. *Not now.* It was a prayer. "What was the attorney's name Tucker mentioned?" she asked, and ignoring Lissa's scrutiny, she looked at Evan. "Do you have his number?"

Evan had his phone out, scrolling the directory. "Yeah, here it is. Mickey Loomis."

Roy made a gesture as if he was washing his hands of them all. He turned on his heel.

"That's right," Emily said to his back, "walk out on your own son, on your own family. It's what you've always done." She was as helpless to keep the caustic edge from her voice as she was to stem the consuming flow of her panic.

"Let him go, Momma." Lissa's voice was shaky. Tears glazed her eyes.

Emily pressed her fist to her mouth, listening to Roy's uneven tread fade up the stairs. It was only a matter of seconds before the door to their bedroom slammed, and she felt the walls, the very floor under her shoes, tremble.

While Evan spoke to Mickey Loomis, Emily made coffee. It was marginally calming, going through the routine. Still, her brain was humming, anxious. She was aware of Lissa, taking sugar and cream to the table, and, that quickly, Emily knew she couldn't protect Lissa, that she had only been fooling herself to think it was possible, or necessary, or even laudable. But motherhood wasn't like other jobs. You couldn't retire or quit, or turn off your feelings like a faucet when your children became adults. She'd made mistakes, grave mistakes; Emily knew that, too.

She filled Lissa's cup. "Your father's right. I interfered when I shouldn't have, when it would have been better for Tucker if I'd forced him to manage on his own." She kept Lissa's gaze, seeing the question there: What did Emily want? She scarcely knew herself. Forgiveness, certainly. Understanding was probably impossible, unless you were a mother yourself, then maybe . . . But even Anna had trouble comprehending Emily's motives. Anna would say she didn't know what she would do if Tucker were hers, as if everything Emily did wasn't suitable or right.

"Tucker isn't easy, Momma, I know that." Lissa stirred sugar into her coffee. "I love him, he's my brother, but honestly, watching what you've gone through with him—it's a big part of why I'm scared to have a child."

Evan caught Emily's eye. "Mickey's talking to someone at the sheriff's department right now. We should know pretty quick about Tucker's status."

Emily nodded and, holding up the carafe, asked if he wanted coffee. "Or pie. I could cut you a slice."

"In a minute, maybe. Thanks," he answered.

"Mom? What about Revel Wiley? You don't know her, do you?"

Emily sat down. "I'm afraid I do."

The look of utter astonishment on Lissa's face might have been funny in other circumstances. "How—?"

"How do you know her?" Emily asked, even though she dreaded the answer, the one she knew was inevitable, that Revel had confronted Lissa with her demand for money in exchange for Tucker's cell phone.

"You first," Lissa said, looking somehow chagrined and worried and annoyed all at once.

"Your brother was arrested last fall, for stalking her," Emily said, and she went on, making short work of the details. "I paid her off so you—so nobody would have to know. I don't know what to think. . . ."

"But how? How did you do all this without Daddy finding out?"

Emily said she felt as if Roy did know. "I think Revel has spoken to him, too."

"Joe helped you, didn't he? Who is he to you, Mom?"

Emily didn't answer. She couldn't imagine what either one of her children would make of it if they knew she and Joe had once been lovers.

"Mom?"

She looked up. "Please don't ask, okay? You're better off not knowing."

Lissa considered this for a moment, holding Emily's gaze in a steady, penetrating way. It's what Roy did, the tactic he used when he wanted to make someone talk. Emily knew it well; she'd been treated to it many times. She clamped her jaw.

Lissa gave up. "Well, what are we going to do? She says she has Tucker's phone, that you have three days to pay her to give it back, or she's going to give it to the police. Do you think she found the photos on it that Tucker took of Miranda? Because she knows Darren assaulted Miranda. She told me—"

"She told me what she found was proof he wasn't in Austin. She didn't mention anything else."

Lissa held Emily's gaze.

"What?"

"It's just she didn't look all that techie to me, as if she would know where to look for that kind of

194

information on a cell phone. Evan thinks she's bluffing."

"Maybe he's right."

"But when she brought all that up, about Miranda, she said there were others. What if it's true? What if Darren hurt Jessica Sweet? What if that's the connection?"

"Tucker's been booked," Evan said.

Emily stared blankly at him, some corner of her mind registering that she had only the vaguest idea, a television idea, of what that meant.

"Happened a half hour ago." Pushing his cell phone into his pocket, Evan sat next to Lissa. "There's nothing we can do until morning when he's arraigned, or at least Mickey hopes it will happen that fast. He said the state will probably ask for an impossible bail amount, but he thinks he can get it down—" Evan broke off.

Emily waited. Lissa said his name.

He met her gaze. "If it comes out that Tucker is in the habit of disappearing, it could go against him. It makes him seem like a flight risk." Catching the glance Lissa darted in Emily's direction, Evan paused. "What?"

"You aren't going to believe this," Lissa said, "but Mom knows Revel Wiley. Evidently, they've done business together."

Evan frowned.

Lissa explained, her voice mixing aggravation with impatience.

As if I were a child, Emily thought, *caught in some unfortunate misbehavior.*

Evan blew out a mouthful of air. "Well, maybe they won't be able to talk about that since the charges were dropped. Let's hope they never find out how."

"If she does have Tucker's phone, don't we have to get it back?" Lissa asked. "We can't let her give it to the police."

"You want to pay her five grand?"

Emily had seldom heard Even speak so sharply to Lissa or to anyone.

Lissa said, "No, but what if it can be used somehow to incriminate him?"

"The cops can and probably will pull Tucker's cell phone records, anyway. It'll take time. They'll have to get a subpoena first, but they don't need the phone or Revel to make it happen."

"She alluded to other women Darren has assaulted. If we could talk to them, get them to go to the police—"

"No, Lissa. We aren't going to do any of that. Tucker has an attorney, the police are investigating. We're going to stay out of it and let the cops do their jobs."

"Evan's right, honey," Emily said. "Tucker has been running with a rough crowd. It could be dangerous to get involved in this any more than we are already."

"We can't cave to blackmail." Evan was firm

about it. "Your mom's already done it once, and it's unfortunate, because if the cops find out, she could be in trouble, too." He looked at Emily. "I'm sorry."

She said it was all right, that she would take whatever was coming. Getting to her feet, she went to the window over the sink as if there was anything to see beyond the reflection of her own face, pale and drawn, in the glass.

"I'll lay all of this out for Mickey when I see him in the morning," Evan said. "Let him know what Revel's up to and why. And that she's looking for more money," he added.

They shared a silence.

Evan broke it. "It should be fine."

He was trying his best, Emily knew, to comfort them. And he was right, she thought. It would be fine, as long as Tucker was telling the truth, and if truth did prevail in the end. But as anyone knew, that wasn't always the case. Sometimes what prevailed were the lies.

It was after midnight. Lissa and Evan had just left, and Emily was alone in the kitchen making a cup of chamomile tea when she heard the ceiling overhead creak. She glanced up. She had assumed Roy had gone to bed. What was he doing in Tucker's room? She listened to his footsteps criss-cross the floor; there was a sound as if furniture was being pushed around.

The kettle whistled, making her jump. Taking it from the stove, she poured the boiling water into her cup and carried it to the table. The noise from upstairs continued for several more minutes, long enough that she thought about going up, but then she didn't move. She didn't want to see Roy. She was too angry at him, still, and too exhausted to fight with him.

She couldn't imagine what difference it would make.

Remembering later, how she sat there, oblivious and indifferent, she would be appalled. She would think if only she had gone to Roy then, it might have changed everything.

15

"I've never heard my parents talk that way to each other. Have you?" Lissa looked across the truck seat at Evan. "Maybe I should have stayed."

"Your mom didn't want you to," he answered. "Like she said, you need to rest, too."

They were stopped, waiting for the light to change at the I-45 intersection. Lissa felt the intensity of Evan's gaze and went still. He was going to bring it up, the possible pregnancy; she could sense it. How could he think that was important now when her brother, her entire family, was in such terrible jeopardy?

"What about bail?" she asked, preempting him. "Did Mickey give you any idea how high it might be?"

The light changed. Evan attended to his driving, the silence riding like a stranger in the space between them.

"There's over a quarter million in the business account, but it might not be smart to take the bail money from there," he finally said.

"Then what do you suggest?" Lissa glanced at him. His face was a geometry of light and shadow, his expression a puzzle. Before tonight she would have said of everyone in the world, she knew him best, trusted him most, but he had changed the rules on her without warning. How could he possibly think that was fair? And then he'd tried telling her what to do. Where had that come from? What would happen if they couldn't agree? Suppose he left her? Now, of all times? Why was she even thinking in such terms? She scrubbed her hands down her thighs.

He was talking about taking out a second mortgage on their home.

"My parents should be the ones to do that. Their house is paid for," she said.

"I doubt Roy would go for that," Evan said, then darting his glance between the rearview and side view mirrors, he said, "Who is this bozo behind us?"

"What bozo?" Lissa looked over her shoulder.

"This guy—I think it's a guy, the one driving that light-colored Camry. See him? He's been following us. He's made every turn, changed every lane."

"Where?" Lissa couldn't pick out the car Evan was talking about, but she wasn't good at identifying cars.

"He's dropped back. Maybe I'm nuts, but I could swear he pulled in behind us when we left your folks'." Evan watched the rearview. "I think I've seen him before, too."

"Who would be following us?"

Evan shook his head. "Hell if I know. I'm

probably crazy." He looked at the mirror again. "I don't see him now."

Lissa settled back, her attention returning to her worry over her parents. "Dad acts as if he hates Tucker."

"He doesn't, Liss. You know better. He's upset, and not just about Tucker. That was kind of a bombshell you dropped about Coe."

Lissa said she knew it; she repeated her apology, and when Evan put his hand on her knee, her heart eased somewhat.

"I'd like to wring the bastard's neck," he said.

"I know."

"The cops should be looking at him for these murders. Sometimes sick bastards like Coe escalate. They go on to commit bigger and better crimes. They're like druggies—it takes a bigger fix to get their rocks off."

Lissa had heard that, too. She said, "If we could get Tucker's phone, find those pictures—"

"I meant what I said before, Liss. I don't want you going anywhere near Revel, or Darren Coe, either. Your mother's right, these people are dangerous. Let the cops handle them, okay? They know what they're doing."

She didn't say anything.

"Lissa, promise me." He squeezed her knee, adding emphasis. She promised.

"It keeps getting loonier and loonier," he said moments later.

"I'm not sure I trust the police, Ev," she said. "It's like you say, why aren't they looking at Darren? They should at least question him."

"Well, maybe they are. Tomorrow, I'll call Mickey and ask him if he knows whether Coe is a suspect."

"You won't tell him—"

"No. What happened to you is none of anyone's business." He looked at her. "You have nothing— nothing," he repeated, "to be ashamed of."

"You aren't angry at me for not telling?"

He took her hand, kissed her palm. "Not angry, no. I wish you'd trusted me. I wish you didn't feel you had to go through that alone."

She pressed her fingertips to her eyes.

"It's going to be all right," Evan told her.

"I'm just so worried about Mom and Dad. How much more of this craziness can they handle?" Lissa lowered her hands. "I couldn't believe it when Mom brought up Dad's breakdown and what he did to Tuck. They never talk about it. Have either of them ever said anything to you?"

"Nope. I only know as much as you've told me."

"Which is almost nothing." Lissa looked out at the road, subliminally aware of the traffic that passed, the stitch of the tires on the pavement. "The family strategy has always been to pretend that day didn't happen, or not so much it didn't happen as that it had no effect. Or if there were bad effects, they were dealt with. Daddy went into a VA hospital to get help, and Tucker and the rest of us went the family counseling route."

Evan allowed the silence.

"I never heard anyone at my house use the words post-traumatic stress disorder while I was growing up, never once."

"Your dad won't even use a cane, for Christ's sake. He's damn sure not going to let anyone call him a head case," Evan said.

Lissa glanced at him. "You know Tucker's innocent, right? You don't have doubts like Dad."

"Your dad doesn't have doubts. He's afraid for Tucker, that's all. He feels like he's got no control. He can't help his own son. Can't protect him. But you know how hard it is for him to show his real feelings. He's just not that kind of guy. He never will be."

"Why not? Just once why can't he let Tucker know he loves him? What is so hard about it?" Lissa didn't expect an answer, and Evan didn't supply one. She looked at the darkened faces of the houses they passed, and thought of the families sleeping inside them, their ordinary lives, their sane normal lives. "He's so much a part of Tucker's problems," she said softly.

But hearing her, Evan said, "They're part of each other's problems."

She couldn't deny it, and neither her dad nor her brother was willing to look head-on at their issues. They couldn't be honest with each other,

203

couldn't even talk reasonably to each other. It would never change between them, Lissa thought. They would never resolve their differences. Not even if one of them was dying.

Inside the house, Evan switched on the kitchen desk lamp and punched the blinking light on the answering machine.

Lissa set down her purse and went around him, and she was hunting through a cabinet for the Tylenol when she heard a voice. "This is Cathy," the voice said. "I'm calling for Mrs. DiCapua."

Lissa jerked her gaze to Evan's. It was Dr. White's nurse. Her heart slammed against the wall of her chest.

"Dr. White put a rush on your blood test, and I just happened to still be here when your results came back."

Lissa knew what that result was by the way Cathy sounded, as if she were on the verge of delighted laughter.

"You need to call the office as soon as you can," Cathy was nearly singing.

Evan switched off the phone. He was smiling.

Lissa gripped the countertop. "Maybe she always sounds that happy."

"I don't think so, babe." He came to her and pulled her into his arms.

"I can't believe we're in this predicament."

"Together. We're in it together. I know I can't be

pregnant for you, but I'll be the best support I can be. You won't have to do any of it alone—not the doctor visits, not the labor, not the night feedings, diaper changes or walking the floor. I promise, and you know how experienced I am, how many times I've been through it."

She took a shuddery breath, biting her lip, trying to swallow her tears. They came, anyway. "I'm so scared, Ev." Her voice broke against his chest.

He gathered her more closely to him, murmuring, "It's okay, babe. It's okay. I'm right here. I've got you," and his breath stirred the tendrils of hair that were loose at her temple.

She grew quiet finally, and stepping out of his embrace, she went to the pantry to find a tissue. "I don't think I'll be a good mother."

"You'll be fantastic," Evan said. "You have so much love to give. You're kind and patient, fun loving and sexy— Well, the sexy part is for me. . . ."

"Maybe not with a baby, though." *Suppose it turned out like Tucker, riddled with issues? How would they stand the stress, the heartbreak?* The questions that framed the true source of her fear rose in her mind. She couldn't bring herself to ask them out loud. It felt mean and disloyal. Neither did she point out to Evan all the unhappiness her parents had endured on Tucker's account, facing nothing but one problem after another. Evan knew all of that already.

"Nobody's family is perfect, Liss," he said, and she sighed.

She wadded her tissue and dropped it into the trash, keeping her back to him.

"This is our baby," Evan tried again, "and forgive me, but I think we'll be better parents than your folks or mine, and I think parenting is what makes the difference."

He wanted her to be persuaded, to agree, to acquiesce, but she couldn't. "I can't talk about this anymore." She faced him. "We have to get through tomorrow, Tucker's arraignment—"

"Jesus!" Evan clapped his head in his hands. "You know, Liss, I love your brother, too, but I'm really tired of sidelining our lives to take care of his, and I'm damn sure not giving up on having our baby because of him. Tucker doesn't always get to come first."

"I never said he did."

"Maybe not, but you act as if he does. You live your life as if he does."

"I'm going to bed." Lissa slipped off her flats and picked them up.

He grabbed her arm when she tried to walk past him. Their eyes locked. "That's it?" he said.

She looked down at his hand that circled her elbow, and he let her go.

"Please promise you won't do it—won't have an abortion, Liss."

"I don't know what I'm going to do, Ev."

"Lissa! For God's sake, it's not just your baby! It's my baby, too. I don't believe this, that you would just get rid of it!"

Lissa didn't answer. She felt numb with exhaustion, an overcoming sense of unreality. This wasn't happening to her but to someone else. She was a spectator, an audience of one watching a play. Soon the curtain would drop, and she would resume her life, the one she'd had before today, that she'd mostly loved and felt safe in.

Evan leaned against the counter. "You can't go off on your own with this, Lissa."

"I won't."

"But you've done it before, you know you have, and if you do it this time, if you do something irrevocable without talking to me, I don't think I can be there for you. You need to know that."

She examined her shoes for a moment, rubbed at a smudge on the toe of one. "I'm going to bed," she repeated. "Are you coming?"

"No," he said.

She left the kitchen, and despite the hard place they were in, she thought he'd follow her. Even after she changed into her nightshirt, crawled into their bed and switched off the lamp, she waited to feel his weight settle in beside her, but he didn't come. She lay on her back, fighting a fresh threat of tears, staring at the ceiling, and after a while she heard him open the door to the linen closet. She heard his steps fade toward the front of the house in the direction of the study that was furnished with an old leather sofa, and she knew then that for the first time in her married life, she would spend the night alone.

Something woke her, or maybe she never really fell asleep. Maybe her mind was working on Tucker's troubles all along as a way of distracting her from her distress over her quarrel with Evan. Whatever the prompt was, it pulled her upright, fully alert, and as if she had a plan in mind, she went from her bedroom down the hallway and into the bedroom she was using temporarily as her art studio. Her laptop was sitting where she'd left it on her art table. Perching on a stool, she powered it on and did another Google search for Sonny Cade's name, hoping there would be an email address at his company's website, and there was. But when she opened the message box, she sat with her hands in her lap, staring at the screen. It wasn't possible to condense her concern, the plea for the help she thought Sonny could provide, into a square half the size of an envelope.

How would she begin? With Revel Wiley? Lissa was still amazed that the woman had approached her. Worse yet, Revel had spoken to her mother; she had threatened her mother. The idea felt suddenly terrifying. Who knew what Revel's agenda was? But it was the same when Lissa thought of Detective Sergeant Garza. Both women gave her the feeling that her family was a pawn in some much larger game that was being played out on opposite sides of the law. It made no sense, not that Lissa could see. She loosened her gaze, thinking of Revel, recalling the woman's outrageously tight clothing, the heavily made-up eyes, her brazen demeanor.

Only other thing I can say is that's pretty much how and when all this shit got started—with those two losers. Revel had said that. What shit was she referring to? And what two losers? Tucker and Darren? Darren and Miranda? Miranda and Jessica? Lissa didn't know anything other than she didn't want her mother involved with Revel; she didn't want her endangered by that woman. If it were not for the risk it might pose to Tucker, Lissa thought, she would call the police on Revel and not think twice.

She began her message.

Dear Sonny, she wrote, I don't know if you'll remember me. We went to high school together. You knew my brother, Tucker Lebay. I would like to stop by and see you tomorrow and would be grateful if you could let me know a time that would be convenient. Lissa paused a moment before tapping out, It's urgent, then signing her name. She closed her eyes and pushed Send.

In the morning, she found Sonny's answer. I'll be at my office and free any time after twelve noon. Look forward to seeing you. S.

16

Emily bolted upright, uncertain at first what had wakened her or where she was. Objects swam at her in the murky light. She recognized Tucker's chest of drawers, his desk and chair. The linen window shade was up, the window itself a shiny, blackened eye. She tumbled her fingers through her hair, remembering now that after finishing her tea, she came up here to Tucker's room, curious to see what Roy was doing, but he'd left. She must have lain down, fallen asleep.

Fishing with her feet for her shoes, she bent absently to straighten the rug, an ivory-and-sage-green dhurrie that was askew beside Tucker's bed, and she was in the process of righting herself when the terrible sound came, shattering the night silence. It was something between a groan and a scream, barely human, ragged with fear, and she froze. *Tucker!* In her sleep-muddled mind, it seemed reasonable to think of him first. That he'd wakened in his cell and shouted out in panic. How would he stand it? Being locked up? Suppose they couldn't get him free? Her throat constricted. She lost her breath.

The noises continued, grew louder, a series of verbal, frightened bleats.

Not Tucker, but Roy, she thought, and the

realization sent her quickly down the hall toward their bedroom. She halted in the doorway, giving her eyes time to adjust, to make sense of what she was seeing: Roy, crouched on the bed, alert to some imaginary horror.

Imaginary to everyone but him.

Emily had learned that from painful experience. The first time his cries wakened her, they were newlyweds. She had naturally reached for him, wanting to reassure him, and moments later, when she found herself on the floor, head reeling, she'd had no idea what had happened, that he'd mistaken her for his enemy and slugged her, blackening her eye. He'd been mortified. As he was months later, when his fist clipped her jaw. By the third time, she learned to get out of his way. When she encouraged him to see someone professional and get help, he refused. What could a doctor do about nightmares? But then that terrible day came when instead of her, it was Tucker who was made to suffer, when Roy, however accidentally and unconsciously, had put his own small son's life in danger, and that had altered everything.

There had been other episodes since then, but none so violent, or even close, and now, standing here, Emily couldn't remember the last time Roy had a full-blown night terror. Not in years, she thought, but he was in the grip of one now, a bad one.

He was back "in country." That was how he'd put it if he could speak rationally. He would say his unit was undergoing constant shelling. Emily knew from the way he covered his ears and moaned that the noise and the action were painfully real to him. If he were able, he would say they had battled for control of this village, or that hill, or some trail, or a bridge, or whatever, for days and nights on end. He would say that after a battle, when quiet first ensued, it would sound as loud as the shelling. And yet it was through that very quiet that he initially heard the little boy's thin wail, his tiny, forlorn sobbing.

On one of the rare occasions Roy had ever spoken to Emily of the events that led to the loss of his leg, he said he acted because he knew a child was in danger, and he couldn't bear it. He tried to at first. He rolled from his belly onto his back and stared up at the vacant sky, pretending it wasn't the sky over Vietnam but over Texas. He plugged his ears and tried to tune out the anguished cries. Still he heard them even as they dissolved and grew softer and more hopeless.

At nineteen, then, Roy was barely out of boyhood himself when he jackknifed to his feet and ran a zigzag path toward the bombed-out village, heedless of his own safety, intent on finding the child, on saving him. He believed the location was secure when he scooped the small boy into his arms.

It was likely the last time he ever considered anything in his life secure.

Emily said his name now, taking a step into the room.

He gave no sign that he heard her, but shifted in a rough semicircle on his bent legs, the one that was whole and the one that was not, eyes rolling and filled with terror. Sweat slicked his face, darkened patches of his T-shirt on his chest and under his arms. His breathing was loud and ragged, almost a sob.

Emily's own throat closed. Her eyelids burned. She knuckled her fist to her mouth, fighting an overwhelming need to go to him. Any minute now the fear would pass. He'd collapse back into sleep as abruptly as he wakened, and in the full light of morning, only she would remember. That was the way a night terror worked; the dreamer would have little to no recollection of their actions. She knew this from talking to the psychologist years ago and from experience, not only with Roy but sadly with Tucker, too. His first episode had come in the wake of Roy's breakdown, when he had been so terrorized by Roy's actions.

Stress was the trigger, and they were under a huge and horrible amount of it now. It would end up killing them if something wasn't done.

Emily took another step. Ambient light trembled over the walls. She felt chilled and, looking toward the closet, thought of her nightgown and robe that were hanging inside. She could change, put them on, she thought, and she was moving that way when a sound caused her to look over her shoulder in time to see Roy drop from the bed to the floor. His back was to her. She heard his labored breath, scrabbling noises.

What is he doing? The thought careened through her mind just as he turned toward her, still crouched, raising his arm. He was holding the gun, the old Colt service revolver, and she blinked, not believing it at first. But it was there, in his hand, the same gun she'd discovered under their bed this morning, the one he had evidently stowed there without telling her. Her heart stalled.

"Roy?" His name was a question.

Emily thought of flipping on the ceiling light; she thought of letting loose the scream that climbed her throat. She did neither. Wherever he was in his mind, she was his enemy. Her eyes darted to the phone, barely discernible, on the nightstand, but if she were to move at all, he would shoot her, convinced he was defending himself, his position, the lives of his fellow soldiers. She had no doubt of that.

"Roy," she said softly. "I'm not armed. Can you see?" She lifted her hands slowly, so slowly, palms facing out.

He watched her, brow knit into a slight frown. Lifting his elbow, he balanced it on the mattress, steadying himself.

She thought it was a sign that he was coming back. "Roy? It's all right now. You're safe. Can you hear me? You're at home with me, Emily, your wife. Do you see me, sweetheart?" Her voice snagged, broke. She held her jaw tight. *Don't cry. Not now.*

Suddenly, he pivoted, and half rising, he switched on the bedside lamp then faced her again. Emily bit down on the tiny shriek that hammered her teeth. His gaze was locked on hers, and as she watched, he lifted the gun again, pressing it now against his temple.

"Roy! No!" She stepped forward.

"Stay!" he told her, and she did. Only her heart raced, battering her ribs.

Time passed. Each second was ticked away on the grandfather clock on the landing in loud, heedless defiance of everything that mattered. Emily could feel the old clock's vibration through the thin soles of her shoes, the walls of her brain. She wondered why this was happening and couldn't think how to stop it. Roy had never threatened her life or his own while in the grip of a night terror. She thought of the stories she has seen on television, where a husband shoots his wife, even his children, and then himself. What will happen to Tucker if she and Roy are dead? She made a sound, something like a whimper. She thought, *Please, don't let it end like this.*

And now, as if he was alone, and she wasn't

here, wasn't a witness, Roy lowered the gun and pushed it under the bed. Then hoisting himself back onto the mattress, he curled on his side, facing the wall, knifing his hands between his drawn-up knees, and for a big man, a solidly built man, he looked so small and as vulnerable as a child. She sat beside him, putting her hand on his hip, lowering her face to his shoulder. "It's all right now, sweet. You're safe, safe home with me." She breathed the words against the cool flesh of his upper arm, taking in his ripe odor. It was the scent of fear, of loss, of guilt and futility. He was still beneath her touch, and she couldn't decide whether he was sleeping.

Before she could put too much thought into it, she slipped out of her shoes and her slacks, and lying beside him, she cupped herself to him, molding herself to his spine, the curve of his buttocks. She wanted to warm him, to bring peace into him. And later, toward dawn, when he rolled over to face her, it seemed right when he kissed her, gently at first, but then his mouth on hers grew hotter and more demanding. She responded, arching against him, suddenly desperate with desire for him in a way she hadn't been in a long while. He found her gaze, and his eyes were intent on hers and clear of shadows. He was here now, with her, and not elsewhere, not gone to some nightmare place. She felt the urgency in his touch and welcomed it when he shoved her blouse aside and shucked her underwear from her. He groaned when he entered her as if in relief. It was as if they had made a pact to lose themselves in this wild need to take their fill of each other, but when they were finished, and Roy lifted himself from her, to lie alongside her, her impulse was to push herself away.

She was somehow appalled. It was mere hours since she was furious at Roy for walking out on her and his family. She thought of Tucker, their son, locked in a jail cell across town. Her mouth was dry, and her head was full of disgust—for herself, Roy, the sex.

"I'm sorry," he murmured, as if he were reading her mind. "About earlier, I mean. I acted like an ass."

She rose on her elbow, surprised by his apology, ready to press the advantage. "We have to be together on this, Roy."

He averted his glance.

"Roy?" she prompted, but he didn't turn to her, and his refusal to meet her eye renewed her aggravation. "I can handle the situation myself, you know, with Evan and Lissa's help. We don't need your blessing or even your permission."

He turned to her, and his face was gray, more haggard than she had ever seen it. "You've got no goddamn idea the kind of shit Tucker's in, Em. Trust me. I'm going to do what I have to, what I can to protect this family, okay? To protect you and Lissa. But I need you not to go messing in it."

She kept his gaze. "What are you saying? That you think Tucker's guilty?"

He didn't answer.

"What about Darren Coe?" she demanded. "He attacked your own daughter."

"If I'd known—"

"Well, now you do. He has a history."

"It's a long way from sexual assault to murder."

Emily didn't respond; she didn't know how, where to go with any of it.

"For all we know the police have questioned Darren," Roy said finally. He closed his eyes. "We should try and get some sleep."

She lay beside him, but she couldn't sleep. She thought of how she had found him earlier, in a panic, thrashing, and how, confronted with the heartrending evidence of his anguish, her pity for him softened her anger. The way it always did and with the same result—that she was constantly torn inside between loving him and hating him.

She thought of how he looked at her when he raised the gun to her face. Suppose he had not been unaware of what he was doing? Suppose in that deranged pocket of his mind, where the terror overtook him, he wished her dead? Wished them all dead? Wished even himself dead? The fine hairs on her neck rose. She felt his presence, the heat from his body, like a thousand hot needles pricking her skin. Was he truly sleeping or was he watching her? Waiting for her to move, to get up, to leave him? What brought the night terror on? Something must have triggered it.

She realized she had no idea anymore what he was thinking, and it frightened her. Her heart jumped. She wanted to fling aside the bedcovers, get up, get away, but somehow, she managed to wait until Roy's breathing slowed and deepened before climbing carefully from their bed. He would sleep soundly now, maybe for hours, after the night they had endured.

She carried her clothes into the bathroom and put them on, donning her old gray cardigan that she found hanging on the door hook. Roy didn't stir when she tiptoed from the bedroom, taking the cordless phone, carrying her loafers. New morning light gilded the banister, while the stairway itself was lost in a bottomless well of black ink. She scarcely noticed. She could find her way through any part of this house blindfolded if she had to. She walked through the kitchen and let herself out the back door. To be safe, she went farther, down the back porch steps, out to the picnic table. She was thinking of Lissa and the danger she could be in from Revel when she sat down and dialed Joe's number. It rang once before she thought to check her watch. Barely six.

His voice was sleepy when he answered. He brushed aside her apologies, listened while she explained her concern about Lissa, and this time, when Joe said he would find Revel and speak to her, Emily didn't argue.

"Before we hang up, there's something you should know," he said, and his voice was soft with concern. "The headline in today's paper . . . it says Tucker was arrested."

"It mentions him by name?" she asked, and she knew it was foolish.

"In the article, yes," Joe said. "I'm so sorry about all this, Em. I would give anything to spare you the heartbreak of it, if I could."

She said she knew, that she appreciated it, and then she sat for several moments after they severed their connection, holding on to her sense of the comfort and strength speaking to him always brought her.

Somewhere nearby, there was a rustle of birds waking, a sleepy song, three notes, six. A breeze twitched the newly budding branches of the old elm. Shadows in pearled shades of gray opened and closed like a dove's scalloped wings across the picnic table's dirty surface. She was buttoning her sweater against the chill when she heard it, the thud of the newspaper, the *Houston Chronicle* with its damning headline. It struck the front porch step, and she flinched.

Joe had told her what it said. He had worked a case most of the night, and he'd seen the news-paper when he got off. She was scarcely conscious of the movement when she stood and, leaving the phone, walked around the corner of the house toward the street. She had no plan to speak of. She would tell Lissa later she had nothing in mind, really. In fact, she wasn't thinking at all when she walked into the yards of her neighbors, and onto their porches, to collect the offending newspapers, as many as she could carry, and when her arms were full, she brought them home and dropped them into the trash can.

Looking down at them, she thought how many more there were, delivered all over the city, all over south Texas, and she knew she couldn't gather them all, any more than she could stop the calamity that was unfolding or keep the media from reporting it. The stories would be based on half truths and conjecture and outright lies. It was the lies that would break her family, Emily thought. The lies were what would be their undoing.

It didn't occur to her then that it was possible for the truth that exposed the lie to be even more deadly.

17

Lissa picked up the *Houston Chronicle* from her mother's kitchen counter and looked at the headline. Boyfriend Held in Strangling Death of Former U.S. Senator's Daughter, it read. Tucker's photo, his mug shot, was underneath it, but the sight of him, connected to this headline, was surreal. Surely, she was dreaming.

"It's a terrible picture, isn't it?" her mother said.

"Worse than terrible," Lissa murmured. Tucker was disheveled and staring, scarcely recognizable. "I don't believe this is happening." She passed the newspaper to Evan, and then handed him a steaming mug of coffee. Their fingers touched; their eyes clashed. He looked exhausted, Lissa thought, as if he hadn't slept, either. She didn't ask. They weren't really speaking. She found her mother's glance. "Evan has to leave in a bit to meet Mickey at the courthouse."

"You'll post bail and bring Tucker home?" her mother asked Evan.

"If the judge allows it." He leaned against the counter.

"You'll ask Mickey about Darren?" Lissa didn't want him to forget.

He nodded.

She looked from him to her mom. "I'll stay

here and wait with you and Daddy," she said, and when her mother's eyes welled, she repeated what Evan had told her last night, that it would be all right, even though none of them knew if it would be, today or ever again.

Her mother pulled out a chair and sat down. She said something about having taken the neighbors' newspapers.

"What do you mean, you took them?" Lissa poured coffee for herself.

"It was dumb, but this morning before it was really light, I was—I was outside, and something came over me. I don't know what. I got all the newspapers I could carry and threw them in the trash can. I'm so sick of the way the media lies about everything. Even that picture of Tucker is a lie."

"What is that all over your pants?" Lissa came to the table. "It looks like blood."

"It's tomato sauce. The last of the homemade. I dropped the jar last night."

Lissa realized the slacks were the same ones her mother had worn yesterday. She was wearing the old gray cardigan, too. One of the cuffs was unraveling; the elbows were baggy, and she'd buttoned it wrong, and somehow it was that detail, the misaligned buttons, even more than the rest of her mother's rumpled appearance, and the deep forlorn shadows in her eyes, that alarmed Lissa. Her mother was ordinarily so tidy. She

223

took pride in being neat. "Did you sleep in your clothes, Momma?"

"They write in the newspapers as if they know us. . . ." She trailed off, her fingers worrying the sweater's crooked neckline. "I shouldn't have done it, taken the papers. People will be annoyed. I know I am when I don't find the paper on the porch where I expect to."

Lissa exchanged a worried glance with Evan. She took her mother's hand. It was cold. "Have you eaten anything?"

"I couldn't. I should make breakfast, though, for your father. I heard him come down. He must have gone into his office. He's in terrible shape, Lissa. He had an awful night. I don't know when I've seen him in such dire straits."

Evan looked down the front hall. "The door's closed." He checked his watch. "I could try and talk to him, but I really need to go."

Lissa shook her head. She imagined her father sitting in there alone, brooding, furious. "What about some toast and juice?" she asked her mother, going to the counter. "You can manage that, can't you?"

"I'm going to take off." Evan brought his cup to the sink.

"You'll call?" Lissa asked.

"Soon as I know anything." He kept her gaze, and his eyes were gentle, but he didn't kiss her, and as she watched him go down the back steps and out to the alley, where they'd parked the truck earlier, tears seared the undersides of her eyelids.

Lissa couldn't coax her father into joining them for breakfast. He wasn't mean, or loud, or rude. He just asked to be left alone.

"What happened after we left last night?" Lissa asked when she came back into the kitchen. "Did you and Daddy argue?" She lowered two slices of wheat bread into the toaster and turned in time to see her mother shiver. "Momma?"

There was no response. She didn't even raise her gaze, as if it were so heavy it couldn't be dragged up, but faint color did rise out of her shirt collar to settle on her cheeks.

Lissa didn't press. She thought she understood. Clearly, her parents had gotten into it, and it was no surprise given how they had spoken to each other last night. She buttered the slices of toast and brought them to the table. She poured two small glasses of orange juice and brought them to the table, as well, and sitting across from her mother, she said, "I'm not hungry, either, but it won't do Tucker any good if we starve ourselves. So let's eat this, okay?"

Lissa was glad for the ghost of a smile that drifted over her mother's mouth. She smiled, too. "We'll get through this, Momma. We did it before, we can do it again. At least Tucker has a lawyer this time."

"It's going to cost a fortune, isn't it?"

"Yep, but Mickey is the best. What else can we do?"

"Your dad—"

"He'll have to get over it." Lissa took her plate to the sink and came back, balancing her hands on the back of her chair. "Momma?" she said. "You know the headaches I've been having?" and then she stopped, before she could say it, before she could deliver Dr. White's diagnosis. It sat in her mind, huge and unthinkable. *It must be a mistake.* The thought appeared, even though she knew it wasn't likely.

"You aren't sick, Lissa, are you?"

She sat down. "No, I'm pregnant."

"What?"

Lissa might have laughed at the look of pure amazement on her mother's face.

"How?"

"The usual way, I guess."

"Well, I know that, honey." Something that looked as if it might be delight hovered in the corners of her mother's eyes. "You've seen Dr. White? You're sure?"

"I talked to him this morning. He's sure, but I'm not."

Her mother was tentative. She leaned forward, and reaching over Lissa's shoulder, she lifted Lissa's braid and set it down, then ran her fingertips around Lissa's ear, patting her cheek, soothing her, comforting her.

Lissa turned her face into her mother's palm. "I'm really scared."

"I'm here, honey. I'm right here."

Lissa sat back, covering her eyes with her fingertips. "Evan is talking as if we should have it. I didn't expect that. He's always said we were enough, you know, just the two of us."

"He's changed his mind? Did he say why?"

"It's the reality of it. Before, we were talking theoretically. But this is real, a real baby. Only it doesn't feel real to me. It feels like headaches and me getting light-headed and passing out. It feels like the worst timing in the world."

"You're fainting? You didn't tell me—"

"I'm thirty-eight, Mom. Evan's forty-two. There's a better than average risk of us having a baby with problems. As if we don't have enough already."

"If you mean Tucker, you can't let his issues interfere—"

"What if I have a child like him? I love him, but when I think of all he's put you and Daddy through, I don't think I could handle it." Lissa hadn't meant to say it and, seeing the flare of regret, of remorse, in her mother's eyes, wished she could call it back. "I'm sorry, Momma. I only mean—"

"No, I know what you mean," her mother said, "but a child is such a miracle, a unique blend of so many different things. No two are alike, not even in the same family. Look at you and Tucker, you couldn't be more different in temperament."

Lissa held her mother's gaze, looking intently at her, and even though she knew it was a terrible question, an unfair question, she asked it, anyway. "If you knew then, before you got pregnant with him, what you know now, would you do it again?"

Her mother shifted her glance, something like annoyance or impatience, crossing her expression. "If I could change anything," she said after a moment, "it would be the day I left Tucker here alone with your father when he had that terrible breakdown. I would spare them both that, if it were possible, and who knows then the difference it might have made? Where we might be now, instead of this awful place where we are?"

"You couldn't have known that would happen, Momma."

Patting Lissa's arm, she said, "You can't know the future, honey. None of us can. All we can ask for is the courage to deal with the situation when the people and circumstances in our lives aren't the way we thought they were or what we planned."

"But having a baby—it seems like you're playing Russian roulette. There's no changing that outcome, either, once the bullet's in the chamber, once it's fired."

"Oh, Lissa, I think that's a little extreme—"

"What if I don't have what it takes, Momma?

The courage, the mothering, nurturing gene, whatever it is?"

"You do. Of course you do. You'll make mistakes. Every mother does. They're inevitable."

"I know everything in life is a risk, including birth, and it isn't that I don't love children. I do. It's just—" Lissa broke off. Her apprehension seemed made up of so many different elements.

"Are you considering an abortion?"

Lissa looked at her mother. "Would you hate me? I'm not so sure Evan wouldn't."

"No, of course not. You have to do what's right for you, but don't base a decision solely on the difficulty your dad and I encountered raising Tucker. You and Evan aren't the same."

The doorbell rang. Their eyes locked. Mutual alarm jolted the air between them.

"I'll go," Lissa said.

"What if it's a reporter? Or one of the neighbors? Suppose someone saw me taking their newspaper?" Her mother clutched the front edges of her sweater.

"I'll tell them they're welcome to look in the trash can," Lissa said.

But it wasn't a reporter or a neighbor. It was Detective Sergeant Garza and her partner.

Lissa's heart paused. "Detectives? Or should I call you both Sergeant?"

"Either or both is fine, Mrs. DiCapua."

Lissa's glance darted over Garza's shoulder to

another man in uniform, and then her gaze traveled farther, to the street, where a Lincoln County sheriff's patrol car was parked at the curb.

"Sorry to trouble you, but we've come for Tucker's car," Garza said. "We have a warrant to take the vehicle and another allowing us to search the premises." She held up a fistful of folded documents, meaning for Lissa to take them.

She didn't. She asked if it was necessary, as if she had a choice. She thought of shutting the door.

Garza introduced her to the man in uniform, explaining he was there to take the vehicle. "We've got a tow truck standing by in the alley."

Lissa stood motionless, but when Garza moved as if she meant to step over the threshold, Lissa blocked her. "I'd like to look at the warrants, please."

Garza handed them over, and Lissa unfolded them, amazed at her nerve. Phrases written in legalese swam at her: *Affiant came before me this day . . . Whereas I have made inquiry . . .* But her anxiety was so strong she couldn't make much sense of the words. She did note the warrants were signed by a judge and stamped with an official-looking Lincoln County seal.

"Look, Mrs. DiCapua, I know this is difficult, but the quicker we get started, the quicker we can be out of your way."

"Lissa? What's going on?"

"It's the police, Momma. They're taking

Tucker's car and searching the house." Lissa backed out of the doorway; she found her mother's hand.

"I need one of you to open the garage," Garza said.

Lissa wondered how they knew Tucker's SUV was in there.

"I'll do it," her mother said.

An image of the rust-colored stain on the floor of the cargo hold flooded Lissa's mind. "Is it really necessary to take the Tahoe?"

Her mother said, "You won't find anything," as if she knew.

"Blood." Lissa said it before she could stop herself, as if she had to.

Her mother stared at her. Garza and her cohorts were riveted, waiting for Lissa to explain.

She darted a glance toward her father's office. Even though the door was closed, he must hear them. Why wasn't he out here, taking control? It was what he was best at. Suppose he'd had a heart attack? "There's blood in back," she said, "on the carpet. It's from a dog." Lissa spoke over her panic and dismay. She argued with herself that it could work in Tucker's favor, that she had volunteered the information. She said to herself that it would show Garza they weren't attempting to hide anything, and if they weren't, then neither was Tucker.

"Tucker rescued a dog a few weeks back.

Someone hit him and left him in the street," said Emily.

Lissa was relieved that her mother knew.

"My son is kind like that," she continued.

Lissa exchanged a look with Garza. *Told you.* The words hung in the air, palpable for all that they were unspoken.

"Yes, ma'am." Garza was noncommittal. "We still have to impound the vehicle."

Her mother nodded and retraced her steps to the kitchen with the deputy trailing in her wake. Lissa was amazed at her mother's composure. She seemed like the eye of the storm, and somehow it settled Lissa, quieted the hammering of her pulse. "Where do you want to start?" she asked Garza, and when the detective answered that they would like to begin with her brother's bedroom, Lissa led the officers up the stairway, conscious of the sound of their tread on the steps, the ribbons of dust swirling in the muted light, the booming tick of the grandfather clock on the landing.

"This is it." Lissa paused in the hallway outside Tucker's bedroom, hesitating, unwilling to move aside, to open his private space to police scrutiny.

"We can take it from here," Garza said.

Lissa stepped back then, letting the detective and her partner cross the threshold. While he went immediately to Tucker's closet, Garza stood just inside the doorway, running only her glance around the room, as if she were studying it, absorbing the atmosphere. Something in her posture, the intentness of her gaze, caused a frisson of unease to loosen along Lissa's spine. After a moment, Garza crossed to the bed and bent to retrieve a stack of magazines from the floor, riffling through them. Lissa saw that issues of *Playboy* were among the collection.

So what? she thought. "All guys read *Playboy*," she said, and she regretted that she'd spoken, that she sounded so defensive.

Garza set the magazines on the nighttable. "Maybe you should go downstairs and check on your mother, Mrs. DiCapua."

Lissa didn't move. "Did Tucker bring you the receipts? If not, they're in the glove box of his car. They'll prove he wasn't here."

Garza didn't answer.

"Have you checked out the security footage at the club where he was in Austin? Talked to the members of the band he was with? What about the club owner? Tucker knows him."

The pity on Garza's face when she looked at Lissa infuriated her. "What about Darren Coe? Have you heard of him? Did you know he assaulted Miranda and threatened to kill her the month before she died? There's a report in Houston. Could you at least look into it?"

"I think I found something." Garza's partner was far enough inside Tucker's closet that Lissa couldn't tell what he was holding. Clothing, maybe—a shirt or a jacket. "What is it?" She started across the room.

Garza held up her hand. "We need you to go downstairs now, Mrs. DiCapua. We'll let you know when we've finished."

Lissa kept the detective's gaze long enough to know she would gain nothing by arguing. On her way to the kitchen, she tapped on her father's office door.

"Daddy?"

No answer.

"Please say something, will you? Just let me know you're all right."

"I'm fine." The syllables were clipped, dark.

"The police are here. They have a warrant to search the house."

No response.

"Daddy? You're going to have to let them in." Lissa balanced her fingertips on the doorknob, thinking of turning it, but she knew it was locked. "Be that way," she said under her breath.

Her mother was sitting at the kitchen table and Lissa joined her. Neither of them spoke. The drag of the officers' footsteps overhead was loud and jarring. It was as if the house had been overrun by aliens or thieves, and they could do nothing about them.

"They took the Tahoe?" Lissa finally asked.

Her mother said they had. She said, "There was a lot of blood in the hatch."

"I know," Lissa said. She didn't say how badly the sight of it had frightened her. She would come undone if she started talking about her fear, and that would undo her mom.

"The deputy said they would run DNA on it." Her mother looked down the disordered front of her sweater, unbuttoned and rebuttoned it. "He told me he couldn't just take our word for it, that it was from a dog."

"I don't know why the police are even looking at that blood. Jessica and Miranda were strangled." Lissa thought a moment. "I bet it's a scare tactic. They do that, you know. They're like Daddy. They think it'll make you talk."

She heard the detectives descending the stairs, and she went into the hall, heading toward the living room, her mother following close behind.

"What's in those bags, do you suppose?" Her mother had stopped to look at the two brown sacks with tops neatly folded over, standing by the front door, and Lissa thought of the discovery Garza's partner had made upstairs, that whatever it had been, it was inside one of the sacks now.

She went into the living room, her mother at her heels. "Sergeant?"

Garza turned from the piano, holding the photo of Tucker and Lissa in their childhood Easter finery. It looked obscene in her hands. Lissa wanted to order her to put it down.

"You aren't taking those, are you?" Her mother's voice was thin with dismay.

"No." Garza set the photo back on the piano.

Lissa looked through the arched doorway into the dining room where the other detective was hunting through the drawers in the sideboard, riffling the stacks of linen, turning over pieces of the family's sterling silver.

Her mother said, "If you could tell me what you're looking for . . ."

Neither of the police officers answered.

Lissa said, "I imagine that would defeat the purpose, Momma. Wouldn't it, Detective Sergeant?"

"What's that door go to?" Garza indicated the office on the other side of the hallway. "We'll need to get a look around in there. The kitchen and laundry room, too, then we'll get out of your hair."

"My husband's in there. He isn't well. I don't want to disturb him."

Lissa said, "We don't have a choice, Momma," and crossing the hall, she knocked on the door. "Daddy? You need to let the police in, okay?"

He pulled open the door so abruptly, Lissa was almost unbalanced, and brushing by her, steps dragging, uneven, heartbreaking, he demanded Garza show him the warrant.

Lissa's breath faltered at the sight of him. He looked awful, raw-eyed, as if he'd been crying. Was that possible? Like her mother, he was dressed in the same clothes he'd had on yesterday.

He hadn't shaved, and the short gray bristle of his beard faded into the gray bristle of his buzz-cut hair, catching the light, seeming to wrap his head in a silvery caul. Lissa exchanged a worried glance with her mother.

Lissa said she had the warrant, and she went to the kitchen to retrieve it. When she returned, the detectives were already inside her father's office, with the gun cabinet open. They were questioning him about permits and whether any of the guns had been fired recently. Lissa handed him the warrant, and he took it, without looking at it. Looking instead at Garza, asking the same question Lissa had. "Why do you care about the guns? The Sweet girl was strangled, wasn't she? The same as Miranda."

Garza didn't answer him. She left the room without the guns. Her father sat behind his desk, but Lissa and her mother followed the detectives into the kitchen.

"When will you return our things?" Lissa's mother asked them.

"Once the investigation is over," Garza said.

But Lissa wondered who would care what became of the sacks and their contents after this was over—especially if Tucker went to prison?

Garza spoke to her mother. "If you could direct us to the laundry room—"

Lissa pointed it out, and when Garza came from there with the basket of unwashed laundry, when she dumped it into the sack her partner held open, Lissa was in disbelief. "What are you doing?" she asked.

"Those are my husband's clothes." Her mother was nearly shouting.

Garza said she was sorry; she mentioned the warrant again, that it stipulated they could take anything and everything that might be useful as evidence.

"My husband's clothes don't qualify."

Lissa slipped her arm around her mother's waist.

"Roy's favorite flannel shirt is in there. At least let me have—" She broke off, taking in a sudden breath, shifting her gaze.

Lissa tightened her grasp. "Momma?"

"Tucker did some wash—"

"When?" Garza asked.

"Monday. He started a load. I finished it for him." She faltered over the words, as if she were examining the memory in her mind. When Garza's brows rose, she said, "There was nothing on his clothes, Sergeant. I would have noticed. I can testify to that. I can put it in writing, or whatever you people—"

"Shut up, Emily."

Everyone, including Lissa, turned toward the sound of her father's voice.

He came into the kitchen, pausing at the foot of the table, holding on to the back of a chair as if he needed it for support.

Lissa's mother stepped out from her embrace. "I'm just explaining—"

"I'll handle this."

Garza set down the laundry basket. "Let's stay calm here, okay, Mr. Lebay. You give us another minute or two, we'll be on our way."

"I'm not giving you a goddamn thing. I want you out of my house."

"I understand—" Garza began reasonably.

But she didn't understand, Lissa thought.

"Now!" her father shouted, stepping toward Garza.

"Stay there, Mr. Lebay." The detective raised her palm to the level of his face, widening her stance, and putting her free hand on her hip, she flipped back the front edge of her suit jacket far enough that Lissa saw the butt of her holstered weapon. Her partner adopted the same square-shouldered stance as Sergeant Garza. Their moves were sharply defined and well-executed, like dance steps.

Like taking the safety off a gun.

"C'mon now," Garza said. "Let's not make this any more difficult than it has to be."

"Lady, you haven't seen difficult." He took another step, and it was meant to be menacing, but the posturing was empty, almost foolish, and it hurt Lissa to see him. He was so disheveled, dilapidated really, weighed down. The whole structure of his face seemed to have loosened overnight into folds that sagged toward his neck.

Seconds passed, and Garza evidently came to the same conclusion, that his threats, like his appearance, lacked substance. She retrieved the laundry basket, returning it to the laundry room. She smiled at Lissa and her mother and said she was sorry. "Truly," she added.

She seemed genuine, but it could just as well have been an act. She said they would see themselves out, and Lissa waited with her parents in the kitchen, listening to the scuff of their footsteps fade down the long front hall. The click of the front door was soft. Lissa looked at her mother. She was looking at Lissa's dad.

"Roy?"

He walked to the back door as if he hadn't heard, as if Lissa and her mother didn't exist. His gait was awkward; he was very nearly staggering, and when he stooped to catch the place on his leg where the stump met his prosthesis, Lissa brought her hands to her mouth. The screen slammed behind him.

"Roy?" Her mother followed him onto the porch, down the back steps.

Lissa went to the screen, holding it open, looking after them, her father lurching across the yard, disappearing into his workshop, her mother faltering in his wake. Lissa watched until her mother, too, disappeared. She should go after her parents, but what could she do or say that would help them? Instead, she hunted through the keys that were hanging on the hook by the door until she found the set that went to her dad's truck.

Before she left, she wrote her parents a short note—*Running an errand. I borrowed the truck. Hope it's okay*—and signed her name.

Pulling out of the neighborhood, she headed for I-45. Sonny's company was located on the other side, the west side, of the interstate. His email had specified he wouldn't be available until after twelve, but she was lucky, spotting him almost immediately through a partially open door behind the reception desk when she walked into the security firm's outer office. He was talking on the phone, head down, leafing through the loose pages inside a manila folder.

"May I help you?" the receptionist asked. She was young, still in high school, Lissa guessed.

She gave her name and explained she had an appointment, that she was early. "It's urgent, though," she added. "He knows that it is."

"Okay. Let me ask if he can see you now." The girl smiled, and went to Sonny's door. A conversation ensued that Lissa couldn't hear, but when the girl came back, she smiled again, and said Sonny would be free in a few minutes.

Lissa was looking at a row of photographs, black-and-white images of men dressed in army fatigues, carrying weapons and all manner of wartime gear, when Sonny said her name. "Lissa Lebay!"

She wheeled. "It's DiCapua now," she said.

"Oh, right. I heard you married that guy who worked for your dad." He came toward her, swallowed her hand in his grip.

"I didn't think you'd remember me," she said.

"Prettiest girl in your class and totally out of my league."

Lissa liked his grin, the humor and warmth in his eyes. She didn't remember that from high school. The other real change in him she could see, other than that he'd gained in height and breadth, was his hair. It was cut short now, a military bristle, like her dad's.

He ushered her into his office, directed her to a chair in front of his desk.

Lissa seated herself, noticing an array of photos on the credenza. A girl in one of them resembled the young receptionist and when Lissa remarked on the likeness, Sonny said it was his daughter. "Pammy's a sophomore this year at our old alma mater. Can you imagine? That high school was new when we started going there."

"It goes by fast, doesn't it?" Lissa said, adding truthfully, "Your daughter's lovely," and she was grateful for this initial exchange of pleasantries. It mitigated the intensity of her anxiety and made Sonny seem regular. He was a dad, a family man, not the smart-mouthed kid she remembered with the swagger and the attitude.

He smiled again. "Good thing she takes after

her mother, huh? She's a good kid. You have any?"

Lissa shook her head. "I'm here to talk about Tucker. You know he was arrested for Jessica Sweet's murder. It's possible he'll be charged with Miranda Quick's murder, too." Mickey had explained the additional charge could be forthcoming.

Sonny sobered. "Yeah, I kind of figured that's why you wanted to see me, but I'm not sure how I can be of help."

"Tucker said you work security at the club, plus you're a police officer."

"Not anymore," Sonny said. "I quit the force last year when the company started making money. I like being my own boss."

"Oh, well, sure. I know what you mean." Lissa ran her fingertips around her ear and smiled briefly. She felt nervous. It wasn't anything she could put her finger on; Sonny was outwardly friendly, but she sensed a reserve. "Tucker didn't kill those women, Sonny. I know how that sounds, coming from his sister, but you know him. You know he couldn't have—" She broke off, afraid of losing her composure, and she didn't have time for that.

"Would you like some water?" he asked, and she ought to have found his solicitude reassuring, but she didn't.

Thanking him, she declined his offer and cleared her throat. She wanted to ask him outright if he agreed that Tucker was innocent. She wanted to demand that he tell her what he knew, because he did know something. His gaze was so intent, she felt under scrutiny. She felt the way she had when she'd sat across the desk from Detective Sergeant Garza, as if there were some agenda working that she knew nothing about. Maybe it was a cop thing, but somehow, Lissa didn't think so, and doubt made her cautious.

"I want to help Tucker," she said. "But I don't know how. I thought maybe you would know— because you work at the club, you would know whether there were other men who— I mean, you must hear things, see things."

"I can only imagine how difficult this is," he began.

"Yes." Lissa cut him off. "My parents are a mess. So is Tucker. Do you remember Darren Coe from high school?"

"Coe? Sure. Why?"

"I heard a couple of things recently about him that make me wonder if he wasn't involved with Jessica and Miranda and not in a good way." Something like interest flickered across Sonny's expression, or did she imagine it? Lissa wasn't sure.

"What couple of things? Who have you been talking to?" Sonny's tone was conversational, not in the least threatening.

Still, Lissa felt the small hairs rise on the back of her neck. Remembering her dad's caveat regarding a man's silence, she didn't answer.

Sonny bent forward on his elbows. "If you're asking whether Coe frequents the club, the answer is yes. He comes around. He's like a lot of guys. Married or not, they've got a thing for the ladies. In Coe's case, they're his after-school sport, if you get me." Sonny laughed at his joke, then his mouth flattened. "I heard his wife doesn't much like it."

"You don't look as if you like it, either."

"The guy's an asshole. We both know that. He's been an asshole his whole life."

"He assaulted Miranda the month before she was killed. Did you know? Was he an asshole to Jessica, too? Did you ever see him get rough with her? Could he have done this, Sonny? Could he have murdered these women?" Lissa was begging; she could hear it, but she couldn't feel badly about it, given what was at stake, and she thought it was worth it when she saw Sonny's expression soften. She saw his guard come down.

"Look," he said, "between you and me, Tucker's problem is Darren's reputation here in town. You ran around with his sister in high school, right? You know she's married to a Houston city councilman."

"But this is Lincoln County."

"Lincoln County, Harris County, doesn't matter. Coe's got family on the force up here, an uncle. Either place, whatever complaints come in about him, they hit the circular file. Are you getting me?"

"You're saying Darren can do whatever he wants, break whatever law, batter women, murder them and get away with it, and my brother can go to prison for it."

"I'm not saying anything, really."

"Because you could get into trouble." Lissa wasn't asking. "Something else is going on here, isn't it, Sonny?"

He regarded her steadily.

"That sting operation—" She paused to pass a hand across her brow as if she might clear it of her disbelief that she was sitting here, having this discussion. She thought if she didn't know better, she would look around for a television camera. She began again. "That sting operation, the one that got Todd Hite arrested. Miranda was the one who told the police what was going on. She was working for them. Were you aware of that?"

"I might have been," he said, shifting in his chair.

"Did Jessica work for the police, too? Could that be the motive in her murder? Because Tucker wasn't involved in any of that, he wasn't arrested. He didn't even know Miranda was a police informant."

"He *was* arrested, though, last fall for stalking Revel Wiley. Did you know about that?"

Lissa's breath left her in a dejected gust. "I only found out yesterday when Mom told me." She met Sonny's glance, looked away, looked back.

"What?"

"I talked to Revel." Lissa didn't know whether to be frank. She couldn't get beyond her sense that she was endangering Tucker, herself, her family, with all this talking. This was what happened when you lost your ordinary life, she thought, and another life was substituted, one for which you had no road map and you were afraid to ask for directions, because you didn't know who you could trust.

Sonny, who had been leaning back with his hands behind his head, sat upright now. He repeated what Lissa said. "You talked to Revel," and she caught it again, that bright note of interest, curiosity—suspicion?—that shiny edge in his tone of voice that made her nervous.

"You know her, right?" Lissa asked.

"She's a piece of work," Sonny said. "Where did you find her?"

"She found me. She came up to me in the parking lot of my office and tried to blackmail me into paying her for her silence about Tucker. She acted as if she knows things about him. At least, it's what she wanted me to believe."

"Huh." Sonny toyed with the edge of his desk blotter.

"She said she has Tucker's cell phone, that there's information or something on it that proves he wasn't in Austin, but he's got receipts that show—"

"She doesn't have his cell phone. The crime lab techs in Houston have it."

"Revel turned it in?"

"I'm not sure how they got hold of it. I don't see how they could have gotten it from Revel, though."

Sonny said this almost to himself, and he did look confused. Lissa would remember it clearly later, the bafflement on his face.

He met her glance. "I heard it was underwater at some point, that they don't know whether they can get any data off it."

"Underwater?" Lissa was mystified.

Sonny didn't respond.

In the pause that came, Lissa heard Pammy talking and thought she must be on the phone.

"There's one other thing I can tell you."

Lissa brought her gaze back to Sonny, who eyed her somberly. "You didn't hear this from me, okay? But the coroner's report indicates he found Coe's DNA on Jessica Sweet's body."

"Really?" Lissa felt hope rise. "Does that mean—? Isn't that good news?"

"It could be. The thing is he found Tucker's DNA, too, so in this case, the DNA doesn't necessarily mean anything. Both those guys had a thing for her. Both of them were seen with her the night she was murdered."

"Tucker has an alibi, though, I started to tell you—"

"Yeah, I heard that, too. He claims he's got receipts, proving he wasn't in the vicinity at the time of Jessica's death, but he never turned those over to the cops that I know of."

Lissa started to say the police had taken Tucker's car; they would find the receipts in the glove box. But suppose they didn't?

Sonny got to his feet, and she did, too.

He said, "I wish I could be more help."

She shouldered her purse. "Tucker didn't do this, Sonny."

"My money's on Coe, but then I think the guy's a son of a bitch and being a son of a bitch doesn't get you convicted of murder in this state."

"What does, Sonny? What will it take?"

"A witness," he said, "or a confession."

Lissa thought about that. She repeated the word *confession* in her mind. Sonny's voice stopped her at the door of his office as she was leaving.

"What was Revel driving when you saw her?" he asked. "Did you notice?"

"Couldn't help it. A brand-new red Lexus. Lipstick red. I always heard exotic dancers made good money. Why?"

"Oh, no reason," he answered.

Lissa kept his glance a moment longer, and somehow, she knew he was lying.

Outside, she hunted for her own truck for several moments before remembering she had driven here in her dad's truck. Sliding behind the steering wheel, she backed out slowly, and that's when she noticed it, the light-colored Camry. At first, Lissa thought the driver, a woman, wanted her space, but then the car fell in behind her. Lissa glanced at it in the rearview. She thought how she wouldn't have recognized, or paid attention to, the make of the car at all, if Evan hadn't mentioned that he thought a Camry followed them from her parents' house last night. But he had said the driver was a man.

Turning left under the freeway overpass, she found the sedan again, traveling in the lane adjacent to hers, several discreet car lengths back. Lissa deliberately slowed, waiting for it to close the gap. The driver directly behind her honked his horn, a long angry blast. Ignoring him, Lissa slowed even more. Traffic made it impossible for the Camry to do anything but pass, and when she caught sight of the driver, her breath stopped.

Revel?

Could it be her? Lissa saw only the driver's profile as she sped by. Still, Lissa was almost positive Revel was at the wheel. She hung back, and it was only as she watched the Camry disappear that she realized she should have taken down the license plate number and called the police. Or Sonny. But then Lissa thought, No; she didn't trust them any further than she did Revel.

18

Emily followed Roy into his workshop, worried for him, needing to know his mood, what he was thinking. The window glass was fly-specked and cloudy from age and rainwater. The stone floor was cool under the thin soles of her flats. The air smelled of wood shavings, linseed oil, an underscore of turpentine. It reminded her of her father. He'd spent a lot of time out here; it had been his refuge.

"Lissa's pregnant." She began with the lesser of her anxieties, and when Roy didn't answer, she said, "I don't know if she'll go through with it. She's afraid."

Roy's silence continued. It was so quiet Emily could hear his breath. She could hear the drone of an airplane overhead. Someone down the street was mowing their lawn.

"Roy?" Emily turned.

"I didn't think she could have kids. I didn't think she wanted them."

"That's what she's said in the past."

"What does Evan say? Does he want her to have it?"

"He does. I think they've had words about it. Lissa sees it as a kind of betrayal, because Evan has always said he didn't care whether they had

251

children. It's the reality, you know? It's different than the possibility. For him, anyway. I think it is for her, too, but she's fighting it."

Roy fiddled with his tools, picking up a whittling knife.

"Are you all right? I'm talking about last night. Do you remember?" Emily wasn't thinking of anything other than the Colt revolver. She saw it in her mind's eye, the way he had held it on her, then on himself. She had half hoped the police would find it and take it, take all the guns. But that one, the revolver, she had to get it out from under their bed, out of their room.

Roy said he remembered, and somehow she knew he was referring to their intimacy.

"I'm talking about before," she said meaningfully. "You were in— You were really struggling. A nightmare, I guess?" Her voice lifted; she was asking, hoping he would say what triggered it.

He wiped a hand over his head. "I'm under a shitload of stress."

"I know. We both are. The whole family is."

"You don't know the half of it," he said, and something in his tone raised the fine hairs on the back of her neck.

"What does that mean?" she asked.

"Nothing," he said. "I'm sorry about last night," he added, and his voice was rough.

"We just have to get Tucker home safe, Roy," she said.

"I know about Joe Merchant," he said, locking her gaze.

"Joe?" The name from her mouth was a question, a protest.

"Don't." Roy raised his hand at her. "Don't come off like you don't know who Joe is, or what I'm talking about, okay? Give me that much, won't you?"

She stared at him, feeling caught, snared; she was a deer in the headlights. "It's not what you— He's a friend, Roy. That's all." She stammered as if she were guilty, but of what? What did Roy know? From whom?

He turned his back to her.

"Am I not allowed to have friends?" Her tone rose, bordering on shrill. Even as she spoke her mental eye was loose and flying over her memories of the hours she and Joe had spent together. There was nothing there, no adulterous act, nothing close . . . other than the truth her heart knew.

The sound Roy made was derisive.

"Are you accusing me?" She was furious now, that he had made her feel guilty, that she had allowed him to have this effect on her.

"Should I be?" He faced her. "You just said it isn't what I think. How do you know what I think? If it's only a friendship—"

"It is," she insisted.

Roy picked up a chunk of balsa wood, turning

it in his hand. It was four or five inches in length, an elliptical shape. A project already in progress. "Here's what I think—know," he amended, setting the blade of his knife against the wood. "You have never been happy with me."

"Oh, Roy, that isn't—"

"Let's be honest, can we? Once?"

"If you're saying I've been unfaithful, I would never do that to you. You should know that about me. After almost forty years together I would think you would know that. After last night, I was with you, there with you, loving you—"

"What I know is that after I got back from 'Nam, I was bullshitting myself when I believed you weren't marrying me out of pity."

She started to object. He cut her off with a gesture, and after a moment, she admitted that maybe she had felt a certain amount of pity. "How could I not? I still feel it—pity, sadness, call it what you will—I call it compassion—for you and all the men who fought in that war, any war. Does that make my commitment to you less, because I hurt for you, because I'm sorry you lost your leg?"

He didn't answer.

"Roy?"

"It doesn't matter anymore."

"Of course it matters." She crossed the floor to stand next to him, to look into his face, and she was shocked to see his anguish. It was carved into the creases that bracketed his mouth; it sharpened the shadows in his eyes. Somehow they fumbled their way into each other's arms, and she felt him clinging to her. He bent his head awkwardly into the hollow of her shoulder.

It wasn't a lover's embrace, but more one of desperation, even of fear. She thought of the ways he had always been at war inside himself. She thought of who he might have been if he hadn't gone to war. The loss of his leg was horrible enough, but it was the loss of his dreams that had crippled his soul. What was a man without dreams?

If only he could accept the rewards from the life he had lived, if he could be content with that, but that, too, seemed beyond his scope.

"It's my fault," he said now, raising his head.

"What is?" she asked.

"Every goddamn bit of what's happening to us, to Tucker, and I'm sorry, Em. Sorrier than I can say, and I mean to take care of it. I'll fix it. I will. I promise."

Emily tightened her grip on him. She had never thought she would hear that promise again, had never imagined they would be in circumstances that would require it. "It's all right," she said, forcing herself to sound calm. He didn't need to know he was scaring her. "You're exhausted," she told him.

Roy broke their embrace, wiping his hands down his face. He said he was fine, but of course, it was obvious that he wasn't, and now, on top of everything else, he was ashamed. She wished she could spare him that much at least.

"I should check on Lissa," she said, thinking that to give him time alone to collect himself was the next best thing. Thinking if she could somehow get by Lissa, she would go straight upstairs to retrieve the gun. But where would she put it?

Roy said he'd be in later. He said, "It was that woman, Revel, who told me."

Emily frowned.

"About you and Joe meeting with her. I know you paid money to get the stalking charge against Tucker dropped. Revel wants more now, which, if you'd asked me, I could have told you would happen when you paid her the first time. But you didn't ask."

"I didn't want to worry you, Roy. You were already dealing with your retirement, and we were just getting through Tucker's involvement with Miranda's death."

"So you called Joe. Yeah, I got that."

She had injured his pride, wounded him more deeply than she could have imagined, or would have ever wanted to do. The harm she'd done him sickened her. "I'm so sorry. I thought—" she began.

"I figure you know she's got Tucker's cell phone," Roy cut her off. "She wants five grand for it, or she's giving it to the cops."

"Evan thinks she's bluffing."

"Well, even if she doesn't have it, she can cause trouble."

"How do you mean? What else can she tell them?"

"Come on, Em. You basically bought her off to get Tucker clear of that charge. You think she won't tell the cops about that and how you did it?"

Emily said she would have to face that when it happened, and she was almost to the door when Roy's voice caught her. "You'll be fine, you know," he said.

When she paused and looked back at him, he shook his head. "I only mean you shouldn't worry."

"You shouldn't, either," she said. "We'll get through this somehow."

"Yeah." He turned from her. "Even the shit in your life's got to come to an end at some point, doesn't it?"

19

It was near one o'clock and Lissa was walking through the front door of her parents' house when Evan called her to say the judge had granted bail for Tucker.

"Thank God." She walked down the front hall to the kitchen. The note she had left was still on the counter. Crumpling it, she crossed to the sink and looked out the window at the workshop. Were her parents still in there? What was going on with them? There was a knot in her stomach like fear, but maybe it was the baby. Lissa put her hand there. How big would it be? she wondered. How many cells high and wide? She opened the trash can and dropped the unread note inside it; she returned the keys to her daddy's truck to the hook beside the back door.

"Lissa? Are you there?"

"Yes. I'm sorry. Mom and Dad are— How much was bail?"

"A hundred and twenty-five thousand, but I only had to write a check for ten percent. Mickey says it would have been worse if the state had any forensic evidence. Also, it turns out the judge knows your mom's family. Evidently the Winter name still carries a lot of weight in this town."

"For some people, I guess. I don't know how much longer that'll hold up, though. What did Mickey say about what Mom did, paying off Revel? Please tell me she won't be in trouble."

"He's working on that and trying to find out about Coe's status with the cops. He said he might issue a preemptive order to get Tucker's cell phone records himself, especially since Tuck says they'll back up his alibi, show he was in Austin."

"The police may already have his phone."

"Revel turned it in?"

"Not exactly, but really, I don't know," Lissa added quickly. She bit her lip, unsure whether to bring up her meeting with Sonny. Evan would be angry, angrier than he already was, that she'd broken her promise not to involve herself. But not telling him meant she couldn't mention sighting the Camry, either, and he should know that, shouldn't he? She touched her temple, confused and still shaken. She was plagued by the sense that they were at risk, that Revel, or whoever it was driving the Camry, and the police posed a danger to them. But what if she was only being overly dramatic? Is that what Evan would say?

She spoke before he could. "How can the phone tell them anything about his location?"

"It records information the same way as a GPS. It's not as accurate, but I think it would be good enough to back up Tuck's alibi."

"Oh, Evan, that would be fantastic. It would be over then, right?"

"It would be strong circumstantial evidence, yeah, but I wouldn't break out the champagne just yet. Tucker is still in some serious shit here."

Lissa sobered, feeling afraid again. "How is he? Did you ask him about Darren assaulting Miranda? Does he still have the photos?"

"He doesn't have the phone he took them with anymore. He said when the cops tried to follow up with her at the time, she wouldn't cooperate."

"Why?"

"He thinks she was scared. But you know this is really not a concern. Like your dad said, he's not charged with Miranda's murder."

Yet.

The word hung between them.

"Anyway, he's not too coherent right now. He's really wrecked, Liss. He looks like hell."

"Poor guy. God, Ev, what're we going to do? What's going to happen now?"

"A trial, it looks like. The judge set a date in June, unless something comes along to prevent it."

Like the cell phone records tracking Tucker's trip that night to Austin, Lissa thought, or what Sonny said, a witness who knew the truth, or even better, a confession from the real killer.

"I've got to go," Evan said. "Tucker and Mickey just came out of the courthouse."

"I love you, Evan. I don't know what I'd do without you."

"See you in a few," he said, and then he was gone.

She stayed at the window, feeling Evan's unhappiness with her, but how could he think they could deal with a pregnancy now? She could barely imagine how they would survive the rest of the afternoon. By June, she would be, what, four months along? Five? And starting to get big. She needed to be working, pulling her weight. If money had been tight before they put up Tucker's bail, it would be even worse now. And his bail was only the beginning. It was going to take all of them working, and even then, they'd be lucky if the business survived.

Lissa turned from the window. She put her fingertips to her temples. Daddy was going to have a fit.

The phone rang, the landline, the sound falling down the stairs.

Lissa's mother came through the back door. "Reporters?" she asked.

"It hasn't stopped. I'm not answering."

"No, I wouldn't," her mother said. "Have you heard anything?"

Lissa repeated the gist of Evan's phone call, and then, because she couldn't hold it in any longer, she confessed she'd gone to meet with Sonny Cade.

"You don't sound as if you trust him," her mother said when Lissa finished giving her the details.

"I have a weird sense about all of it, Momma, even Detective Garza. It's as if we're being watched or something." Lissa went on, describing how she and Evan felt they'd been followed last night. She said, "I'm not sure it was the same driver, but I'm pretty sure the same car followed me from Sonny's office."

"I think I've seen it, too, yesterday."

"You're kidding." Lissa kept her mother's gaze. "Did you see who was driving?"

"No, it passed by in the alley, twice. I didn't really register— It was a woman, I think."

"Revel? Could it have been Revel?"

"Oh, I hope not, Lissa. It worries me so much that she confronted you. Now if she's following you— Why would she do that?"

"I don't know. The whole thing is scary. You have to be careful, Momma."

"It's not me I'm concerned about. It's you."

"I thought of telling the police, but I don't want them to know about our connection to Revel. Who knows what they'd make of it."

"Maybe the best thing would be to tell Mickey."

"That's what I was thinking," Lissa said.

"And Evan. You have to tell Evan, too. It's no good keeping secrets in a marriage, Lissa." Her mother traced her eyebrows with her fingertips.

Her hands were shaking, and there was something working in her eyes, a kind of fervency. She was still so disheveled, in her ratty sweater.

Lissa resisted the urge to go to her and straighten her out.

"We should make sandwiches." She went to the pantry. "There's all that leftover chicken."

"I'll get it," Lissa said.

"It's the blue platter." Her mother got out the bread.

"Is Daddy coming in?" Lissa set the platter on the counter and returned to the refrigerator for lettuce, tomato and condiments.

"In a while," her mother said. "I think he needs a bit of time to get himself together."

"He's not okay, is he?"

"Not so much at the moment, but he will be," her mother answered.

A kind of apprehension crossed her expression that made Lissa ask, "What is it?"

"He knows about Revel. Everything. All of it, and he's upset, mainly because I involved Joe Merchant, I think."

"I knew it. Joe *did* help you get Tucker out of jail last fall. Why are you so secretive about him, Mom? I can tell he means something to you."

A flush warmed her mother's face; she ducked her head.

"Mom?"

"No, Lissa, honey, I'm sorry, but I don't want

to talk about Joe right now. Okay? Can we drop it?"

"Is he an old boyfriend or—or—" But now her mind stumbled at the idea of her mother having an affair.

"Lissa, please?" she begged. "If your dad should walk in, I don't want him overhearing. He's had enough, okay?"

Chastened, Lissa picked up the knife and went to work on the chicken, feeling unsettled. If it was an old love, why was it still such a sore spot?

Lissa would have asked, if the sound of the back door opening hadn't distracted her, if she hadn't caught sight of Tucker walking in.

His eyes teared when she met his gaze. He looked from Lissa to their mother. "I'm so sorry," he said.

And they went to him and folded him into their embrace, and for a long moment, he leaned into them. Lissa had the sense that he would fall without their support. She had the feeling that she and her mother were all the defense, all he had in the world. She felt her mother's anguish and knew she was crying.

The three of them broke apart clumsily.

Her mother went to find a tissue.

Lissa looked around Tucker at Evan, where he stood apart, leaning against the counter. She didn't hold his gaze more than an instant, couldn't read his expression.

Her mother offered the sandwiches.

"I don't think I can eat, Mom," Tucker said. "I just want a shower and to go to bed, if it's okay. I'm so damn tired, I can't think."

She cupped his face, took him into her arms again, murmuring.

"Tucker?" Lissa said. "Do you think it's possible you might have left your phone in Galveston? Were you on the beach? Could you have dropped it in the water?"

"Was it found?"

Lissa didn't look at her mother. "I was just wondering."

"I guess anything's possible," he said, coming to hug her. "I've got to crash." He left the kitchen, and they watched him go.

Upstairs, the phone rang.

And rang.

Lissa went to the window over the kitchen sink. She guessed her dad was still in the workshop. A piece of the alley on either side of it was visible, and she half expected to catch a glimpse of the Camry passing by, Revel at the wheel. She thought again of what Revel said, her line about how this had started—*with those two losers.* What did that mean? Where was Tucker's cell phone? Did Revel have it? Or was Sonny telling the truth when he said it was at the crime lab? And who was following them? Who owned the Camry? Evan had seen a man at the wheel, but it had been dark. He could have been mistaken. Lissa and her mom had seen it in daylight, and on both occasions, a woman was driving. Lissa was convinced she wasn't wrong in guessing it was Revel. Who else had a reason to follow them?

Behind her, Evan and her mother were talking about the media. "Reporters have been calling all morning," her mother said.

"There's a news van out front," Evan said. "I don't know what station, whether it's local or Houston. We came down the alley. I guess they don't have that figured out yet."

"They will sooner or later." Lissa turned from the window.

Evan said he was going out to the site. "I guess I'll swing back by and pick you up later?"

"No, I'm coming with you," Lissa said. "You'll be okay, Momma, won't you?"

"Of course, honey. I know you both have to work. Lord knows we're going to need the money."

"You'll call if anything happens?" Lissa kept her mother's gaze.

"Go on. Don't worry. Get some rest, if you can. You have to take care of yourself now."

"You told her?" Evan asked.

Lissa didn't understand him at first. Then she remembered she was pregnant. Pregnant! she thought, and it shocked her all over again. "I didn't think you'd mind. You don't, do you?"

He looked disconcerted, as if he didn't know what he thought.

"Whatever you decide, Evan, whatever you need, I'm here for both of you," her mother said.

Lissa kissed her cheek. "Thanks, Momma."

Evan gave her mother a hug, but he didn't speak until he and Lissa got into the truck, and then he asked if she was riding with him, out to the site.

She said no. "Would you mind dropping me off at home? I want my own truck, then if Mom or Tucker need me, I can drive myself there." And she left it at that, because he would argue if she told him her intention was to go into Houston, find Revel and somehow make her talk. Evan would say, again, she should leave Tucker's defense to the professionals, but Lissa had no faith in the effort they'd made on his behalf so far.

"I hadn't thought of that," Evan said, and she was relieved.

"I may run by the grocery store before I come out to the site." Lissa invented a bit more fiction, buying herself extra time if she needed it. "I have to pick up some things for dinner."

Evan pulled into their driveway, and she got out.

"I was surprised that you talked to your mom about the baby when we haven't really discussed it ourselves yet." His voice caught her before she could close the door.

"Well, I guess I didn't think you'd mind. I mean, she is my mom."

"But it's our baby, our decision."

"She isn't going to interfere, Evan."

"She'll support you, Liss. Whatever you decide. It won't matter how I feel."

"Of course it matters! I'm not going to do anything without telling you first."

"Anything like an abortion, is that what you mean?"

"No, Evan. I just said—"

"Yeah, you'll consult me first. Thanks a lot for that. It's a real goddamn comfort to know you'll give me a heads-up so I can pencil in your appointment to get rid of our kid. But don't expect a get-well card, okay?"

She stared at him, astonished. The sting of his words, his ugly tone, were like a slap across her face. "We probably shouldn't have this discussion now."

"You're right. Somebody's got to keep the work going, because it's going to take a shitload of money to get Tucker out of the jam he's in this time."

"That's exactly my point, Ev. How can we think about having a baby now?"

He recoiled. "My God! You're really serious. You really are going to use the trouble Tuck's in as an excuse to terminate your pregnancy."

She opened her mouth, not knowing what her

response would be, but he cut her off, saying he didn't know why he was surprised, repeating what he'd said last night, the accusation that Tucker always came first with her. He shifted his glance and said, "I was stupid for thinking it would be different this time, that once, just once, you might consider putting something else, someone else, first."

"That's unfair, Evan! What's happening to Tucker isn't my only concern, and you know it." She stopped. "We aren't going to get anywhere this way, Ev."

He leveled his glance at her and asked her to close the door.

"Evan—"

"Please. I have to go. I need to go."

She slammed the door and watched him back out of the driveway. How had this happened? Only days ago she'd been a happily married woman, and if life wasn't perfect, it was close. Now she and Evan couldn't speak to each other without fighting, and Tucker was facing a murder charge, maybe two murder charges. But standing here in the icy shade of her incredulity was of as little use as her tears or her remorse. She dug her keys out of her purse, got into her own truck, following in Evan's wake. What did he expect her to do? Abandon Tucker? Leave him to a legal system that seemed hell-bent on convicting him?

She couldn't do it; he was her brother. And there was something very wrong with what was happening to him and to her family. They were being blackmailed and threatened, lied to and followed. Reflexively, she checked the rearview, searching for the Camry, almost wishing to see it shadowing her. It would save her the trip into Houston, the hassle of finding Revel. But if it was back there, she couldn't pick it out of the heavy flow of traffic.

What am I doing? She was close to the freeway, heading into the far right lane that would take her south into the city, when the question rose in her mind. Somehow her direction didn't feel right, and she yanked the wheel left now before she could half think about it, and amid the blare of horns and a veritable forest of fingered complaints, she crossed three lanes and entered the northbound interstate feeder, cringing, whispering, "Sorry, so sorry."

She was thinking of what Sonny had said, that it would take a witness or a confession to clear Tucker. If that was true, the killer was the best witness, and the very same person who would make the confession.

And that wasn't Revel Wiley.

It was Darren Coe.

20

She knew exactly where she'd find him, given that it was March and the height of the public school baseball season. He'd be at the practice field behind the junior high school, unless the team had a game. Lissa prayed they didn't, not that she had any idea what she would say. She wanted this over, that was all, the right person punished, and she had little faith in the police effort, centered as it was on Tucker. What did that leave? Who except her?

She thought of what an unlikely candidate she was to pursue Darren. She thought how she had imagined she would never have to see him again. She wondered if she was thinking clearly, or if she was even a good judge of that. What if the stress and her fear had made her crazy?

The dark ribbon of asphalt that led to the network of athletic fields was printed with tire-worn images of helmeted warrior mascots carrying lightning bolts. Stenciling them onto the road was a huge project, one the student members of the spirit club undertook before the start of every school year. Lissa remembered the last time she'd done it, her senior year. She and Courtney Coe had come out here together. They'd done everything together then, they'd been like twins, but that had changed after the party in Galveston. Lissa had never told Courtney about it. She'd been too ashamed, too certain she'd brought Darren's attack on herself. The secret had loomed between them; it had begun the ruin of their friendship. Lissa had known it, but looking back now, she could see telling would have ruined it, too. Courtney would never have believed her, the same as she hadn't believed Holly. It would be so hard to face it, Lissa thought, something so horrible and twisted that your brother had done, and she was sorry for Courtney suddenly, sorry that it wasn't only Darren, but his whole family, that would suffer when the truth came out.

Rounding the corner of the junior high, she saw the boys on the practice field, and she drew in a small, sharp breath, thinking, *Perfect*. Thinking, *I can do this*.

She didn't go right up to the fence behind home plate as she might have. Instead, she pulled the truck near the screen of a small wooded thicket. Parents did this sometimes when they wanted to check out their sons' performance without being obvious.

Lissa put down her window and propped her elbow on the ledge. She could see Darren in the batter's box, hitting fly balls into the outfield. Above the infield chatter, she heard him shouting encouragement. She heard the bat crack against the leather of the ball, too, and she was oddly comforted by the sound. Her memories of Darren weren't all bad. When she was a kid, she'd come out here to practice with him and Tucker and her dad. She'd brought out the equipment, fetched water, shagged balls. Sometimes Courtney had come, too, but only if she was bored.

Summers, when Tucker took off for baseball camp, her dad had sometimes brought her out here by herself and they'd knocked the ball around. Once, he'd taught her about pitching. She can still remember the feel of his hands on hers when he'd worked to position her fingers around the ball: two stretched along the seam made it curve, knuckles curled under and thumb just so, you had a fast break. She remembered the summer wind and the smell of their sweat, the earthier smells of sun-warmed grass, glove leather and dust.

But there was no way back to that simpler time or place, she thought.

She looked through the windshield at Darren Coe, watching him, the easy rise of his bat, his effortless swing. He had all the moves. He was a ballplayer, all right. A natural born athlete, her father said. It was true. Anyone could see it, but it had been wrong for her dad to compare them, to so thoroughly favor Darren and so constantly find fault with Tucker.

Tucker hated their dad for it.

Lissa hated Darren.

She got out of her truck now, not quite closing

the door, and walked up to the backstop fence. She hooked her fingers into the wire mesh. A couple of the outfielders looked at her and then at Darren. He tapped a dribbler down the third base line that the baseman scooped out of the dust and tossed to first. The pitcher snagged a second hit, a high pop-up fly. Lissa had the feeling Darren knew she was there, that he'd known it from the moment she drove under the trees, but when he finally turned around, he widened his eyes as if she were the last person he expected to see.

"Lissa Lebay. What brings you here?" he asked. His smile was rote.

She'd forgotten how good-looking he was, and it annoyed her. "It's DiCapua," she said for the second time that day. "It has been for nine years. Can we talk?"

He lifted his cap, wiped his brow and resettled it, a gesture that was oddly reminiscent of Tucker. Lissa's heart fisted.

"Hey, Jordie?" Darren hollered at a guy near the dugout. The assistant coach, Lissa thought. "Can you take over for a few minutes? I need to talk to this—" he hesitated, locking his gaze with hers. "Lady," he said finally.

Bitch, that's what he was thinking. Lissa saw it on his face. She let go of the fence, telling herself to settle down, to breathe. But he knew she was nervous. She saw that on his face, too.

Jordie said it was fine, giving Lissa a considering

look, one that made her think he knew who she was, the sister of Tucker Lebay, the guy who'd been arrested for murder.

She tucked the cold tips of her fingers into the back pockets of her jeans, and when Darren joined her, they walked a little way off in the direction of her truck. Her pulse was loud in her ears. *What is your plan now?* asked some desperate inner voice. She didn't have an answer.

"I'm amazed you'd come out here, that you'd risk being this close to me," he said. His tone, his demeanor, were casual, too casual, and raised the fine hairs on the back of Lissa's neck.

He flashed that fake smile again, as if they'd been discussing the weather not murder. Goose-flesh rashed her skin.

"It's not that I mind that you came. It's just I'd like to know why. Maybe you want to pick up where we left off, is that it?"

"I came because you knew Miranda Quick, Darren. You assaulted her and threatened her and then you killed her. Now you've murdered Jessica Sweet."

"I don't know where you're getting your information, Liss, but it's dead wrong."

"You knew both those women, Darren. You dated them. You cheated on your wife with them."

"So? Who's telling you all this? Tucker?"

"Your friend Revel," Lissa said, lying bald-faced, watching his expression.

"That bitch? Are you kidding me? I thought you were smarter than to believe what some whore says." He walked a few steps away, walked back. "What the hell do you want from me, anyway?"

"I want you to man up and tell the truth."

He stared at her like he couldn't believe what she'd said. His mouth twitched, and she wondered if he was going to laugh. She glanced past him at the ball field. No one was looking in their direction. They'd been forgotten. She doubted anyone would pay attention if she were to scream.

"You want me to man up." Darren repeated her words, and his voice was low and soft, a caress. He touched her cheek, traced a path to the corner of her mouth. "Are you giving me permission now? You think you're ready for a real man?"

She stepped sharply back. Panic gripped her shoulders, tracked her spine. "I wish I'd reported you, you bastard!"

He grinned and as suddenly sobered. "I'm not saying those bitches didn't deserve what they got. They were like you, a couple of prick teasers." He stepped toward her again as he spoke, ran his hand around the shell of her ear, managed to whisk the pad of his thumb across her lower lip before she got out of his reach.

She wiped her mouth. "Miranda filed charges on you, Darren. The police know you threatened her. There's a report. I also know the police found your DNA on Jessica's body. I'm going over to the station now and tell Detective Garza what you did to me. I'll get in touch with Holly McPherson, too. Between us, we can make the police listen. They'll investigate, they'll find others. You're going to be arrested."

He guffawed and, lifting his hands, said, "Ooooh, I'm so scared," in a high, breathy falsetto. "Give me a fucking break. Like the cops are going to pay attention to some hanky-panky that went on twenty years ago. Are you kidding me?" He looked over his shoulder, asking, "Is she kidding me?" as if they had an audience, as if he'd never heard anything so stupid.

It was pure impulse that drove Lissa toward him, a consuming need to hurt him, to claw his eyes out. If she could she would grind him into dust under her heel. A moment sooner, and she might have caught him off balance, when he was addressing his imaginary audience, but as it was, he caught her wrists, and yanking her close, he bent his mouth to her ear. "I knew you liked it rough. I knew it that night in Galveston. What do you say we finish what we started, hmm?"

She writhed in his grip, panicked and furious, and it was a moment before the small, defiant noises in her throat finally found shape. "Let go of me!" She spit the words through her clenched teeth.

He obeyed, releasing her so suddenly she staggered, and nearly fell.

They stood, gazes locked, he eyeing her sardonically, she breathing in ragged, enraged gulps.

Suddenly, he raised his arms and lunged at her, calling out, "Boo!" and he laughed again when she backpedaled, this time losing her balance and sitting down hard.

She bit her lip, tasting blood. The threat of tears was more from panic and humiliation than anything else, but she'd be damned if she'd cry. "Bastard."

"Yeah, that's what my wife says." He walked off a few steps, as if he intended to leave her alone, and she started to feel relieved, to get up, but then he came back. "You know, I'd be a lot more pissed off at you if I didn't know why you're doing this."

She didn't answer.

"You're just like Courtney, always running your damn interference, thinking you know best, thinking you know how to help. Courtney thinks a person can change. Like that." Darren snapped his fingers. "I keep telling her it's not that easy. Some stuff can't be changed, and some people can't be helped." His stare was penetrating.

Lissa kept still, weighing the odds of escape. Could she get to her feet and run fast enough? It seemed unlikely. As clear as her plan had appeared to her before, now she couldn't imagine what she'd been thinking, coming here, confronting him alone. Had she expected he would simply acquiesce when she accused him? That he would accept her offer to drive him to the police station, where he could turn himself in and write out his confession?

Bending, he scooped a pinecone off the ground and tossed it hand to hand, looking down at her. "If it's any consolation," he said, "I'm with you. I don't believe Tuck killed those fucking sluts, either."

Darren's defense of Tucker caught Lissa off guard; the ensuing rush of gratitude, of vindication, confused her, but she thought it was meant to. She thought it was the effect he wanted.

"Bitches played us. It's how they got their kicks. We weren't the only ones they screwed over, either, so I'm thinking one of their other chumps took them out. Like they messed around with the wrong guy, some really sick bastard who wouldn't take their shit."

Lissa got to her feet, not taking her eyes off Darren.

He tossed the pinecone toward the playing field. "All I've got to say is my hat's off to the murdering fucker. Damn sluts. The only thing they were ever into was each other. Now they're dead." He put out his hand as if he meant to brush Lissa off or straighten her shirt.

She flinched from his touch.

"Have it your way," he said. "You Lebays,

bunch of freaks," he muttered, and he started back to the ball field.

"One thing, Darren?"

He met her gaze.

"You may think you've gotten away with this, that you've hidden all the evidence, but that's wrong, and we both know it." She waited for him to laugh at her, to mock her again, but he didn't.

He said, "You know, this might have been funny before, but I'm not seeing the humor in it anymore."

"I never did." Lissa didn't know where the bravado came from to stand her ground, but she was glad for it.

He took a half step back in her direction. "Listen up, little girl. If I hear you're talking to the cops about me or anyone in my family, I'll shut you down. Do you understand? No one is going to pay attention to you, much less believe anything you say, but I don't like it. You can't go around accusing people of shit like murder. It'll get you into trouble, trust me." He grinned abruptly, as if it were all a joke. It was unnerving. He was still smiling, still alarmingly affable, when in his next breath he reminded her that he knew where she lived; he knew who she loved, including Evan.

She backed away, carefully, keeping him in her sight.

Anyone watching them would have thought they were friends. They would have seen Darren wave, would have heard him tell her it was good seeing her.

She reached her truck, got in and drove away so fast the rear end fishtailed. At the last moment, she looked into her rearview mirror half expecting to see him, to find that he had followed her, but he was nowhere in her view, and somehow she found that even more frightening.

21

He couldn't afford for her, or anyone, to think he was scared; he couldn't so much as be seen breaking a sweat. He thought he was doing pretty good, but now he was worried about the god-damned box, the one that contained the *evidence*. He kept hearing that word; she had said it, and it could only mean one thing, that it had been found. Was it possible? Or was he just being paranoid? He had to check. The only way he'd relax was if he went to the house and looked, if only to reassure himself it was there. He hung a right, took the feeder road onto the I-45 interstate, thinking about the box, picturing it in the place where he'd left it with the items he'd collected stowed inside. He told himself there was no way, no fucking way, anyone could have found it there.

It was small, handmade from walnut, and inside, the lining was emerald velvet, tufted with tiny amber beads. He liked the fact that the box was handmade. It was probably the main reason he'd chosen it to house his mementos, the silken locks of their hair, their plastic laminated driver's licenses, a lipstick, a dangly turquoise earring, the souvenirs he'd kept to remember them by—the evidence.

He should toss it, but every time he tried, he couldn't go through with it. He knew it was sick, that he had to be one sick bastard for wanting to hang on to the shit. You'd have to be blind, deaf and dumb not to know it was sick, but still he kept it. Sometimes, he looked at the stuff, and he remembered. Their smell, mainly some amalgam of dirt, sweat and fear. Their eyes, white in their heads. The flash of teeth, polished, glistening, clenched tight enough to break bone. He'd sat beside them awhile afterward, too shocked by what he'd done to move, but somehow satisfied, too, knowing they belonged to him, only to him.

He parked now and made his way into the house, quietly at first, uncertain if anyone was here, excuse ready on his tongue if they were. But the place was deserted. He'd gotten lucky, but really it was because they were so dumb. He stepped inside the room where the box was hidden, taking a moment to look around, to study whether anything appeared out of place, but if there were anomalies, he couldn't pick them out. The room looked the same to him, static, untouched.

People could be such fools. They could think you were good. Good to your core. They could see you as their fucking hero. They were too stupid or ignorant to figure it out, that it wasn't you they were looking at; it was an image.

On his knees now, he lifted the floorboard, and on seeing the box, that it was still there, untouched, undiscovered, he felt the glow of satisfaction and of relief.

22

Lissa was still rattled from her encounter with Darren an hour later when Evan got home. But there was all the other business between them, too, the harsh feelings that were left from when they'd parted earlier. Evan's eyes when they met hers were ragged with that history, dark with the burden of it, of carrying it all day. Lissa wanted to go to him, to burrow into his arms, to give comfort and take it. But it wasn't that simple anymore, and she was too unhinged.

"I saw Darren," she said, and she blurted out the details, all of them, except the part about where it had gotten physical. She said, "He threatened me—us, my entire family. Can you believe it? Should I call Sergeant Garza, do you think? I'm not sure I trust her, but—"

"What I think is you were crazy for going there, Liss. What the hell is the matter with you? You promised not to interfere!" Evan yanked off his jacket, flung it over a chair. "If half of what you believe about the guy is true, why would you want to mess with him? Get him stirred up? Good God!"

"I don't know. It was stupid. I see that now."

"Jesus. You lied to me yesterday about going to the Merrills' and lied to me today—you said you were going to the grocery store, then coming to the site. I called and called. I left messages. I was worried you'd passed out again at the wheel or something." He passed a hand over his head, and Lissa realized how shaken he was.

Tears rose in her throat. "I'm sorry I lied, sorry I scared you. I am, Ev, it's just— What are we going to do? We're the only ones who know the truth."

"We don't know, Liss. We suspect."

"*I* know," she insisted, and then she stopped, and with her eyes, she implored him.

"What?"

"Sonny Cade, the security guard at the club, the one Tucker knows—"

"No! Say you didn't go see him, too."

She didn't answer.

"I don't believe this."

"He thinks Darren could be guilty, Evan."

"He probably is, but—"

"If you could have seen him today, if you'd heard how he sounded. It was scary."

"That's my point, Lissa. You have got to stop putting yourself in danger. Let the system work."

"No!" She walked in a circle, hands clapped over her ears. "I don't trust it. What if it fails? Innocent men go to prison all the time."

Evan didn't answer.

"I saw the Camry again," she said.

"Where?"

"When I left Sonny's office, it followed me. A woman was driving. I think it was Revel."

"Revel? What the hell?"

"Mom saw it, too, and a woman was driving."

Evan pulled out his cell phone.

"Who are you calling?"

"The cops."

"No, Evan, think about it. You'll have to tell them Revel's connection to Momma, that Momma bribed her. Besides, I'm not one hundred percent positive it was her. Call Mickey instead. There must be some way he can find out who that car belongs to."

But when Evan dialed him, the attorney didn't answer. Evan left a message and pocketed his phone.

His silence made her anxious.

He blew out a sigh, plowing his hand over his head. "I did talk to Mickey earlier," he said.

"And?" Lissa prompted.

"He told me there's a possibility the D.A. will ask for the death penalty, if they can prove premeditation or if kidnapping came into it. They're going to go hard because Jessica was a senator's daughter. It's how it works."

Lissa couldn't breathe; her head felt light. Evan eased her into his embrace, walked her to the table, lowered her into a chair and knelt beside her. He was prepared for her tears, but she was too stunned, too frightened, to cry. He looked into her face and said Mickey wasn't certain yet.

"I wouldn't have said anything, but I didn't want you to hear it on the news." He waited a half second, and added, "All this stress you're under, it worries me for the baby."

"The baby? The baby?" She had to repeat herself before she could grasp the sense of his concern, and then she bolted from the chair, pushing by him, turning to stare at him. "Good God, Evan, my brother could be put to death for something he didn't do! How can you even think about that?"

Evan straightened. "How can you not?"

"I don't want to be pregnant. I don't want to have a baby. I never lied to you about it."

"But now it's happened. Do you know how it makes me feel to hear you say that you don't want it? Why don't you just say what you really mean? That you don't want me."

"That's ridiculous, one thing has nothing to do with the other."

They regarded each other, and she saw something working in Evan's eyes. She thought he might be debating how to respond; she thought she was prepared for whatever he might say, but she was wrong, and when he told her, "I can get an attorney," when he said, "I can fight you for our baby's right to live," she was caught so off guard, her knees loosened.

She reached for the countertop, bracing herself.

Her ears were ringing. She had known this morning, in the driveway when they'd argued, that he was angry at her, terribly angry, but she hadn't imagined it would come to this. "You'd do that?"

He held her gaze for a long moment. "I love you," he said. "You are my heart, Liss, but I would leave you. Know that. I would have to, and I would ask you then to have our baby and give it to me. I believe in a woman's right to choose, in your right to choose, but I'm the baby's dad, and I have rights, too." He waited, and when she didn't answer, he went on. "I'm sorry for the timing. I'll help Tucker any way I can, always, but you've got to understand that I'll do whatever it takes to make sure our baby is safe."

She stared at him, speechless, breathless in her sheer amazement at his equanimity. When did he have time to think it through so thoroughly, this plan for his life that didn't include her? It panicked her, infuriated her. How dare he? How could she live without him? She wrapped her arms around herself, her abdomen, subliminally aware that the gesture was protective, proprietary, born of pure instinct. She was shaking so hard he must see it, but he made no move toward her. He meant her to know that he wouldn't back down, she thought.

He apologized again for the timing, for putting additional pressure on her, but he felt he had to act immediately, before she did something irrevocable. He said it was a lot to take in. He offered her that, a bone to the dog. "If it makes any difference," he said, "I'm as surprised as you are about the way I feel. I never expected to look forward to changing another shitty diaper. I thought after raising my sisters and brothers, I'd had my fill."

A silence came only to be broken a moment later by the merry chime of the doorbell. Evan said he'd go, and when he came back, Tucker was with him.

If anything, he looked more haggard than before. Lissa saw nothing familiar in his eyes when he found her gaze. All the silliness, the brash foolishness, was gone, the light extinguished. He seemed lost, like a bewildered child, and she went to him, flinging her arms around him, furious at herself when the waterworks started.

"I hope it's okay that I came," he said. "I'd have called, but as you know, I don't have my phone."

Lissa swiped her eyes, pinched her nose, exchanging a glance with Evan.

"Look, Liss, I know about Revel," Tucker said. "She's playing games. I'm sorry she's coming after you guys, but no matter what she says, she doesn't know anything, okay? Don't give her any money."

"No, I wasn't planning to. She may not have the phone, anyway. Did Mom tell you?"

"Yeah. I heard you saw Sonny, but just so you know, I wouldn't trust that guy, either."

"But the other night when we got you from jail, you said—"

"Yeah, well, things change."

Lissa didn't know what to say next.

Tucker broke the silence. "I was hoping maybe I could stay with you guys for a while."

"How did you get here?" Evan asked. "Don't the cops still have your car?"

"Mom loaned me hers, but I've had it pretty much all afternoon. I need to take it back."

"We can follow you," Lissa said, "and bring you back here."

He pulled her braid over her shoulder and held her gaze. His eyes were reddened with his sorrow and regret. "I'm really sick about all of this, Liss."

She glanced sidelong at Evan. Couldn't he see it? Tucker's terrible vulnerability? He was in a fight for his life. *His very life!* It would take more than money. It would take everything they had—everything *she* had—to save him. It would use every ounce of her courage and strength to keep her brother going through this. And she wasn't brave or strong, not the way Evan was. How could she handle being pregnant, too?

Evan went to the sink, washed his hands. "So, I guess you're staying for dinner, Tuck? I don't know what we're having."

"Yeah, if it's okay. Listen, I would just stay through the trial, 'cause, you know, I don't think I can handle being at home with Pop the way he is."

Evan turned his back.

"What happened?" Lissa asked. "Did you two get into it again?"

"No, and as crazy as it sounds I almost wish we had." Tucker raised his ball cap, and when he resettled it, he pulled the bill low, shading his expression. "It's just the way they look."

"Mom and Dad?"

"Yeah. Like they're half-killed. Pop's a mess. He's in so much damn pain, but he won't do shit about it. He just sits there. I can't take it. Knowing I'm the cause, I mean."

"It's not your fault."

"Yeah, right."

"You can't help that this is happening, Tucker. For whatever reason the police have fixated on you. They won't look at anyone else. God!" Lissa bounced the heel of her hand off the counter. "It's just so unfair and wrong."

"Did Evan tell you? The state's asking for the death penalty."

"He told me, but it's not certain, right? Isn't that what you said, Ev?"

"It'll only happen if they can find concrete, physical evidence," Evan answered. "So far, they've got nothing. You heard Mickey, Tuck. Their case is strictly circumstantial."

Lissa looked a question at Evan. "You saw Mickey?"

"I sat in on Tucker's meeting."

"I called you first." Tucker found Lissa's gaze. "I wanted someone to go with me to Mick's office. I didn't want to ask Mom or Dad."

Lissa admitted she'd been to see Darren, and Tucker was as unhappy about it as Evan. Why had she gone? Tucker asked. Didn't she know the guy was dangerous?

"Plus the dude hates my guts," he added.

Lissa said she understood that. She started to bring up Miranda, the reported assault. It bothered her that Tucker hadn't told her about it when it happened. She wanted to know why, but he or Evan, one of them, would only remind her Tucker wasn't charged with Miranda's murder. They would only go on and on about how she shouldn't interfere.

Tucker went to the table, asking if he could sit down. He asked for water, and Evan brought him a bottle from the refrigerator. Uncapping it, Tucker took a long swallow. His hand tremored. He was as pale as frost. Lissa had to look away. It hurt too much, watching him, seeing the signs of his terrible fear.

"Do Mom and Dad know?" she asked, looking back at him.

"What? That they might put me down? I

couldn't tell them. I guess somebody should, though, before they hear it on the news."

Evan said, "Maybe we should table all of this for a little while, try and relax, and have dinner. You hungry, Tuck? Could you eat a steak? Lissa, don't we have some T-bones in the freezer? It would only take a sec to thaw them in the microwave and get a fire going. What do you say?"

"I love you, man, that's what I say." Tucker went to Evan, and they grabbed each other clumsily the way men do when they're overwhelmed and feeling awkward with emotion.

Lissa wanted to be there, too, with her arms around them both, but she was afraid Evan would reject her, that Tucker would notice, that she would have to say why, and she wasn't ready. It was difficult enough facing the thought of calling her mother. How could she tell her that her son was facing possible execution? How could she say Evan might leave her?

She waited until after dinner, and while Tucker and Evan did the dishes, she took her cell phone outside. The night air was crisp and as tart as the first bite of a fresh, chilled apple. A breeze scattered splinters of light from a full moon across the yard. Lissa perched on the edge of an old wooden porch rocker that had once belonged to Hiram Winter, and hugging herself, she looked at the sky, delaying the inevitable, finally dialing.

Her mother answered, and as quickly as she could, Lissa said Tucker was fine, and that he wanted to stay with them for a while, and then she stopped because she didn't know how to go on, how to say, Oh, by the way, your son could be put to death by the state.

But her mother knew already.

"It was on the news?" Lissa asked.

"I don't know. We aren't watching it. A reporter came up to your dad outside and told him." Her mother's voice was flat, carefully devoid of emotion.

Sensing the effort it took, Lissa matched her mother's reserve, saying it wasn't certain. She went on, dishing out a stream of comfort, and her mother returned the favor. They agreed the blood in the Tahoe would lead the state nowhere, and in fact, that alone could end their case. They didn't mention the cell phone or the other unknown evidence that might have been packed into the bags the police had taken from the house, or Lissa's meeting with Sonny, or the Camry, or Revel Wiley and her blackmail scheme.

Lissa decided against telling her mother about the trouble with Evan, too, and when her mother asked her how she was feeling, she said she was fine and left it at that. She didn't mention Darren, either. She had no idea where her own breaking point was, much less her mother's, and she had no wish to find out. Not tonight.

She said, "We'll bring your car back after dinner."

"How will Tucker get around?"

"I'll take him to the office to get the company van. It'll do until he can get his car back from the police." *Assuming they give it back. Assuming he's free to drive it.* The thoughts were there, alive in the air between them, but they wouldn't say them.

"Have you told Tucker about your pregnancy?" her mother asked.

Lissa said she hadn't. "I think I should wait until I know what I'm going to do."

Her mother agreed.

A silence hovered. Lissa looked out over the yard. The only sound was the cool breath of an evening breeze. It whispered through the greening blades of grass, sighed along the row of pink-blossomed oleanders that served as a fence line. "Momma," she said finally, "how can this be happening to us?"

But her mother couldn't answer that, and after a moment, they said good-night.

A little later Lissa followed Tucker to their parents' house and waited while he went inside to give their mother the car keys, then she drove him to the office to get the van. When they came home, Tucker followed her into the guest room and helped her shift her art things around—a big table, her easel and boxes of her art supplies—to make a path from the bed to the doorway.

Lissa shook out the bottom sheet and Tucker helped smooth it over the mattress corners.

"At least while I'm here I can finish the floor in your real studio. Then we can get your art stuff moved in down there."

"If you feel like it." Lissa unfolded the top sheet.

"I'll go crazy if I don't have something to do. I'd work out at Pecan Grove with you and Evan, but Pop doesn't want me there. I'm already scaring away the customers."

Lissa looked up. "What do you mean?"

"A buyer backed out today."

Her heart fell; she ducked her face, not wanting Tucker to see her dismay. "Does Evan know?" she asked even as other frightened thoughts crowded her mind. How would they make it? How would they manage if they couldn't sell those houses? And they'd pulled all that money out of the business account to get Tucker out of jail. There hadn't been an alternative.

Tucker answered that Evan did know and that he'd told Pop earlier in the afternoon.

Lissa didn't ask how their father had reacted. She didn't want to know.

Tucker said, "I'm sick about it. All of it, the cash you laid out for bail, horning in here on you and Evan. I thought of going to Morgan's, you know, the girl who gave me a ride when my car broke down the other night, but I didn't think that would be smart under the circumstances."

"No, it wouldn't be. I'm glad you came here, Tuck."

"I just don't want to be a burden. I promise it won't be for long. I'll get my own place."

"It's okay. You know you can stay as long as you need to." Lissa wondered how he thought he would get his own place. She wondered how Evan would take it, her offer that Tucker could stay with them as long as necessary; she wondered where Evan would sleep tonight.

Tucker stood in front of her easel. It held a half-finished painting of a garden landscape, one she'd started weeks ago. She'd been working on the light that fell over the path. It wasn't right, and it frustrated her. She usually painted in the evenings after dinner, but she hadn't in the past few days, not since Sunday. It seemed as if it had been much longer than that—weeks. Months, even. She wondered if she would ever get back to it. If she would ever feel like it again.

Tucker touched his fingertip to the painted moon gate. It was standing ajar, a sunlit invitation. "Pretty," he said. "You are so talented, Liss. Maybe you'll paint something small to hang on my cell wall."

"Don't even talk like that," she said.

"I don't think I could do it, you know? I couldn't survive in a prison, especially not on death row—

just sitting there for years?" He found her gaze. "I'd rather they'd pull the plug."

After her shower, Lissa wrapped herself in a towel and peeped into the bedroom. Empty. She stepped across the threshold, paused to listen. She had left Tucker and Evan in the kitchen talking the Astros' preseason stats, but now the house was silent. Moon-flushed shadows layered the hallway walls. Had Evan gone to bed without saying good-night?

The threat of tears caught her off guard and annoyed her. She pressed her fingertips to her eyes until the urge passed, then, dressed in her nightshirt and sweats, she found her way through the quiet house in the dark. The guest room door was closed, and she hoped Tucker was sleeping.

She crossed the great room to the study. The wood-framed windows there were clear of drapery, and she could see Evan from the door-way, curled on his side on the leather sofa, still dressed except for his shoes. His arms were crossed over his chest, hands flattened beneath his elbows. She wondered where he'd found the old chintz-covered bolster he'd stuffed under his head; she'd made it years ago and hadn't seen it in ages. She wondered why he had no blanket. He appeared to be dead asleep, and it both maddened and relieved her.

She rested against the door frame. Outside, the

fitful night wind rippled the newly flowering canopies of three redbud trees they'd planted two weeks ago. Their shadows trembled over Evan's body, bringing his face in and out of darkness, first whitening the ridges of his cheekbones, now blackening the hollows beneath his eyes. She imagined the tender softness of his skin there, under his eyes. She imagined tracing the blade of his cheekbone with the tip of her finger—

Abruptly she went from the doorway, and retrieving a quilt from the linen closet, she brought it back with her and laid it carefully over him, jumping when he grasped her fingers. Pure reflex made her draw back, but he kept her hand and her gaze, and the moment stretched with the two of them watching each other in the night silence with only the sound of their breath between them.

After what seemed an endless time, when he released her hand, she left him without a word.

23

She cooked a huge breakfast the following morning—bacon, eggs, homemade biscuits and hash browns—and at one point, wiping her brow, she thought, *I'm turning into my mother.* But that was exactly why she was doing it, because it felt normal.

She tensed when Evan came to the counter and poured his coffee, waiting for a word, a clue about his mood. She glanced sidelong at him and found him looking at her. There were dark smudges under his eyes and a red scuff mark near the back of his jaw where he'd scraped the sensitive skin while shaving.

"Good morning," she said, feigning a neutrality she didn't feel.

"I hope you aren't cooking any of that for me," he said. "I've got to get going."

"You have to eat, Evan. Please?" She didn't care about neutrality now, but she did refrain from saying her effort was for Tucker, that she thought it would help him, help to reassure him, if they could sit down together.

She was grateful when Evan acquiesced, and even set the table, taking three plates from the cabinet. He gathered napkins and silverware. She wanted so desperately to go to him, to put her arms around him and pour out her feelings that were jammed in her throat. She wanted to say she was sorry, so sorry.

She wanted to tell him she loved him.

She checked the biscuits and broke the eggs into a bowl.

Tucker came and pitched in, pouring the orange juice. He turned the golden-topped biscuits into a napkin-lined basket, brought the platter of scrambled eggs to the table. He asked if they could say grace, and they did. Lissa fought the lump in her throat. None of them ate much. She would throw most of it into the woods later for the critters.

Evan left. He didn't kiss her goodbye.

"Evan's pissed," Tucker said, passing a Coke can between his hands while they sat at the table.

"He's just worn out, is all," Lissa said. She'd poured herself a second cup of coffee that she didn't want. "I need to go to the grocery store," she said. "Want to come?"

"He slept in his study last night." Tucker looked at her. "What's that about? It's because of me, isn't it?"

"No. Don't worry about it. I've been restless at night, because of the headaches and stuff." She kept his gaze, willing him to drop it.

He took a swallow of the soda. "I wish you guys didn't have to be messed up in this."

"It's okay."

"No, it isn't."

She started to interrupt again, to protest. She wanted to question him about Revel, the cell phone, the charge of assault Miranda had leveled against Darren, Miranda's work with the police. She wanted to talk about what was happening to him, to them, but as if he sensed what was in her mind, her fear for him, her anxiety, he held up his hand.

"You aren't responsible for me, Liss, for anything that's happened to me, ever. I mean, I love you for how you've always had my back. It means a lot. A lot," he repeated. "You know that, right?"

"Yes, but you've done it for me, too, Tuck. We've helped each other."

He put up his hand again. There was something working on his face, a complication of emotions, regret, she thought, anguish even, and something sharper. Was it anger? She started to ask, but he interrupted her.

"You ever think about that day when Dad lost it, when he checked into rehab—what was going on in his head, how fucked up it was?"

A taut silence fell between them, a thin-shelled egg on the lip of an abyss. Lissa knew the direction Tucker was going in, and as much as she wanted to know what had happened on that day, as much as she swore she wanted to hear the truth, now that it was coming, she wondered if she wouldn't really prefer to keep her illusion.

"I didn't even understand it was post-traumatic stress until I was in high school," she said. "I think there's a certain amount of that he's never gotten over."

"You remember his service revolver?"

"The Colt?"

"Yeah." Tucker sucked in a breath.

Lissa touched his arm. "What is it?"

"I don't know. Can't shake that old shit in my head. I keep seeing him, that gun—"

"What do you mean?"

He locked her eyes with his. "Do you have any idea what it's like to have your old man put a gun to your head?"

"What are you saying? He didn't—"

"It was the glass, when I dropped the glass in the bathroom that day, he came off the bed like he'd been shot. He thought he was back in the war, in 'Nam, fighting. He was yelling like a wild man. I tried to run, but he grabbed me and jerked me down on my knees. I had my hands like this." Tucker laced his fingers behind his head. "I thought he was pissed because of the glass. I cut my foot and blood was everywhere. I said I was sorry, that I would clean it up, but he kept yelling, 'Stay where you are,' and 'Don't move or I'll shoot.' Stuff like that."

"Oh, my God, Tucker . . ."

"It was my dad, you know, but not my dad. When he got his old service revolver and put it to my head, I figured that was it. I was going to die. I asked him for Itsy. Down came the rain, right?"

Lissa had a sudden memory of her dad pulling Tucker and Itsy onto his lap, tickling Tucker with Itsy's long spider legs, making him laugh. She could see the love in her dad's eyes. She could feel it in her bones, all that love. It had made her feel safe.

But this other thing? Her dad holding a gun on Tucker? She couldn't see it, couldn't get her mind around it.

"I didn't know," she said, and the words came hard.

Tucker said he was sorry. He never meant to tell, to wreck her day. He'd wrecked everything in her life enough already.

"Whatever happened to Itsy?" she asked.

"Pop destroyed him. Swore there was contraband or some shit inside it. He ripped it to shreds."

"What happened, Tucker? What stopped him?"

"Mom. She came home. By then Pop had locked me in the front hall closet. I heard her voice—" He stopped and something like shame darkened his eyes for a moment. "I hate to admit it, but I wet my pants."

"Oh, Tucker, oh, God, I'm so sorry." She seemed incapable of coming up with anything else to say.

He pinched the bridge of his nose, and she knew he was close to crying.

She thought of the day shortly after that, when

their dad had already gone away to the VA hospital, when she'd walked out on the porch to find her little brother missing. She wanted to tell Tucker about that and about how terrified she'd been. In her mind, she saw it again, the wrought-iron gate yawning open on its hinges; she felt the hollow sensation of disbelief that he was gone and the hotter bite of panic that had come later. But instead, she rubbed his arm, and said nothing.

The silence lengthened; she thought the day might pass and night fall before either one found the ability to speak again.

Then Tucker looked at her and said, "Stuff is happening in my head, Liss. I don't know—I can't—can't hold on to this by myself anymore," and his eyes were so bleak Lissa's heart faltered.

She took her hand away.

"There's this way Dad looks at me, even now, where I wonder if it's me he's seeing or am I still his enemy. It's like I remind him of—I don't know—the fucking war or something." Tucker doodled circles on the table.

Lissa watched his finger going around and around. She could feel his fear, the child's fear, and she wanted to comfort him; she wanted to run so she wouldn't have to hear whatever came next. She wanted to put her hand over his mouth and stop him from speaking, but it wasn't about her. It was about his pain, and inside, a hope grew that if she could listen, then maybe that would make it possible for him to let go of the darkest edge of the nightmare. Maybe some part of this terrible wound, the wound she had sensed existed at the heart of her family nearly her entire life, could be healed, even for her father.

"I was the most scared when I was in the closet," Tucker said. "I could hear him, you know, like crashing around the house. He was yelling orders, 'Get down! Get down!'—stuff like that. But then, sometimes he just . . . howled. Now I know he was crying." Tucker clicked his tongue against his teeth. "Man, that kind of pain—shit, I don't know. What do you do with that?"

Lissa didn't answer; she couldn't.

"He still pisses me off." Tucker's smile was unbearable.

"I wish we could talk about this."

"We are talking about it."

"No, I mean as a family. If Dad understood how you felt, if we could all talk about what happened—"

Tucker hooted as if she was crazy. "Lissa, come on. You're living in a dreamworld if you think the old man would ever listen to anything I had to say. You, maybe, but me? Never. As far as he's concerned, I'm the biggest screwup to walk the earth. He'd rather Coe was his son than me, and that's even if the bastard is a killer."

"No, Tucker—"

"It's true." He was having none of Lissa's protest. "I was never the son he wanted. He gave up on me the day he figured out I wasn't going to be the man he was."

"You're projecting what you think onto Dad, Tucker, not what's real. It's everything horrible that you think about yourself that's in your head, not his."

"Do you have any idea what my life has been like? It's one shitty thing after another, you know? Then boom—" Tucker struck the side of his head "—the only real, goddamned woman I ever loved gets murdered, because I wasn't man enough to get her the hell out of that shitty world she was living in and keep her safe. But how could you know how bad it sucked? You never asked. All you and Mom and Pop ever did was tell me how wrong I was to care about her."

"You're right," Lissa answered, even though she wasn't sure of what she was affirming, or her feelings about it. He was referencing more than the day of their dad's breakdown now, widening the scope to include Miranda's death and every other bad thing that had happened to him in his life. She felt the prickling heat of aggravation that he was so willing to make her and their parents into ogres and cast himself as their victim. Still, it seemed better to go along, and it was easy when she kept her focus on the little boy he'd been and the little boy's terror that lingered, which colored everything he was.

"I'm sorry if it came across that way, Tucker, but sometimes, I've been so scared for you, especially when you disappear. I'll never forget the first time, how relieved I was when they found you."

"I wish I had the guts to keep going. I wish I could make myself over, be somebody else."

"I wish I'd been home with Dad that day, and not you. I was older. I could have handled it better."

"No, Liss." Tucker was adamant. "I'm glad it wasn't you."

She went on as if he hadn't spoken. "I knew you were hurt then. I could see that, but I really didn't understand about the damage, not until I was older." Lissa stopped, while the memories swarmed and stung like a handful of sand flung in her face. "I remember being really scared, too. You and Momma were so quiet after Dad went away, and then you disappeared, and I thought I would die, I was so afraid. I think it's why it's so awful now every time you go. I wish you wouldn't. Mom has such a hard time with it. It nearly kills her."

Tucker didn't say anything.

"She can't keep getting you out of trouble, either, you know? I hate to pile all this on you, but I think she and Dad are at the end of their rope. They can't take any more."

Tucker said he knew it; his eyes teared, and he wiped roughly at them.

Lissa's annoyance softened. "I know it isn't easy, Tuck, but I also know we can work it out, if we work together, as a family."

He flicked his glance at her, and there was something agitated in his eyes, some raw edge of accusation, or pain, or loss—Lissa didn't know. It was as if he was looking at a place she couldn't see.

He said, "She left me with him, Liss. Mom knew how bad off he was. I heard her telling the doctor afterward that she knew Pop was close to the edge, but she left me there with him, alone—" Tucker's voice cracked. He coughed. "I was fucking four years old."

Lissa got up and went to him, wrapping him in her arms as best she could, staggering when he drove his head into her shoulder as if he might bury himself there. The sounds that broke from his chest were ragged and dry. She held on to him, rocking a little, humming nonsense, and when it fell into the opening notes from the "Itsy Bitsy Spider," the child's song, the child's game, that he'd loved when he was small, she was scarcely aware when she picked up the words, ". . . crawled up the waterspout. Down came the rain and washed the spider out . . ." She wasn't holding the man, singing in her teetery voice to the man, but to the little boy, and she was relieved when she felt his tension ease.

When he pulled free, he was sniffing and red-faced. Lissa got him a tissue.

"Pop would have a field day," he said after he mopped himself up.

"There's nothing wrong with a man's tears, Tucker." Lissa blew her own nose.

He didn't answer.

"You aren't any different than Dad, you know."

He looked at her bemused.

"You have symptoms of post-traumatic stress, too, because of what happened. I know you and Mom and Dad got help before, but maybe you need to talk to someone again. Maybe we all do."

"No, it's too late."

"It's not," Lissa insisted.

"I know you mean well, Liss, but really, it doesn't matter anymore." He stood up. "I'm not going to beat this murder rap."

"You will! Of course you will."

"Even if I did, somebody's going to get me one way or another. The cops'll lock me up, and there's no way I can take that again. No fucking way. I'll slit my own throat first."

"I won't let it—"

"Come on, Liss. My own goddamn father thinks I'm guilty."

"He doesn't," she said. "None of us think that. We have to trust Mickey, trust the system." Lissa was offering a plea for faith, the one her mother

310

had offered, and it sounded as foolish and inadequate now as it had then. But what else was there?

Tucker reached for her braid and pulled it forward over her shoulder; he touched her cheek. "Out of everybody, I could always count on you, no bullshit, Liss. I wish I was good enough with words to tell you what it's meant to me. I wish I'd ever been good enough to be your brother."

"Oh, Tucker . . ."

He pushed his chair under the table, heading for the door.

Lissa stood up, too. "Where are you going?"

He looked back at her. "I meant to tell you—I gave those receipts to the cops."

"Really? When?"

"After we unloaded the tile, I stopped by the police station on my way home."

"Tucker!" She felt a surge of happiness. "They'll check them out. You'll be cleared, right?"

He lifted his cap, brought it down and inspected it. "Maybe," he said. "But I doubt it'll be that easy so don't get your hopes up, okay?"

She went to him and laid her hand on his arm. "Come with me. I have to go to the grocery store."

"I've got an appointment with the Mickster."

"I'll take you into town. We can grocery shop after."

"No," he said. "Thanks for a great breakfast."

Something made her go after him, made her ask again. "Tucker, please, come with me. We can go out to lunch, take in a movie, like we used to, my treat."

He shook his head, and she let him go, thinking there was time, that they would have tomorrow. It would haunt her, later, that she let him go. She would remember they hadn't even said goodbye. She would wonder if in her lifetime she had ever said to him that she loved him.

24

Emily was with Anna in Anna's driveway when she spied Lissa's truck turning the corner, and she waved, catching Lissa's attention. "Is everything okay? Tucker?" Emily asked when Lissa joined them.

"He's fine." Lissa gave Anna and then Emily a hug. "I was just on my way to the grocery store, and I thought I'd come by—" She broke off, looking uncertain, as if she was wondering how much she could say.

"It's all right, honey," Emily said. "Anna knows pretty much everything."

Anna squeezed Emily's hand, and she gratefully returned the gesture.

"Tucker didn't have so much as a toothbrush when he came last night," Lissa said. "I thought maybe you'd help me pack up a few of his things? I don't want to cut your visit short, though."

"I was on my way home, anyway," Emily said. "I don't want to leave your dad on his own for too long."

"I'm so sorry this is happening, Lissa," Anna said.

"Me, too." She crossed her arms, holding herself, looking worried, too worried, Emily thought.

They said goodbye to Anna and climbed into

Lissa's truck, and they weren't inches from the curb before Lissa said, "Tucker told me everything that happened the day Dad had his breakdown. It's so much worse than I thought." She rounded the corner and pulled in behind Roy's truck.

Emily sat staring at the disabled-vet license tag. She thought of how Roy nearly gave his life for a child in another country; she thought of the act of courage it had taken for him to do that and to survive. She said, "No one could feel more awful than your dad. It was a horrible thing and my mistake for leaving them alone."

Something crossed Lissa's expression that made Emily add, "I know Tucker blames me, but not any more than I blame myself."

"How could you have known, Momma?" Lissa said, and Emily loved her for it. Lissa went on. "He thinks—he believes, believes to his core, though, that Dad hates him."

"What your dad hates is that he terrorized his own child."

"All these years, it's been eating Daddy alive, hasn't it?"

Emily made a sound that wasn't yes or no. So many things had eaten Roy alive, she thought. Maybe some day she should make a list. She wiped her fingertips across her eyebrows.

They heard the sound of a car engine behind them. Lissa glanced in the rearview mirror, while

Emily turned all the way around to peer out the back window.

A dark blue sedan, a Mercedes, was pulling to the curb. The door was thrust open, and a woman got out, jaw set, mouth a grim line.

"My God," Lissa said. "It's Courtney."

"Courtney Coe?"

"Rickman." Lissa offered her married name. "I wonder what she wants."

Nothing good, Emily thought.

Lissa opened her door.

"I don't know if talking to her is such a good idea," Emily said.

"I'm not backing down from her, Momma." She stepped out, and if she said anything to Courtney by way of a greeting, Emily didn't catch it.

Something was said about Darren. The words *restraining order* and *slander* rose on the razored edge of Courtney's voice.

Emily slipped quietly from the truck, joining Lissa on the sidewalk.

Courtney looked at her, and at first Emily thought from her hard expression that she was only very angry, but there was a sheen of something like tears in her eyes, and her jaw was trembling. There was a lot more going on with her than anger, Emily thought. "Is anything the matter?" she asked.

Lissa glanced over her shoulder. "Courtney says she's getting a restraining order against me,

Momma. I'm to keep my distance from Darren and the rest of her family. It's hard to imagine, isn't it, that once we were best friends."

Courtney scoffed. "You Winters," she said, as if the name were a curse. "You think you can say anything, do anything, that you're somehow immune. . . ." She straightened, sniffing, wiping her eyes. "That might be true in this town, but I'm married to a Houston city councilman. Glen has the ear of the mayor, the governor, people with more money and influence than you'll ever see. You don't know the trouble that can come down on you. A restraining order is only the beginning."

"Are you threatening us?" Lissa asked.

"I'm telling you to leave my brother alone. I'm warning you to keep your baseless accusations to yourself or suffer the consequences. We are prepared to take you to court. We will sue you for every last dime. We're sick of it. Do you understand me? You crossed a line this time, accusing him of being a rapist and a murderer—"

"It's the truth, Courtney," Lissa said strongly. "Do you remember Holly McPherson?"

"Oh, please tell me you are not going to bring up all that old business. Darren didn't do one thing to that girl that she didn't want done."

"He tried to do the same thing to me, the summer before," Lissa said, and told Courtney what had happened.

"I don't believe it," Courtney said when Lissa finished.

"Of course, you wouldn't," Lissa answered.

Courtney looked out into the middle distance a moment before bringing her gaze back. Emily thought she looked resigned or discouraged, some combination. "We have both held on to an illusion when it comes to our brothers, Lissa. We let our loyalty to them come between us. I'm sad when I think about it. You were my best friend, and I've missed having one, missed you. But you're wrong about Darren and wrong about Tucker, and I'm sorry for you that you can't see it."

"I'm sorry for you," Lissa said, "for the very same reason."

Courtney turned up her palms; she apologized again and said nothing had changed. Her family still intended to sue, and then she climbed into her Mercedes and drove away.

"Can you believe her nerve?" Lissa asked, coming with Emily through the gate. "She's sorry for me. As if I'm the one in denial."

"Let's not tell your father about her visit, okay?" Emily led the way into the house. "The idea that she's gotten a restraining order, that she intends to sue . . ." Emily paused at the foot of the stairway, feeling overwhelmed. She felt as if she were standing on an ocean shore watching a huge wave rocket toward her, knowing there was no use attempting an escape, because she could never outrun it.

"It's nothing but talk, Mom. I could tell by the look on her face. She was so nervous. Did you notice?"

Following Lissa into Tucker's bedroom, Emily said, "Honey, I truly believe she meant it when she said she was sorry."

"No, Momma, she didn't." Lissa found a canvas tote in the closet and set it on the bed. She pulled T-shirts, socks and underwear from Tucker's dresser drawers and crammed them into the bag. "It was an act, plain and simple. She's a manipulator and a bully, like Darren, like her mother. We've always said so, right?"

Emily didn't answer. When Lissa disappeared again inside Tucker's closet, she took out the wad of his clothing and repacked it.

Lissa handed her a blue hoodie. "He might need this. It's still cold out nights."

Roy was in the kitchen when they came downstairs, standing at the window, looking out. Emily was dismayed to see him. He'd been in his workshop when she went to Anna's and she had hoped he would still be there. She cast an anxious glance at Lissa, hoping she wouldn't mention Courtney.

"I'll call you later," Lissa said, heading for the back door.

"You're not speaking to your old man, is that it?" Roy asked, facing them.

318

Emily saw that he was leaning heavily on a cane, and her eyes widened.

"What?" he said. "You've never seen a man use a cane before?"

"I've never seen you use one, Dad."

"Well, you have now."

"Roy? Is the pain that bad? Shouldn't you—?"

"Don't bring up the doctor business again, Em. They can't do a damn thing for me."

She crossed her arms.

Lissa said something about his hard head. She indicated the tote and said, "Mom and I packed up some of Tucker's clothes. He wants to stay with me and Evan for now. I'm sure you agree it'll be better for everyone." It was almost but not quite an accusation, an indictment.

"Your mother told me your news." Roy's glance fell to Lissa's midsection. "You'll make a fine mother, honey, if you choose it."

"You really think so?" She sounded amazed, and perhaps she should be, Emily thought. Roy could be sparing in his praise.

He nodded at the tote. "You've been mothering your brother a long while now, whether he needed it or deserved it."

"He thinks you hate him, Dad. Do you know that? This morning, he opened up to me about the day of your breakdown. I didn't know what to say, how to help him. I don't know how to help you, either."

Emily stepped toward Roy. "Lissa, maybe this isn't the time."

"Then when? Tucker's a mess, so's Daddy."

"I don't hate your brother," Roy said. "How could I? I'm responsible for him. Whatever issues he has, whatever business there is, it's on me. It doesn't concern you or your mother." He took a step and then another, staggering a bit, gripping the back of a chair to steady himself.

Emily's heart lurched. She should say something, assist him in some way. She didn't move.

But Lissa crossed the floor to him. "That's the problem, Dad. You take it all on yourself. You won't talk about what troubles you or ask for help. Look where it's gotten us, where it's gotten Tucker!" Her voice was high, pleading, offended and laden with concern all at once.

Emily caught her elbow. "Let it go, honey," she said. She didn't want a protracted discussion now, an argument that involved pointing fingers and assigning blame.

Lissa's long sigh was an indication of her impatience with her parents, what she saw as their refusal to confront the facts. She retraced her steps to the door, but then she paused, and turning resolutely, she went to her dad's side and set her arm around him, awkwardly.

He turned to her, and cupping her cheek, he told her he loved her.

Watching them, Emily brought her tented fingertips to her mouth. She couldn't recall that Roy had ever said that aloud to either of his children, not since they were very young.

"I love you, too, Daddy," Lissa said, and her voice faltered, and then she left swiftly, closing the door, even the screen, without a sound.

She didn't want us to see her cry, Emily thought, and it worried her that Lissa would be driving when she was so distraught.

"I thought he would get over it," Roy said.

Emily looked at him.

"That day, what I did to him. I thought he would forget. I was hard on him, I know, but I wanted him to grow up strong. A man wants that for his son."

"All Tucker ever wanted from you, Roy, was your love and respect."

He stared blindly at a point above her head, face wrenched into an agonized knot. Tears leaked from his eyes, glazing the deep grooves in his cheeks.

Emily was stunned. Picking up a kitchen towel, she went to him. "Roy?" she said, and dabbed his face. He didn't respond to her ministrations, her murmuring, and only tolerated the attention for a few moments before taking her wrists and moving her hands away from his face.

"I don't need your pity," he said, pulling a wad of tissues from his pants pocket.

Looking at it, Emily had the sense he had been

crying earlier. "It isn't pity. I want to help you. If it's the pain—"

"I thought if I was soft on him, even after that day, it would make him weak, and I didn't want that. Because if you're weak, this world will eat you alive, you know? It will eat your guts out."

She held his gaze, feeling at a loss and frightened on some level deeper than any she had experienced since this whole nightmare began. She wanted to step back from Roy, but at the same time she wanted to cling to him. Instead, she clenched the towel in her hands.

The awful silence was pierced from outside by the song of a bird, a wren from the sound, and the series of notes rising from its tiny throat were so high and lovely and clear she felt as though her heart would shatter from their beauty. And when the song stopped, she thought how pain and beauty are often so inextricably woven together they seem to be of the same cloth.

25

Lissa was stowing the groceries she'd bought on the way home from her mother's house when Evan came in. She closed the refrigerator door and waited for some cue from him, a hint to his mood. They hadn't spoken all day except in her imagination, where she had rehearsed a dozen different conversations. She wondered if he felt as awful for how wrong things were between them as she did.

"Hey," she said, because she didn't know how else to begin.

"I figured there would be reporters outside." He shrugged out of his jacket. "There weren't any at the office, either. It's weird."

"Maybe it's because there's some good news for a change."

"Such as?"

"First, the blood in Tucker's Tahoe turned out to belong to a dog just the way Tucker said it would."

"Okay. There's more?" he asked, but not as if he cared. Not as if she or her news or Tucker mattered to him.

Her smile faded. She told him about the receipts, that Tucker had given them to the police. "Mickey's asked the D.A.'s office for them. He can use them to build Tucker's defense."

"Where is he?" Evan hung his jacket in the mudroom.

"In the studio, working. When I talked to Mickey, he told me he thinks the state may have acted prematurely when they arrested Tucker, that they figured on finding something concrete when they searched the house and car, but they didn't." Lissa kept Evan's gaze.

"What?" he prompted.

"You know Mickey's been looking for information on Revel and the Camry, and so far, he's saying there's not much of anything to be found on either one."

"I wonder what that means."

"I don't know. He said to let him know right away if we see Revel or the Camry again, or if anything strikes us as suspicious," Lissa said.

"That's it?" Evan asked.

"He'll get back to us with anything further."

"Jesus." Evan ran his hand over his head. "Tuck knows all this, I guess. What did he say?"

"Not much. He doesn't look at any of it as good. I think he feels too sick about it. Look, I know you don't want him here, but he's got nowhere else he can go."

"It's not that I don't want him, Liss. You know me better than that."

"I thought I did."

"What is that supposed to mean?"

She didn't answer. She gathered the empty

324

grocery bags and put them in the recycle bin. "Mickey said it looks as if the state still intends to go through with the trial, as idiotic as that sounds."

"It doesn't surprise me."

"Do you know how long this could take?" she asked. "Not just the trial but all the preparation? Months. A year, even. Mickey said it's unlikely either he or the state will be ready to go to trial in June. They'll ask the court to postpone."

"We'll just have to deal with it, each day as it comes. It's the same with the money." Evan pulled out a chair and sat down at the table. He had his cell phone in his hand, scrolling through his messages.

Lissa picked up the dishcloth, dampened it and wiped the already clean countertops, the top of the stove, the oven hood.

"We're losing clients."

She paused. "How many?"

"Four so far." Evan toyed with his phone, not looking at her. "New sales inquiries are down, too. I don't even want to tell Roy how bad it is."

"How can we do this, Ev? It's only going to get worse." Lissa sat next to him, catching his glance, holding it. She was thinking of Courtney, her threats to get a restraining order, to sue Lissa, that Evan didn't even know about yet. There was so much piled on his shoulders already, how could she tell him?

"We'll find a way," he said. "Whatever it takes, we'll do everything we can to get Tucker out of this mess."

"I know, but I'm talking about the pregnancy. Even aside from all the stress, is it fair to bring a child into this? What if we lose the business? What if we have to cancel the insurance?"

"I'll get work somewhere. We'll manage."

"How, Evan? Think about it." She touched her temple. "What if we lose the house?"

He looked at her, floored. "You're willing to go that far?"

"You're the one who said whatever it takes."

"So, what you're saying is that you would sacrifice our child and our house, in essence everything we have—"

"Where do you want to draw the line, Evan? Can you put a dollar amount on my brother's life? Because that's what's at stake here. Could you keep this house if the cash from selling it would mean the difference between whether Tucker was acquitted of these charges or imprisoned and possibly put to death for them? Could you sleep nights all tucked up in our bed here if that happens?"

"You're way ahead of yourself, Liss."

"I can't see bringing a baby into it. We can always try again after this is over, if that's what you want, but right now, for me, anyway, the focus has to be Tucker."

Evan stood up. He pushed the chair to the table. "I'll just pack a few things, then, and I'll see an attorney in the morning. I can't let you do it. I can't stand by while you get an abortion. Taking our baby's life isn't going to save Tucker—"

"What the hell is he talking about?"

The shock of Tucker's voice, affronted, disbelieving, brought Lissa to her feet. She stammered something about not realizing he was there.

But he wasn't listening; he was shouting. "Did I hear you right? You're pregnant and you're getting an abortion because of me, the shit I'm in? Tell me you're kidding!" Tucker ripped his cap from his head.

"Don't yell at me, okay? I'm not sure. Everyone keeps acting as if I've made up my mind, and I haven't." Lissa looked at Evan.

He shrugged. "It sounded to me like a done deal."

"You can't do it, Liss." Tucker was white-faced. "It's wrong, just wrong."

"But you know I never wanted— Never thought I was— That I would make a good mother, and anyway, it's just not a good time now with everything that's in front of us."

"Bullshit!" Tucker was shouting again. "You can't let how I've fucked up be any part of a decision like this. I heard Evan say we lost more business today because of me, what people think I did, what they think I am, a fucking monster.

Don't make me the bad guy in this, too." He stared hard at her, pleading, terrified.

"Oh, Tucker . . ." Lissa breathed his name. She reached for him, but he stepped back from her, eyes reddened and glimmering with tears.

Slapping on his cap, he dug in his pocket, pulled out the company van's keys. "I never should have come back here. When I went to Austin, I should have kept on going."

"No, Tucker—"

Evan said something about sitting down to talk, but Tucker paid no heed. He strode to the back door, yanking it open.

"Wait!" Lissa called. She followed him across the back porch, onto the driveway, but he was already in the van, keying the ignition and then he was gone.

Evan didn't touch her; he didn't pull her into his embrace as he might have. "He'll be back," was all he said.

Lissa went into the house. Evan followed her.

"I guess you're leaving, too," she said, but she left him before he could answer, going swiftly from the kitchen into the bedroom. She didn't want to have one more word of discussion or to even think of what more there possibly might be to say. She was tired of being judged, of being a disappointment. Tired of Evan's refusal to look at the situation from her point of view. She moved mindlessly about the room, straightening the bed linen that Tucker had left in a coil. She emptied a drawer in the chest that held mainly her art supplies and stowed Tucker's clothes that she'd brought from her mother's.

With nothing else left to do, she stood in front of her easel, looking at the unfinished painting. The path that led through the open moon gate curved to accommodate a lush floral border planted with clumps of Japanese irises, foxgloves and lobelia before losing itself at the edge of a meadow that faded into a summer sky. The air felt alive, effervescent. The drone of bees was audible. But the light was wrong in the foreground, where it was closest to the viewer. She had worked hours on that aspect of the work without success, but she realized now that the trouble wasn't the light but the murkier depth of the shadows.

She saw how to fix it, and going through her tubes of paint, she selected the colors she needed, squeezing them onto her palette. She chose a brush from the collection she kept in an old, crazed milk pitcher and set to work. The world and her thoughts telescoped to include only her field of vision. It was what painting had always been for her, a means of transporting herself from her life to her field of dreams. When she was finished, she stood back, wiping her fingers on a rag, looking at the result, and she was satisfied. She would show it to Evan, she thought.

Evan, who had said he was leaving. Following Tucker, who was already gone.

She bent her head. How long had she been working? How many hours had she spent lost here, in her painted reality? She left the bedroom, walking through the dark, quiet house. In the kitchen, she checked the time. After ten. She thought of eating, but she wasn't hungry. She tried calling Tucker's cell phone. No answer. It was the same when she dialed Evan's number. She could call her mother, but if Tucker wasn't there, she would only worry. Lissa leaned against the counter, pressing her fingertips to her eyes that burned with the hours of work and lurking heartbreak. Her back ached, too, from standing at the easel, and her head hurt. She thought of taking Advil, but knowing it would be bad for the baby, she didn't, and it surprised her to feel pangs of concern, of defense. Instead, she took a shower and washed her hair, not knowing what else to do, and then got into bed. After a while, lying there, sleepless, she remembered something her daddy used to say when she woke up terrified from a bad dream: that life would look better to her in the light of a new morning.

She did finally doze off only to waken some-time later, unsure why. She lay for a moment, listening, hearing nothing more than the sound of her heart, her pulse in her ears, and then she got up and went through the house to the study. She knew Evan was there before she reached the doorway, and relief loosened her knees when she saw him lying prone on the sofa, one arm flung over his eyes, head resting on the old floral bolster.

"What's wrong?"

The sound of his voice startled her, but she came into the room a little way. "I can't sleep."

He said he couldn't, either, and he scooted over and patted the coverlet she'd brought him the night before as if to indicate she should join him. But remembering earlier when he said he would leave her, she didn't go to him. She pulled out the desk chair instead. "I thought you were gone."

"I was," he said.

"Why did you come back?"

"I need to be here for you. With you," he added, and her heart shifted. "I don't mean I've changed my mind about our baby," he said after a moment.

Lissa pulled up her knees and rested her cheek on them. She had unbraided her hair, and it fell around her, making a dark curtain. "I really haven't decided about it, Evan."

He made no response.

"He told me what happened the day Daddy broke down."

Evan propped himself on his elbow. Moonlight iced his cheekbones, the blade of his jaw. His eyes were dark pools. "Do you want to tell me what happened?"

She did, and when she was finished, she only

realized she was crying when Evan came to her and brushed her cheeks.

"I don't know how to stop caring for him or about him." Lissa's voice was muffled against Evan's chest. "How am I supposed to do that? I can't abandon him. If our positions were reversed, if it were me charged with murdering those women, Tucker wouldn't abandon me. He would fight. He would fight with everything he had."

"I know," Evan said.

"He can't go to prison. He'll die if he's confined to a cell. After what Daddy did, locking him in that closet? He couldn't take it. There's no way."

"We'll work it out," Evan said. He swung her into his arms and carried her to the sofa, laying her down. Settling beside her, he cradled her against him, and her throat tightened with her gratitude and her love. She thought maybe it would be all right between them, after all. She thought maybe they really would find the way to work it out.

It was still dark when Evan rose later and, taking Lissa's hand, led her into the bedroom and lay down with her in their bed. She thought they must have dozed. When they wakened and reached for each other, pale light was seeping through the blinds, a glow the color of opals, the color of dreams, she'd think later in all the unrelenting madness. They began without words, their movements coming from the music of shared memory and mutual need. She twined her legs with his, closing her eyes, giving herself to him, giving herself to the touch of his hands on her breasts and in the hollow where her rib cage dipped into the curve of her waist. His palm slid along the smooth contour of her thigh. His gaze was locked with hers when he came into her, moving slowly, waiting, she knew, to see that she was with him, that they were together, and she loved him for it, for his care of her.

When they were spent, they lay facing each other. He brushed the heavy weight of her hair over her shoulder, running his fingers along its length. "I don't want to lose you," he said.

She set her fingertip on his mouth, and he seemed to understand her wish to have this time, this hour before dawn, untroubled by fear or anger or worry. But when he fell asleep, as much as she wished to, she could not. She couldn't fight the whirl of her thoughts, her anxiety over Tucker, and she slipped quietly from their bed.

In the kitchen, she started a pot of coffee and turned on the television, a morning talk show. She didn't register which one, didn't pay any attention, not until they cut to the local news, and she heard a reporter say something about a woman who was missing. Now Lissa looked at the screen; she upped the volume.

"A witness has come forward," the commentator was saying, "one who believes he saw the missing woman, Suzette Bowers, late last night, in the company of Tucker Lebay. As you might recall from previous newscasts, Lebay was recently arrested for the murder of—"

"Oh, no, no, no." Lissa tented her fingers over her mouth. Her blood rushed in her ears.

"Lissa? What's wrong?" Evan asked from the doorway.

She found her cell phone, dialed her mother. No answer. She tried her dad's phone and then Tucker's. Nothing.

"Lissa?"

She turned to Evan, mind reeling. "Another woman has turned up missing. We need to go to my parents' house, Ev. I'm afraid for them."

26

Morning wasn't more than a silver thread of light on the horizon when Emily heard Roy in the bedroom overhead—Tucker's bedroom. She glanced at the kitchen ceiling. What was he doing in there—again? Turning off the fire under the teakettle, she went to the bottom of the stairs. "Roy?" she called. "What are you doing?"

No answer.

If she'd had a choice, she wouldn't have gone up, not that it would have changed anything. As it was, when she reached Tucker's doorway and looked in, she was shocked by what she saw, the signs of disturbance, even of frenzy, that confronted her. The dresser drawers she'd closed so carefully yesterday after Lissa packed Tucker's clothes were emptied of their contents, and his bed linen was in a heap on the floor. Clothing from his closet had been flung from the hangers.

Roy looked up from where he sat in the midst of the turmoil on his knees. His eyes were heated with some fevered intensity, not in the way of a night terror or a post-traumatic stress episode, but in the way of a man obsessed, a man who was panicked, one who had thrown reason and caution to the wind.

"There is something here, something to tell if

Tucker did this, Em. I know it," Roy said. "I can feel it, and I have to know. I don't want to wait for a trial, to hear from some jury that doesn't know Tucker from fucking Adam that he's guilty." He finished rolling the dhurrie and shoved it against the bed frame. "There's a loose board here somewhere. Do you remember it?"

Emily did. Tucker had kept his treasures there, an Indian arrowhead he'd found, a baseball signed by Nolan Ryan, a small gold nugget on a chain that had belonged to Emily's father, the set of transformers that McDonald's had put into their Happy Meals once upon a time. She didn't know when or how the floorboard had come to be loose, but they'd left it because it was important to Tucker, having this secret place. "It's nearer the center of the room," she said, "but he cleared all the things out of there, I think." Her heart was faltering, beating an uncertain rhythm in her chest. She brought her hand there, watching as Roy worked his way on his knees toward the center of the room, where her direction had guided him. He ran the tips of his fingers along the floorboards, studying the path they made intently, hunting, she guessed, for the single board with the missing nails.

"Here, this is the one." The wooden slat lifted easily, but Roy only raised it an inch or so and then lowered it back into place, glancing at her. The look in his eyes seemed to question her, to ask for her permission. She felt cold and, crossing her arms, hugged herself, shrugging. "There's nothing there," she said.

But she was wrong, and she knew it in that last final moment of relative sanity and hope, knew it in some prescient way before Roy lifted the small wooden box from its hiding place. They recognized it at the same time. Handmade out of walnut, and lined in emerald-green velvet. The box had been her wedding gift to Roy. He had used it to hold his jewelry. How had it come to be here? Her eyes collided with his.

"What the hell?" he asked, as if she could explain, as if she were even capable of speech. If she could have uttered a word, she would have forbidden him to open it. She would have reminded him of Pandora and her box of horrors.

"I wondered what had happened to this," Roy said. He was bearing the burden of the box across both palms now, staring at it. "I thought you put it away."

He hadn't kept much of anything inside it. He wasn't the sort of man who wore a lot of jewelry. He wore his wedding band, almost never taking it off, and he left his watch on top of his bureau nights before going to bed. Emily honestly couldn't remember what the contents of the box had been. She didn't want to know what they might be now.

She gestured vaguely and said, "Maybe it's only

your stuff in there. Maybe he wanted to keep it, who knows why."

Roy stood up; he carried the box to Tucker's bed and, shoving aside a pile of clothing, sat down. Emily sat next to him. They looked at each other, sharing their bewilderment, their terrible reluctance. Panic snapped in the air between them. It was as if they knew, already knew. Roy lifted the lid, and they saw the contents—the locks of hair, the turquoise earring, the lipstick and the two driver's licenses that had belonged to Miranda Quick and Jessica Sweet.

"Ah, Jesus," Roy cried out, and Emily moaned softly.

"No . . ." She tore the box from Roy's hands and flung it across the room, shouting, "No! No! No!" Turning to him, she hurled herself against his chest, sobbing, "Oh, Roy, please . . ."

He did his best to comfort her. She felt his hands smoothing her back. He half carried her from Tucker's bedroom into their own and sat her down on their bed. Then he sat next to her.

"Our son could not have done this," she said.

"But he did," Roy said.

Emily looked at him. "You knew, didn't you? You've known since Miranda—"

"He's never been right, Em. Not since that day, after what I did. Ah, Christ." The words came out, a half sob. "I held a gun to his head. How could I do that, to my own kid?" Roy picked up her hand, bringing it to his mouth. "I am so sorry, so, so sorry."

She felt the words, his breath damp and warm against the flesh of her palm. "No, it can't be only that. There must be some other reason."

"It twisted him, Em, in worse ways than we knew."

She wasn't convinced or maybe she didn't want to be.

"What other reason is there?" Roy asked, desperately looking to her for an alternative, a last-minute reprieve from the burden of his guilt, even as he knew there wasn't one. That knowledge sat deep in his eyes, too.

"I don't know," she said. "Genetics? Some brain anomaly? Oh, God . . ." She caught her lip, rocking her head back. The pain in her heart was fierce, searing. She prayed she would die of it.

"It doesn't really matter now why or how it happened."

She jerked her glance to his.

"He has to be stopped, Em."

You wouldn't keep a dog you couldn't trust in your house, would you? You would put that dog down. Roy's voice, his statement from a few days ago, ran through Emily's mind, and she flinched from it, not wanting it there. "We have to talk to him, Roy, don't we? We have to give him a chance to explain before we turn him over to the police."

"Who said anything about the cops? I don't

think I could do that. What would be the point, anyway? They've already said they want to execute him, and we'd be there with him, too, every goddamn step. Could you stomach that? Could you watch them kill our son?"

Emily looked into her lap, feeling tears bite the undersides of her eyelids. How could one set of parents make two so very different children? Was it possible that a single traumatic event could have so much impact? She remembered their last visit with the child psychologist that he had said Tucker seemed to have come to terms with the terrible thing that had happened. He seemed able to separate the actual event from the man who was his father. The psychologist had said Tucker understood his dad hadn't meant to hurt him. The doctor had claimed he'd done all he could, that he didn't believe Tucker would benefit from further counseling.

So, they had come home and put it behind them, far behind them. They had resumed life as usual, assuming Tucker was fine when he wasn't. Had she known that he wasn't? Emily hugged her knees. How could she accept this, the terrible facts, the ineluctable proof of what Tucker had done, of what he'd become? What had she missed? Her fear of her own culpability was like a hot coal burning in the center of her chest. Were these women dead because of her refusal to see the truth and to act on it? What if there were others as Lissa insisted, as Emily herself believed?

The questions cried out for answers she couldn't give. Her mind was sluggish with grief and the fatigue of so much unrelenting calamity. She wanted it to end; she was ready for that.

"Mom? Pop? You awake?" Tucker's voice, sounding agitated, rose from the landing.

Emily heard his step on the stairs and got to her feet, fumbling to button her robe. She was aware of Roy, standing beside her. She felt the tension in him; she felt his fear, a force not separate from her own.

"What the hell happened in here?" Tucker's voice boomed, and Emily knew he was looking at the chaos in his bedroom.

"Tucker?" Roy called. "We need to talk. We can work something out, son. Okay?"

He came into their bedroom, and his eyes, when he brought them to Emily's, were torn with misery.

"I thought you were at Lissa's," she said.

"She's pregnant, Mom. Did you know?"

"That doesn't concern you," Roy answered before Emily could.

"It goddamn sure does." Tucker didn't sound angry so much as hurt and bewildered. "She's getting an abortion because of the shit I'm in. Did she tell you?"

"What else would you expect?" Emily's voice rose. "She believes in you, in your innocence, but you aren't innocent, are you?"

Tucker stretched out his hands. "She can't do it, Ma. You have to stop her."

Emily stared at him. She loved him and yet was sickened by the sight of him, and now, in spite of herself, she was frightened for him and of him. Her own son. A murderer. How? How could it be true? And yet it was. This wasn't a nightmare, or the hideous calamity you might watch unfold on the news from your sofa, while congratulating yourself that it wasn't happening to you. No. She would never waken from this, she thought. The terrible sound, a cry she could feel breaking from her core, some interior and bottomless well of sorrow, climbed into her throat, and she bit down on it, holding it in with her teeth.

Roy said, "We found the box, the evidence. We know what you did, that you murdered those girls."

"Momma?" It was a child's appeal, thin with anguish.

"Oh, Tucker, what have you done?"

Time seemed to stop and the silence that filled the room was punctuated by the sound of the grandfather clock on the landing, each separate tick swelling and detonating, a bullet fired from a gun.

Tucker folded onto the side of the bed; he held his head in his hands.

Emily fisted her hand and pressed it to her stomach.

"All I ever wanted was to make a life with Miranda. I know you hated her and thought she was trash, but she wasn't. She was the one for me, the only one. We could have had a life together, you know? Like Lissa has with Evan. We could have been happy."

"What happened, Tucker?" Roy asked.

"I went there to talk to her, and Coe was there. I saw them through the window in her bedroom. She'd been with him before, but she swore, after he beat her up, it was over."

"You never told us," Emily said.

"Because you thought she was wrecking my life."

"Your mother and I wanted you to be happy, Tuck. We wanted to keep you safe." Roy's voice was ragged. "We were wrong—about so many things."

Emily sat next to Tucker. "I know about Miranda's assault. I know you went with her to the police station, that you took pictures of her injuries."

"She said she would press charges. She promised me she wanted him out of her life."

"She lied to you," Emily said gently.

Tucker met her gaze; his eyes were dark pools of anguish. "After I caught them, I waited for Coe to leave and then I—I only wanted to talk, Momma, but Miranda wouldn't listen. She kept pushing me and yelling at me. I put my hands around her neck. I just wanted her to stop yelling. I didn't mean to hurt her, I swear."

"What about Jessica Sweet, son?" Roy asked.

"I don't know. She kept on me about Miranda, for months afterward, asking who did I think killed her. She was so heartbroken. I kept trying to comfort her, you know? It made me feel so bad." Tucker addressed his dad, looking up at him. "Then when we were in Galveston, she went off on me. She said she knew I killed Miranda, and she was going to the cops. I was so damned scared, Pop. I couldn't let her."

Roy put his hand on Tucker's shoulder.

"I thought if I put them in the woods, in the same place where the other bodies were left—" Tucker paused, wiped a hand down his face. "I didn't figure the cops would single me out like they have, or the news reporters—they act like they hate me. Everyone does. I don't know why."

There was real bewilderment in his eyes, and longing, Emily thought, the same longing everyone has to belong to someone, to be loved, and it occurred to her in that moment that somehow, no matter how much attention they gave Tucker, how much they cared for him and about him, for whatever reason, he couldn't feel it where it counted, in his heart and soul. She had loved him from the moment he was conceived, in the only way she knew, with her whole being, but the connection, the means of receiving that love inside him, was broken. How or why, who could say?

Her throat ached with her sorrow when she moved to take him in her arms, but he shifted to the floor, and before she could register what was happening, he stood up holding the Colt, Roy's old service revolver.

He put the muzzle to his head.

"Tucker, no!" Emily half rose, wondering how he'd known it was there, lamenting anew her oversight in not moving it.

"Give it to me, son," Roy said quietly.

Tucker lowered the gun. "Ha, ha, almost had you," he said, but his eyes were flat now, devoid of expression. Cold. "If you give me some cash, I'll get out of town. I'll disappear. You won't ever have to hear from me or see me again. It'll be like I'm dead. I wish I was, anyway."

"The cops will only come after you," Roy said. "You can't outrun this."

He sounded so calm, Emily thought. It was as if he was simply stating the plain facts, which she supposed was true. For all of them. If they were to go to the earth's end, the knowledge of what Tucker had done, the roles she and Roy had played in it, would be waiting there, hulking and dark.

"I can't go to jail, Pop. You know that, and you know why."

"Give me the gun," Roy repeated. "We'll find some other way."

Tucker stared at him. He raised the barrel to his head again.

The moment spun out.

Emily felt time slowing, the air thickening. She thought of the day Tucker was born, remembering the nights she'd walked the floor with him bundled in her arms. She could feel the crown of his head, its downy softness, where it was tucked just under her chin. Another memory came, an image of Tucker and Lissa when they were young, kneeling at the coffee table downstairs in the living room, heads close together. Lissa was teaching Tucker to write his name. Oh, the concentration in their small faces, Emily thought. The two of them had been so delightful as children; they had been the light of her heart. She was half smiling when she stood up now, and as if in a dream, she shot out her arm, and closing her fingers around the gun barrel, she jerked the Colt from Tucker's grip.

She could scarcely believe she'd gotten possession of it, but she saw it, very clearly, in her hand; she felt its weight, but then it was gone as Roy grabbed it, and at the same time Tucker lunged for it, too, and she jumped away as they fell to the floor. Looking wildly around the room, she found her cell phone, and she was dialing 9-1-1 when she heard a woman's voice, one she recognized.

"Don't move," the voice said.

Emily turned. "Revel?"

27

They found the company van parked in the alley behind Lissa's parents' house, pulled in close to the back gate, driver's-side door hanging open. Lissa and Evan exchanged a glance. They looked into the van as they walked past it, but there was no sign of Tucker. Still, every nerve, every fiber of Lissa's being, was alive and tingling with a horrible sense of doom. She knew something awful was happening, but not what it was or how to prepare herself for it.

With Evan in her wake, she climbed the back stairs, but suddenly she couldn't face it, couldn't take another step, and she stopped so abruptly Evan collided with her. In the distance, she caught the rising wail of a siren. Was it coming here?

"I can't go inside," she whispered.

"I'm right here, babe," Evan said. "Do you want me to go in first?"

She shook her head and, taking a breath, walked into the kitchen, and she was immediately struck by the pervasive quiet, the air of desertion. There were no signs anyone had been downstairs yet. The curtains over the sink were still closed; the countertops were immaculate. A hand towel printed with chickens was precisely folded over the oven door handle the way her mother always left it. Above it, the teakettle sat on a burner. The tick of the grandfather clock on the landing was audible and steady, the beating heart of the house, as it had always been in Lissa's memory. She turned to look at Evan, who was a little behind her, and that's when she caught sight of someone on the back porch, outside the door. Evan saw, too, and he moved in front of Lissa, shielding her, and the sharp intake of his breath matched Lissa's own when Detective Sergeant Garza stepped into the kitchen with Revel Wiley on her heels.

Sergeant Garza brought her fingertip to her lips.

"What are you doing here?" Evan asked.

Lissa stepped out from behind him. "What is *she* doing here?" Lissa was looking at Revel, who looked nothing like she had the last time Lissa saw her. She was dressed now in a black turtle-neck, black denim jacket and jeans.

"We think your brother is here. Have you seen him?" Garza asked.

"No," Lissa said. "How do you know he's here? What's going on?" She struggled against a fresh wave of panic.

"We were following him and lost him near the interstate." Garza kept Lissa's gaze. "But then we saw you in the underpass and figured you weren't out driving this early for no reason, that you must have heard something from him or your folks. Where are they?"

"I don't know. Upstairs, I guess. What are you doing here? Why is Revel here?"

"I'm a cop," Revel said, "a detective. When we met I was undercover. My real name is Devon Stowe." She pulled her jacket aside to reveal her badge that was pinned to her belt. Lissa caught sight of her holster, too, and the butt of her gun.

Other movement out on the porch drew Lissa's eye. More officers were gathering there, at least four that Lissa could see, all dressed in uniforms.

"What the hell is going on, Sergeant?" Evan demanded.

But a sound now, something like a crash overhead, had them looking upward.

The detectives pulled their weapons.

"Stay here," Stowe said. "Let us handle this." She motioned for two of the uniformed officers to come inside, and along with Garza, the four, with guns drawn, moved into the hall.

Lissa watched them, ears ringing, her head hollow with disbelief. She felt Evan's arm around her.

The seconds ticked, punching the thick silence, and then Lissa heard Detective Stowe talking, asking Tucker to put down the gun. "Nice and easy," she said. "You don't want anyone to get hurt, right?" Lissa heard her ask.

"Do what she says, Tucker, okay?"

At the sound of her mother's voice, Lissa broke

from Evan's grasp. "Momma?" She flew up the stairs, pushing by the uniformed officers who tried to stop her, halting only when she reached her parents' bedroom doorway. Sergeant Garza grabbed Lissa's arm, but she shook free, stepping over the threshold, her breath uneven, her heart beating hard in her chest.

"Oh, Lissa, no, you shouldn't be here."

She looked across the room when her mother spoke. "Momma? What is happening?"

"Your brother— Tucker murdered Miranda and Jessica. We— Daddy and I found proof."

"Proof?" Lissa frowned. "No, you must be mistaken."

"Go back downstairs, honey," her dad said gently from where he stood near the foot of the bed.

"Do what he says, Mrs. DiCapua."

Lissa looked from her dad to Sergeant Stowe when she spoke, her glance falling quickly from the sergeant's face to her hand that she held cupped over the butt of her holstered weapon.

"Get out of here, Liss," Tucker said. He was standing several feet beyond Devon Stowe, between the side of the bed and the bathroom doorway, holding their dad's old Colt service revolver to his temple.

"What are you doing?" Lissa asked him in a voice not much above a whisper.

"Get out of here," he repeated.

"I will," she answered, "when you put the gun down."

"You don't want to do this, Tucker," Sergeant Stowe said. "Life is never as bad as you think."

He jerked the revolver in her direction. "Lady, you don't know shit about my life."

"I do, Tucker." When their dad spoke, Tucker whipped the Colt in his direction.

But their dad didn't flinch. He went on quietly, keeping Tucker's gaze. "I know how bad it is, the way I know what you did isn't your fault. It's mine. As a dad I really fucked up with you. I failed you on so many levels, and I'm sorry. If I could go back, if I could do it over, I would give anything—" His voice broke.

Lissa tented her fingertips over her mouth. She felt the other police officers and Evan close behind her, but they would be as afraid as she was of taking any action, of setting into motion something that couldn't be undone.

"Tucker, please," their mother begged.

He wheeled on her, his eyes wild, unfocused, the Colt raised to her face, and even though the movement was small, Lissa registered it when his finger bore down on the trigger. She was aware of Devon Stowe to her left, holding her weapon in a two-handed grasp, and in the second before the sergeant shot at Tucker, Lissa was aware of her father, coming at her from the right, shoving her from harm's way, pushing past her and into the path of the bullet Stowe fired, stopping it from hitting Tucker, saving his son in the only way he knew how.

Did she scream? Lissa would never know. The blast from Sergeant Stowe's gun was so loud that it deafened her. She watched, horrified, as her father fell, and then time spun out and nothing moved, as if this room, life, the earth, the universe itself, had lost its power.

The spell broke when Tucker fell to his knees. "Momma?" he said, and his voice was high with confusion and fear.

The other policemen rushed through the door, tackling him, pushing him down until he was prone on his belly on the floor.

Evan pulled Lissa against him, steadying her. "Are you all right?" he asked.

"Yes, but Momma and Daddy—?" She turned in Evan's embrace, and her heart paused when she caught sight of her father. He lay on his back, unmoving, near the foot of the bed. A bright swath of red bloomed high on the left side of his chest. He was pale, as pale as ash. Her mother and Devon Stowe knelt beside him. The sergeant was shouting into her cell phone for an ambulance.

"I'm sorry, Momma." Tucker cried the words.

Lissa shot a glance at him, and she didn't know him. The man in handcuffs who was being led from the room was a stranger, a monster, a murderer, and all this time, she had seen him with someone else's face. The truth took her breath; it chilled her to her bones.

"He's not dead, is he?" Tucker made his escort stop before he walked out of Lissa's sight. He searched her gaze. "Jesus Christ, did you see what he did? Crazy bastard. Why did he do that? Why didn't he let them shoot me?"

Lissa didn't answer him.

Neither did their mother. She was bent over their father. Lissa went to kneel beside her. "Are you all right? Did Tucker shoot you?"

"No, something happened. I don't think the Colt fired."

"My God, Momma. I can't believe he even aimed it at you."

"He doesn't know what he's doing."

When her dad spoke, Lissa dropped her gaze to his.

He was looking at her mother. "I unloaded it."

"The Colt?" her mother said.

"After what I almost did to you the other night—" He couldn't finish. His breathing was labored.

Lissa watched his chest work as he took air in shallow sips. "Daddy, don't talk. An ambulance is coming."

Beside her, her mother was shaking badly, and thinking she was going into shock, Lissa whipped off her jacket and draped it over her mother's shoulders. She found her dad's hand

and held it. His eyes were still open, but already the light was fading from them.

Evan knelt beside her. He touched her dad's shoulder. "Hang in there, big guy. Help is coming."

Her dad's smile was more grimace.

Her mother touched his brow; she smoothed the hair at his temple. Her tears speckled his cheeks. "Don't go," she whispered.

He smiled at her and then at Lissa, making another effort to speak. She would always think if only it had been quiet she might have heard his last words, but they were swallowed in the sound of approaching sirens. Lissa felt the final pressure of his fingertips, and then his hand went loose in hers.

28

There was a police investigation into Lissa's father's shooting, but ultimately Detective Sergeant Devon Stowe was cleared of wrongdoing. She had only been trying to wing Tucker, to stop him from shooting anyone, including himself. Public opinion was overwhelmingly in her favor. She was doing her job, people said, protecting the public from a killer. Lissa heard one man being interviewed on the car radio who said it was a shame the detective's bullet hadn't found its mark, that a bullet was a hell of a lot cheaper than what it cost to house a murderer. There were other publicly aired comments, too: *What kind of parents don't know what their own son is up to? Couldn't they tell there was something wrong with the boy? Why didn't they get help for him? Why didn't they get the guns out of the house? They should have taken better care, taken control. They should have stopped him. . . .*

It infuriated her. She wanted to defend her parents and herself, but how could she, given the proof of what Tucker had done?

A couple of days after her father died, she was alone in her kitchen when Sonny Cade called to convey his condolences. "I'm shocked," he said, "but I know I can't be more shocked than you must be."

"I can't make sense of it," she admitted. She felt she would spend years trying to. Even her emotions were a forest of sensations from anger to grief to utter despair, a landscape that heaved and sank, that was different every day.

"I thought I knew Tucker," Sonny said, and then he made a sound, something rueful. He said he was sorry, but not for what.

He might not even know, Lissa thought. "It's hard," she said.

"Have you seen him?"

She walked outside onto the patio, looking down the path toward her art studio. Evan was there, finishing the floor. She would go help him, she thought, when she was finished talking to Sonny. "I don't know what I would say to him," she said. "Neither does Mom. He's asked us not to come, anyway, through his attorney." Mickey had said Tucker was too ashamed and so broken with guilt and grief over his dad's death that he'd been put on suicide watch. She wanted to hate him, but somehow her heart ached for him. "At least there won't be a trial."

"I heard he pled guilty."

"Mickey said he wanted to spare us. I'm grateful to him for that." She bent her head back, blinking into the sky, which was overcast, netted in scallops of white and gray. Before sentencing,

Tucker had written to the court, asking to be given the death penalty, but the judge had denied his request, sentencing him instead to life without parole. A fate that for Tucker would be worse than death. Hadn't he said he couldn't take it, being closed up? Lissa stood up abruptly. She couldn't go there, couldn't allow images of where he was now into her brain. She would lose it, if she did.

As if sensing her distress, Sonny changed direction, saying how fooled he'd been by Revel Wiley.

"I'm surprised you didn't know she was working undercover," Lissa said, remembering the curious look Sonny had given her the day of their meeting when she'd mentioned meeting Revel.

"You mean because I'm an ex-cop. We don't always recognize each other, and her disguise was damn good."

"She did a great job. Momma and I totally bought into the whole routine."

"They did tell you it was staged, because they weren't sure if you were involved somehow, maybe protecting Tucker."

"Yes, but when I heard that, I thought it must be a joke."

"Family takes care of family, right?"

Until they don't, Lissa thought. Hadn't her own brother betrayed her?

When she didn't say anything, Sonny changed direction again, this time asking Lissa if she knew that Revel aka Devon was at the party in Galveston the night Tucker was seen with Jessica.

Lissa said she hadn't heard that. She walked back into the kitchen. What they did know, they'd learned from Mickey. It turned out the police had been building their case against Tucker, bit by circumstantial bit, until the D.A. felt confident they had enough evidence for a conviction. The warrant for Tucker's arrest had been issued after the club owner in Austin, where Tucker said he hung out, denied seeing him. The owner, who knew Tucker well, said he hadn't seen him in months. There were the cell phone records, too, that while they showed usage during the week-end Jessica was murdered, all of it had taken place in the vicinity of Houston, Galveston and Hardys Walk, not Austin. And there were the receipts. It turned out they didn't exist, that Tucker had lied when he said he had them, when he said he'd turned them over. "No one's told us much about any of the investigation that led to Tucker's arrest," Lissa said.

"Well, it was really an accident that Devon was involved at all," Sonny said. "She was working another case, similar to the Todd Hite sting. You remember?"

"The whole money laundering, prostitution, drug thing, you mean?"

"Yeah, but when Tucker showed up at that party, she knew who he was, that he was a person of interest in Miranda's murder, so she kept an eye on him. She was there when Tucker and Jessica got into it, and Jessica dropped his cell phone in the toilet."

"In the— Are you kidding? That's how it got wet?"

"Yeah. I guess she was pissed. Anyway, Devon recovered it. She fished it out." Sonny waited, but Lissa had no idea what to say. Nothing about the police end of this was relatable; it wasn't her family he was talking about. It couldn't be.

"Maybe this is too hard—"

"No," Lissa said. "I want to hear it."

"After the blowout, Jessica left. Tucker followed her, and Devon followed him. She just had this gut feeling, you know? She lost them in traffic, though, once they got into Houston."

"You mean she could have stopped him?"

"Yeah, maybe." Sonny paused. "But they would have gotten him eventually for the other."

"Miranda."

"Yeah."

Neither of them said that if Tucker had been stopped, Jessica would still be alive.

"Before I let you go," Sonny said, "I do have one more piece of news."

"Oh?"

"According to Devon, our mutual friend could

be feeling the legal heat himself pretty soon, although if you were to repeat that, I'd call you a liar."

"Are you talking about Darren Coe?"

"Who?"

"Okay," she said. "I get it. I won't be sorry if he's in trouble, though," she added.

"Keep your eye on the news," Sonny said.

"I will," Lissa answered, and she thanked him; she appreciated that he'd taken the trouble to call.

"No problem," he said. "You let me know if I can do anything."

After they hung up, she thought how people changed, how much Sonny had. More than she would have thought was possible.

The following week, after the coroner released her dad's body, Lissa, her mom and Evan held a graveside service for him. Anna helped them plan it, and somehow, the media didn't get wind of it. But in the initial days following the tragedy, they were kept under scrutiny, the objects of curiosity and derision. Even when the woman who was reported missing the day of Tucker's arrest was found alive at a boyfriend's house, there were people who didn't believe it, who were convinced Tucker had kidnapped and killed her, too. The amount of misinformation that was passed around was maddening, intolerable after all they'd been through. The business suffered. Home construction at Pecan Grove was at a standstill. They had nothing new coming in. Under the circumstances, there was no question of Lissa's mother going anywhere but home with Lissa and Evan.

Lissa shadowed her. She could almost not bear to have her mom out of her sight. Some nights, she left Evan, sleeping, and went to lie down beside her mother, and they held each other. They talked about what her dad had done, stepping into the path of a bullet that was meant for Tucker.

"Was it suicide?" Lissa asked once.

"I don't know," her mother said. "Possibly. He felt so horrible for how he terrified Tucker when he was small, you know? He suffered for it every day. In so many ways, he could never get past it. But he suffered with so much. Tucker caught the brunt of his misery, I think."

"Dad put too much pressure on him. First he pushed him to play baseball, then he pushed him into working construction—"

"He gave his life to save Tucker's," her mother said softly.

"Oh, Momma, I know."

They lay still for several moments. The window was open slightly to the night breeze, and Lissa watched the curtain rise, billowing, and fall, like breath. A lone cricket tweedled a few notes that then died. She remembered the night Tucker showed her his folder filled with clippings about the murders that had taken place along the southern stretch of I-45. She remembered his admiration of John Douglas, the FBI profiler. She had thought nothing of Tucker's interest then, but now, in hindsight, it seemed chilling. Had it been or did it only seem that way now in light of all that had happened? Lissa thought she would probably never know.

"We should have talked more," her mother said.

"As a family, you mean?"

"Yes, but at the very least, I could have talked to Tucker myself about your dad's issues. It just seemed best not dwell on them. I mean in the way it's best not to pick at a wound once it starts to heal. I have so many regrets, though, I wonder if I'll ever come to the end of them."

Lissa could name her mother's regrets; the list was similar to her own. They wished they had not judged Miranda so harshly. They wished they had rid the house of every gun. They wished Daddy was alive, and Tucker was right in his mind.

They were cleaning up the kitchen one day after breakfast when Lissa asked her mother what she would have done if the police hadn't arrested Tucker. "Would you have turned him in?"

Her mom picked up a towel to dry her hands. She took so long to answer that Lissa thought she wouldn't, but then she said, "It's horrible, but I'm relieved I was spared that. It's going to be hard enough to know daily that he will grow old in that place, caged and locked down like an animal—"

Her voice broke; she drew in a breath. "I can barely stand the thought of it."

Lissa turned from her mother to stare out the kitchen window. She wondered, too, how they would stand it, but a few minutes later when she asked, her mother said all they could do was to live it.

"One day at a time. It's what your dad would want and Tucker, too, if he could say. They would want us to try and be happy."

A pause fell, and when Lissa felt her mother's hand on her back, she somehow intuited what was on her mother's mind, and she stiffened.

"The timing is terrible," her mother said by way of prefacing her concern, "but there is one thing you're going to have to do, and fairly quickly now, and that's to decide about the baby. Either way, I'm here for you, and either way, you'll need medical attention."

Lissa covered her eyes with her fingertips and started to cry; she couldn't help it. She felt her mother's arms come around her and turned into her embrace. "I'm so scared, Momma. What if the thing that made Tucker do this is genetic? What if it's in me, and I pass it to the baby?"

"Oh, honey, a child is more than its genetics." Her mother rubbed circles on Lissa's back. "You and Evan are loving people. You love each other. You will love your child. That's what's important."

You and Daddy loved Tucker, but it wasn't enough. The thought flared in Lissa's brain, but it would be cruel to say it, to add more to the burden of guilt and grief her mother was already carrying.

Evan hadn't mentioned the pregnancy. Lissa had the sense that he was giving her time, and she was grateful to him for it, but she knew her mother was right, that there was little time left.

In the end, it was only a handful of days later when the decision became clear to her. She would never really know why or how. It was a rainy afternoon, and she was sitting on a stool at her art table that Evan had carried down to her studio for her earlier, idly doodling in her sketchbook, thinking of another long-ago rainy day when she and Tucker had lain flat on their bellies on the front porch, coloring. The air had been damp then, too. It had smelled of crayons and moss and of something more astringent. Maybe the huge chaste berry tree planted near one corner of the porch had been in bloom. And there they were, the two of them, in her mind's eye, so joyfully content, so involved. So happily absorbed.

She looked up when Evan tapped on her door and came inside to tell her that lunch was ready, and he must have seen something in her eyes, because he came and knelt beside her. She cupped his face in her hands, a fresh image crystallizing in her mind of the two of them bent over the side of a crib, watching their baby sleep. In her imagination, Lissa reached out her hand, stroked the sweet softness of one round, flushed cheek, and her heart was pierced by such yearning, she almost cried out.

She held Evan's gaze. "I want our baby," she said softly, "more than anything."

His eyes widened. "Really?"

"I'm still scared."

He stood up, pulling her into his arms. "I've got you, babe," he whispered against her hair. "I'm not going anywhere."

In the end they decided to relocate to Denver, where Evan's younger brother, Connor, was opening his own residential construction company and was thrilled to learn that Evan and Lissa would join him. Lissa hated to leave the house they'd built, but as Evan pointed out, they could build another. They needed a third bedroom, anyway, with the baby on the way. She thought how much she would miss her studio with the lovely north light, and the gazebo, where she'd last sat, reminiscing with Tucker. But she knew moving was for the best. Even if people in town had been kind, and very few were, they needed a fresh start for themselves and for the new life Lissa carried. She couldn't bear the thought that anyone, remembering Tucker, would watch for signs of something horrible and twisted in her baby. She prayed she wouldn't do it. She held fast to the belief that with enough love, if such tendencies were present, they would be transformed. From the research she did, it seemed even science agreed it was possible that such things could be overcome.

Her mother turned down Lissa and Evan's offer to join them in Denver, instead taking Anna up on her invitation to camp out there for a time. She wanted to see to it that the lake house was finished and to oversee the sale of the house in Hardys Walk. Thankfully Joe Merchant had found some-one to clean up the carnage so that, although the memory lingered, there wasn't a physical trace of it left. But there was still the ordeal of sorting out what do with all the furniture and the rest of what the old house contained, four generations of belongings. Lissa took a few of the furnishings with her, and she brought more back to Denver after every visit home. She came as often as she could until the doctor banned her from travel the week before Thanksgiving. The baby was due the week of Christmas.

The last time she walked through the house in Hardys Walk, the house her great-great-grandfather had built, was in October. By then most everything had been packed and sold, moved or stored. It was a warm day, and leaving her mother and Anna in the kitchen, Lissa walked outside, into the backyard. She sat in the old swing, idly shifting it with the toe of a shoe that was nearly blocked from her view by the huge mound of her belly. She thought of her dad and wondered what he would make of her now. Tucker would tease her; the Tucker she knew would laugh that goofy laugh. She could almost hear it, and the rush of warmth she felt, something akin to affection, surprised her. But Tucker's laugh was the best thing about him; it must have been a gift from the clear, healthy part of his brain. She missed his laugh; she missed him and her dad.

Blinking, she looked up through the branches of the old elm at the sky that was clear of every blemish, an immaculate sheet of cerulean blue, and she wondered if she could hold on to the gift of Tucker's laughter, and if she could, would it soften her anger? Would it allow her to remember only the love?

It was the day after New Year's, and Emily was alone in the old house, a final walk through before she handed the keys over, at the closing tomorrow, to its new owners, a retired architect and his wife who were relocating from Chicago.

She rested her hand on the carved newel post and found herself looking to the grandfather clock on the landing. But, of course, it was gone. Sold like many of the other antiques her family collected through the years. Climbing the stairs to the second floor, she felt both lighter and heavier. She had taken a few of the other furnishings to the lake house, where she was living for now.

She liked the solitude there, and the quiet was balm to her soul. She knew most everyone, including Lissa, thought it was a bad idea, but it was the only way she would survive, by retreating into a corner, where she could nurse her wounds away from prying eyes. She was in touch with Anna and Joe, and that much company was enough for now.

Reaching the upstairs hallway, she stopped. The light was uncertain, the silence deep. Fragments of memories loomed from the shadows. She imagined she could hear their voices, those of her children and Roy, her mother and father. She went to the doorway of the bedroom she had shared with Roy, empty now of everything but the dust moats that sifted through the air.

Was it suicide?

When Lissa had asked her, Emily hadn't been sure, but standing here now, she thought, *No.* When Roy stepped into the bullet's path, it had been an act of reconciliation, of atonement. She hoped he had found peace. She hoped that her son would, as well, but she thought the possibility for that might lie beyond this world.

Turning from the doorway, she thought she would gather her courage and peek into each of the other rooms and then go. Walk out the front door and lock it for the last time, walk away and not look back. But it was proving to be harder than she expected, and she was near tears when her cell phone rang. She checked the caller ID. Evan! Her tears vanished; her heart soared. "Tell me you're finally a daddy," she said by way of answering.

"I am," he answered. "Lissa is fine, wonderful, beautiful." He said this in a rush of elation and joy.

"Boy or girl?"

"A girl," Evan said. "The tiniest, most perfect little daughter in all the world. Next to Lissa, that is," he added.

And Emily laughed. "Tell my darling daughter I'm on my way," she said.

Acknowledgments

The evolutions of a story can be many and varied, and it was certainly the case with this one, but they were not as numerous as the people I have to thank for getting it to this magical place— between the covers of a real, live book!

Thank you more than I can say to my steadfast critique partners, TJ Bennett, Wanda Dionne, Joni Rodgers and Colleen Thompson, who listened to draft after draft of many pages of manuscript. Thank you also to early readers, Jo and Susan, and to David and Christie, two of the best plot sounding boards in the world. Thanks also to John, Michael and Heather, for their continuing faith in me. All of you share in the celebration and always know even when I don't that there's a way, and I'm so grateful for that.

Of course, none of this would be happening at all without my brilliant agent, Barbara Poelle. There is no better sounding board or plot strategist in the world. Never mind her patience, her faith, her kind heart and her unflagging encouragement, not to mention the funny stuff, the sparkles of laughter. I may never get over the stroke of good fortune that joined us as partners.

It is with the same immense gratitude that I mention my lovely editor at MIRA, Erika Imranyi.

It's really difficult to describe the exact nature of what she does with my words—some sort of alchemy happens. She's so generous and giving of her time and patience, and then there's the care she gives to every detail—it's exacting, but there is always room left for the story to grow, to evolve in the right perfect way. Having her faith and support and her expert guidance is another stroke of good fortune and I'm so thankful for it.

Thank you, too, to MIRA editors Lenore Waldrip and Michelle Meade, and a huge shout-out to the entire MIRA marketing and PR teams, especially Lisa Wray and Michelle Renaud, who have educated me in all things PR, patiently answering my endless questions.

And, once again, I could never say thank-you enough to readers everywhere. Without you my dream of living the writing life would have never left the ground! Love and joy to all of you!

Safe Keeping

Barbara Taylor Sissel

Questions for Discussion

1. Emily regrets that she didn't put a stop to Tucker's relationship with Miranda when it began in high school. How would you handle it if your son or daughter became romantically involved with someone you believed to be a bad influence?

2. Emily and Roy are at odds over how to handle Tucker's lingering dependency on them. In their situation, which side would you choose? Would you be inclined to give Tucker more latitude as Emily does, or do you think Roy's "tough love" approach would be more effective?

3. As siblings, Lissa and Tucker seem close, although she doesn't claim to know and understand her brother on every level. In fact, he mystifies her in certain ways. Do you share a bond with your sibling? Did the bond survive childhood or did you drift apart once you were grown and left home? Discuss the ways you might have kept this bond intact. Discuss the ways the bond may have been broken and the reasons for that.

4. Do you feel a mother can share as tight a bond with her grown son as she might with her grown daughter? How much do you feel gender is a factor in the context of creating tightly knit family relationships?

5. How do you feel about Roy's gun collection? He kept it locked in a cabinet, but do you feel that was sufficiently safe gun practice? Would the tragedy at the story's end have been avoided if guns hadn't been in the Lebay home?

6. Emily does a lot of cooking, finding relief from stress in the occupation. Lissa paints. What do you do when you're under pressure, when your heart is troubled, to find peace?

7. Emily shares a deep bond of friendship with Joe Merchant, a lover from her past, and while she doesn't conceal her friendship with Joe from Roy, she doesn't talk to him about it, either. Do you feel it's a betrayal of Roy and their marriage vows? Does the nature of Emily and Joe's relationship feel morally ambiguous to you or do you feel she has a right to have whomever she chooses as a friend, man or woman?

8. Lissa is deeply conflicted about her pregnancy, concerned her baby will be born with

psychological and emotional issues, in essence that the baby might turn out to be troubled in the way Tucker is. Do you feel her concerns are valid? What are your thoughts about nature versus nurture?

9. Lissa and Emily are uncertain where to lay the blame for Tucker's issues. Are they the result of the tremendous fear he experienced as a child when in the throes of an episode of post-traumatic stress? Or is Tucker's troubled nature the result of faulty genes? Do you believe a person can simply be evil and there is no explanation?

10. The difficulty of forgiveness is a theme in this story. Could you forgive a family member who had committed a heinous crime?

11. Emily and Roy make tremendous sacrifices in order to keep Tucker safe. Discuss some of those sacrifices. How far would you go to protect your own child? Would you act as Roy does in the final scene?

12. Discuss the significance of the title.

A Conversation with the Author

Safe Keeping is about a family that is forced to confront the very real possibility that one of their own might have committed a horrible crime. What was the genesis for the idea and characters in the novel?

It grew out of a fascination with the I-45 serial killings that plagued Texas for a number of years. There was a lot of coverage over time of the parents of the young women who were murdered, and while my heart breaks for them, for some reason, I wondered about the person or persons who committed the crimes. I imagined a man and a troubled family history. I imagined what might happen if he were caught. At the time, a number of men were looked at as suspects, and even though they were later cleared of every shred of suspicion, they were shunned. One man who was questioned extensively committed suicide. So then I wondered: What if that were my son or my brother, charged with such a heinous crime or crimes? Suppose I believed with every ounce of my being he was incapable of such violence? How far would I, as a mother or a sister, go to prove his innocence? I also wondered about violence itself. Is the tendency a matter of genetics or does it lie in how we are parented? What science is beginning to uncover in regard to answering this question, the nature versus nurture debate, is fascinating. A gene, referred to in everyday parlance as the "warrior gene," has been identified, and its presence can predict the tendency to aggressive behavior.

For those readers who are interested, there was a series conducted on NPR radio about neuroscientist Jim Fallon, who has made the study of the criminal brain his life's work. When he learned from his mother of his family's violent ancestry (Lizzie Borden among them), since he had all the tools, he conducted brain scans on a number of his relatives and found nothing out of the ordinary. Then he did a brain scan on himself and discovered that he does have the anomaly that his own scientific investigations have shown can predict whether someone is capable of violence and even murder. The intriguing fact is, though, that, according to his mom and the rest of his family, he's never exhibited violence, or even the tendency. Turns out it requires a triggering event. To listen to the entire program, visit NPR, the special series, Inside the Criminal Brain.

Your previous novel, *Evidence of Life*, also features a woman whose seemingly perfect family life is unhinged. Is motherhood a common thread in all your writing? What is it about this theme that inspires you to write, and what is the message you're hoping readers will take from your books?

Motherhood is indeed a theme in all my novels, mainly because, although I've had many jobs in my life, being a mom has been the most challenging, the most arduous and rewarding, of them. It's a journey that isn't over, although my sons are grown and we're not sharing the same roof. There is still a bond that while invisible is no less invincible and compelling and even fascinating to me. I think the relationship to one's children is probably as close as it might come to experiencing unconditional love on earth. If this is true, then it stands to reason that—and some of us do tell our children this—no matter what happens, we'll always love them. Mistakes, bad choices and errors in judgment are inevitable in families. I think the source of my inspiration for writing my novels is rooted in this reality, and in themes of love and forgiveness, especially as they evolve through sibling and parental relationships when these relationships are under pressure. If there is anything I would want a reader to take away from the stories I write, it would be the idea that regardless of the nature or size of the mistake and its inevitable and often horrible fallout, love and forgiveness are possible, as sentimental or even mawkish as that may sound.

In the novel, the bodies of Miranda Quick and Jessica Sweet are found in an area you refer to as "the killing fields." Is this a real place?

Unfortunately, it is. The actual "killing fields" refer to a section of Texas's Interstate 45, roughly the fifty miles of highway that links the southern edge of Houston to the Galveston Bay area. Over a period of years, beginning in the 1970s, more than thirty (some claim the number is over forty) girls and young women have been found brutally murdered in mostly remote locations along that stretch of roadway. At one time, some years ago, when bodies began to be found along the same interstate north of Houston (the setting for my novel *Safe Keeping*), it was rumored that the serial killer responsible for the murders of the women found on the southern end of the highway had moved his base of operations north. I don't think it was ever established that was actually the case. A movie was made a few years ago about the I-45 serial killings titled *Texas Killing Fields*, starring Sam Worthington. It was based on true events.

Evidence of Life and *Safe Keeping* are both set in Texas, and although you currently reside there, it's not where you're originally from. What about the state of Texas are you drawn to?

I actually grew up in the Midwest and was brought to Texas as a teenager by my mother, who took on the job of overseeing oil royalty interests in the state for my grandmother. I'll never forget my first sight of a drilling rig or of the pump that's set in place once the well is brought in. The fields in north Texas where I lived at the time were littered with this odd-looking equipment. But lest you think this is a rags to riches story à la *The Beverly Hillbillies*, it's not! There was black gold in that flat land, but it didn't exactly gush out of the ground. I did like to go with my mom, though, when she talked to the drillers. It was such a wildcat business then, and the people involved in it were such characters. I loved hearing their stories, but I have to confess, I was very sick for my home up north. I wasn't all that enamored of living in Texas, not until we took our children to visit the Texas Hill Country, west of Austin, where I set *Evidence of Life*. Some people—and I saw this a while back in the *New York Times*—compare the region to the Napa Valley or even Provence. All I know is that for me there is something very special there.

What was your greatest challenge in writing *Safe Keeping*? Your greatest pleasure? The biggest surprise?

The greatest challenge was in focusing the plot. I began with too many elements and so much had to be cut away to even find the real plot of the story. I thank both my agent and my editor for helping me with this. Looking back, it is as if I had this huge rock, and we just kept chipping away through draft after draft to find the essence of the gift the rock contained. But it was worth every ounce of effort and feeling that way, that level of satisfaction, when we finalized the last draft—that was the greatest pleasure. I think the biggest surprise was in how the elements finally did mesh, as beautifully as well-oiled gears. I despaired it would never happen!

How did you know you wanted to be a writer, and when did you actually start writing? What was the first thing you ever wrote?

My sister taught me to read before I ever started school and she and my mom both had a love of books and reading. My mother taught us respect for written words. She taught us to value them, to choose them wisely. She taught us to think about and discuss what we read, too. I loved all of that, but the exact moment when all of that love crystallized into the desire to write happened when, at age eleven, I was reading *Wuthering Heights* under the bedcovers with a flashlight. Some one scene in that story, I've forgotten which one, was so affecting that it caused me to poke my head up out of the covers and to say to myself that I wanted to do this. To write a story that would so reach inside of people they would forget everything else, forget even themselves. I considered writing while I was in high school, but the idea didn't really take flight for many years, not until my youngest went off to school, then the old dream resurfaced. Before that, along with whatever I wrote in college, I kept a journal and wrote poetry and a handful of character sketches. I suppose the earliest story I ever created was when I taught ballet to some neighborhood kids. I think I was around twelve or thirteen, and I offered ballet lessons as a way to earn money. At the end of the summer, my students performed a ballet I choreographed. I think the story was something about a little lost girl, basically a favorite children's book *The Wizard of Oz* as it might be rendered in a classical ballet. I don't remember what music I used. I do remember choreographing a short ballet to the theme from Exodus, too.

Who are your favorite writers and why?

The Bronte sisters for sure. The Russian authors, Dostoyevsky and Tolstoy. W. Somerset Maugham, Edna Ferber, Samuel Butler, Edith Wharton, Edgar Allen Poe, William Faulkner, Daphne

DuMaurier, Willa Cather, Rudyard Kipling, Oscar Wilde. There are so many. I loved them for similar reasons, the humanity of their stories, the virtual worlds they built that I could live in as long as the story lasted. The characters they wrote about so vividly that I was in their skin, experiencing their lives. That these authors could write and bring such color to life from a mere mix of black and white words simply fired my imagination. It still does. Today, I love Anita Shreve, John Burnham Schwartz, Andre Dubus, Annie Proulx, Elizabeth Berg and I just fell in love with Elizabeth Strout. Again, so many authors to love and the reason for loving them is mainly to do with character more than plot, I think. Marilyn Robinson is another who does beautiful characters. I wish I had more time to read!

Can you describe your writing process? Do you write scenes consecutively or jump around? Do you have a schedule or a routine? A lucky charm?

I begin every morning by revising yesterday's work and then go on to write new material, usually working for four to five hours, then afternoons are spent on the commercial aspects of the business. When it comes to writing the story, I do work consecutively. For me, one detail hinges on another. The slightest change can unhinge everything that comes after, like a domino effect, so the story has to be right from the beginning, or as right as I can get it on that day, before I move on. As for a lucky charm, I think it's my muse, whom I envision as an adorable but capricious child and often, when I get stuck, when I can't find her or the inspiration and creative flow she brings me, I go out to the garden and find her there, waiting for me.

Center Point Large Print
600 Brooks Road / PO Box 1
Thorndike ME 04986-0001 USA

(207) 568-3717

US & Canada:
1 800 929-9108
www.centerpointlargeprint.com

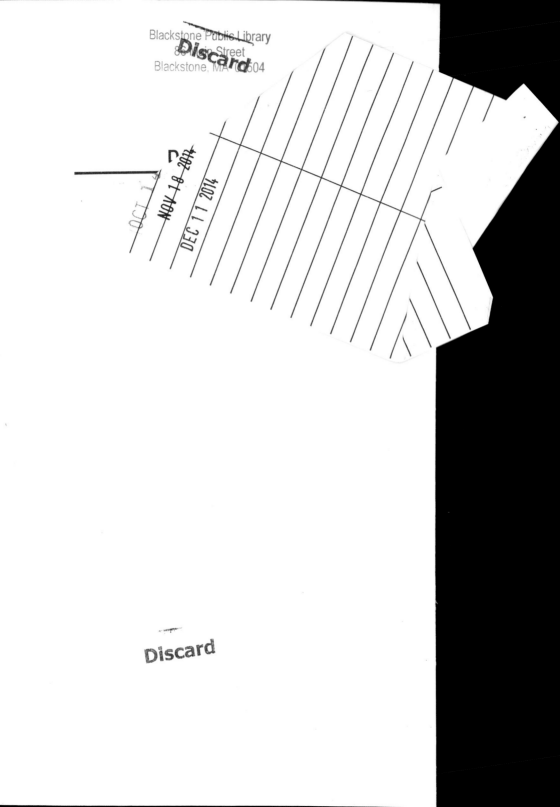